P9-CKE-474

Praise for John Dickson Carr and *The Witch of the Low Tide*:

"There is always something engaging in reading a Carr. . . . His books have an authentic flavor." —*New York Times*

"Only John Dickson Carr, the master of suspense novels, could write this."—*Chicago Sunday Tribune*

"A superlative detective novel."—*Denver Post*

Also by John Dickson Carr available from
Carroll & Graf:

John Dickson Carr
The Witch of the Low Tide

Carroll & Graf Publishers, Inc.
New York

FOR
NORA AND KENNETH REDDIN

Copyright © 1961 by John Dickson Carr
Copyright renewed 1989 by Clarice M. Carr, Bonita Marie
Cron, Julia McNiven, Mary B. Bowes.

Published by arrangement with Harold Ober Associates, Inc.

First Carroll & Graf edition 1990

Carroll & Graf Publishers, Inc
260 Fifth Avenue
New York, NY 10001

ISBN: 0-88184-672-4

Manufactured in the United States of America

PART I

THE ENCHANTMENT

We need hardly caution newcomers against the artifices of pickpockets and the wiles of impostors, two fraternities which are very numerous in London. It is even prudent to avoid speaking to strangers in the street. All information desired by the traveller may be obtained from one of the policemen, of whom about 16,000 (some 260 mounted) perambulate the streets of the Metropolis.

—BAEDEKER'S *London and Its Environs* FOR 1908

1

The train reached Charing Cross towards dusk of a fine evening in June. David Garth, outside the station, had been about to hail one of the new motor-cabs when he first saw the man whose words led him into nightmare.

All the way up in the train from Fairfield he had been thinking about Betty Calder. It was a nuisance having to leave her, if only for a few hours. And a professional appointment made under such outlandish circumstances, for so outlandish a time, disturbed the routine of his apparently stodgy life.

He was more than David Garth, M.D. He was David Garth, Harley Street specialist, spoken of as "the" coming man (whatever that might mean, as Garth's sardonic humour often mused) in the practice of neurology.

Before leaving Fairfield he had put on evening-clothes, as though there were some mystic boundary between Kent and London. His white gloves and glossy top-hat shamed the dust of the train. He was thirty-eight years old, lean and stately despite a mocking intelligence; and, for all this parade of dignity, as wild a romanticist as ever lived. "Hah!" Garth said to himself.

Afterwards he never forgot the air or the texture of that evening: the tarry smell of wood-paving after a day's heat, the remnants of sunset beyond Trafalgar Square, and a soft traffic-rumble punctuated only by the jingle of hansom-bells or the *putt-putt* of an occasional motor-car.

These familiar noises poured at him in an unreal twilight

round Charing Cross. His closest friends, Vincent and Marion Bostwick, might have been surprised at his meditations.

"For the first time," he was thinking, "I am in love. By God, I am."

"My dear fellow," said another voice in his mind, "these biological urges—"

"You and your biological urges," said a furious mimicking. "You and your accursed scientific terms. Shut up, do you hear me. *Shut up.*"

He had left Betty at Fairfield, or, to be exact, near Fairfield at the seaside cottage with its bathing-pavilion built out on the beach. The long surf thundered through a hot summer. Whenever Garth pictured Betty Calder, that eminently respectable young widow of twenty-eight, his mind brought an image which (in the literary sense, anyway) was embarrassing. He thought of Betty as a water-nymph. But the year was 1907. For an unchaperoned young widow to have rented a seaside cottage at all, he conceded, was rather a daring move.

So the South Eastern and Chatham Railway whisked him up to London. He was crossing the station courtyard towards the cab-rank when a voice hailed him out of gloom.

"Oi! You! Sir! . . . Dr. David Garth?"

"Eh?" said Garth, and stopped short. "Yes?"

At the other side of the Strand, beyond caked mud and blowing dust, a few shop-fronts showed a gleam of the new and dazzling electric light. But it was only a gleam. Horse-drawn omnibuses, white and green, bumped past in a dwindling parade that shook the arc-lamps of the station yard and seemed to shake the whole street as well.

Of the newcomer Garth could see little except that he was a thickset man with a fat face and a curly-brimmed bowler hat. He had a confidential manner and a large gold watch-chain, and breathed as though he had been running.

"You *are* Dr. Garth, aren't you? May I ask, sir, whether you've been summoned to Scotland Yard?"

"Summoned to Scotland Yard? No, I have not. Is there any reason why I should be?"

"Now let's not argue the matter, sir," the newcomer said persuasively. "If you're not going there now, Doctor, may I ask where you are going?"

"Who are you? What do you want?"

"I'm a police-officer, sir. Name of Twigg."

"For your information, then, I am calling at my office to keep an appointment with a patient. Afterwards I shall have a very late dinner with some friends of mine, Mr. and Mrs. Bostwick, and return to the country by the eleven-twenty train."

"Isn't it a bit late in the evening, Doctor, to be keeping an appointment with a patient?"

"The circumstances are unusual—"

"They are, Doctor; they are for a fact. So I think, sir, you'd better come along with me to the Yard."

"Oh? Why should I?"

"Now let's not argue the matter, sir." With a knowing air, all weightiness and unconcern, Garth's companion held up his hand and drew the air through a hollow tooth. "Here's my warrant-card, if you'd care to see it. George Alfred Twigg. Detective-Inspector, Criminal Investigation Department. As to why we'd like a word with you, it might be (mind, I only say it might be!) about somebody who's been leading a double life."

Hansom bells jingled in the dusk. Garth spoke sharply.

"A double life? Who has been leading a double life?"

"Ah! That's as may be. If you'll just step into a cab, now, we can be there in half a tick."

"Inspector," Garth told him with great courtesy, "we had better understand each other from the beginning. Unless you are prepared to tell me what you want of me, I am afraid I can't accompany you to Scotland Yard or anywhere else. Are you prepared to tell me?"

"The object of them questions, sir, will be disclosed in due course."

"Then so will my answers. Good evening, Inspector Twigg."

"Now I warn you, sir . . . !"

"You warn me of what?" asked Garth, stopping again and turning round.

Silence stretched out under a welter of noise. When his companion did not reply, at least for the moment, Garth gestured towards the driver of the nearest motor-cab and got into it. The driver, setting in motion a shaky clocklike innovation known as a taxi-meter, sprang down from the cab and swung hard at its starting-handle. Inspector Twigg said something which was lost as the motor exploded into life. Thudding, vibrating throughout all four fenders, the cab rolled out into the Strand and bore left towards the moving carriage-lanterns round Trafalgar Square.

Hansoms, four-wheelers, private equipages seemed to rush at them from their own speed. The driver of one four-wheeler, with a look of extraordinary ferocity, bent down to curse the motor-cab as it passed.

"Brrh, yer ruddy hell-wagon," he screamed almost into the chauffeur's ear. "Brrh, yer swindling turncoat. Brrh! Brrh! Brrh!"

And he cracked the whip, startling his own horses, while the chauffeur looked lordly without deigning to notice.

Of course, you might reflect, these jarveys had more cause for wrath than noise or speed or the reek of exhaust-fumes. What they really hated was the taxi-meter, which prevented a cabby from overcharging you. No longer could they make a scene in public, so that most Englishmen would pay almost any fare to shut them up. Cabbies hated the taxi-meter; they refused to accept it. And yet, unless they did accept it, in thirty years' time their whole horse-drawn world might be swept away.

Incredible! But that was progress. David Garth, sitting bolt upright in the tonneau, conceded all this even as he worried over different matters.

That remark about a double life had disturbed him more than he cared to admit. Certainly he had been leading a double life, in one sense at least. His friend Cullingford Abbot, the Commissioner of Police's private secretary, must somehow have guessed or discovered.

Confound the whole business!

It was no very guilty kind of double life. It did not concern Betty Calder; still less did it concern Vincent and Marion Bostwick. It was only that Garth had no wish to be laughed at.

True, he wouldn't have minded if Vince Bostwick learned about it. He had grown up with Vince, who was just his own age. Vince was fully as amiable as Garth was grave. Vince had the look of a typical outdoor man, with thin cheeks and weatherbeaten complexion and crisp hair parted in the middle, though as a matter of fact he seldom ventured farther from town than a Scottish grouse-moor or the baccarat tables at Ostend and Trouville. Vince's careless air concealed an agile brain as well as much sensitiveness. To all outward appearances he and Marion, married just two years ago this month, were exactly the sort of fashionable, well-to-do couple for whose pleasure this Edwardian age seemed to exist.

But Garth wondered.

Then he cursed himself for wondering. He was very fond of Vince.

Marion, the daughter of an Army officer, had been born and brought up in India. When both parents died of cholera, her guardianship fell to her father's close friend and commanding officer. And Colonel John Selby, Royal Bengal Artillery, was nothing if not dogged and conscientious. He paid for the girl's schooling. He put her in charge of a stern courtesy-aunt named Mrs. Montague. Then, when he retired on half-pay, Colonel Selby took them both to England and to a starched, gloomy house on the heights above Hampstead. Vincent Bostwick, meeting Marion there, proposed marriage less than three weeks after he met her.

"My dear old boy," Vince had almost shouted, "I tell you I know what I'm doing. Nobody can say a word against Marion or her family."

"Steady, Vince. Nobody is saying a word against the young lady. You're in love with her, I take it?"

"My dear old boy, she's the only woman on earth. I never knew I could feel like this about anyone."

"And she is in love with you?"

"Yes. Yes! Strangé as it may seem, she is."

"Then what's troubling you?"

"Well, Marion's young. She's only eighteen. She's just half my age. But that's all right, isn't it?"

Garth had said nothing. At this time he had not yet met Betty Calder, or realized how he himself could go overboard. He met Marion only once before the wedding, on an evening when Vince took him to dinner at Hampstead. Of "Aunt Blanche and Uncle Sel," otherwise Mrs. Montague and Colonel Selby, he kept only the haziest memory. Marion's striking good looks blotted out most other impressions.

There was a glitter about her: a sheen on her dark red hair and a flush on her high, clear complexion. At eighteen she seemed as poised and self-assured as though she were ten years older. If a pang of disquiet shot through him, he still said nothing. If Marion were getting married to break away from elderly people and the fustiness of discipline, he had not the heart to intrude on Vince's obvious happiness. Nor had he quite cared for the atmosphere or feeling of that house at Hampstead; Colonel Selby bought it quite cheaply, Vince said, because it had a bad reputation and three people had committed suicide there.

Thick lace curtains muffled the windows. In a big cavern-like drawing-room, heavy with golden-oak furniture, Marion's ready small-talk flowed and her quick laughter rang and fascination lurked at the corners of her eyes.

"Well, old boy?" Vince had demanded at the end of the evening. "You liked her, didn't you?"

"Yes, of course."

"Damn it all, David, you needn't play the cautious juggins with me. Either you did like Marion, or you didn't. Which is it?"

"I do like her, Vince. She's a charmer. I congratulate you."

For in any case, after some initial embarrassment—their wedding, a rather hasty affair in the registry-office at Hampstead Town Hall, was attended neither by Mrs. Montague nor Colonel Selby—he had no reason to intrude on his friend's happiness.

Vince's wealth smoothed the way. After a honeymoon journey as far as Athens and Constantinople, they took a house in Hyde Park Gardens and entertained a good deal for younger people. That, in a sense, was the paradox.

If Marion developed certain disturbing airs, if at times she tended to nag and to remind Vince that he *was* rather older than herself, yet it was she who became the dignified one of the pair. Within two years she had bloomed into a stately, beautiful woman. Garth forgot most of his qualms because of what happened to him at Ostend in the summer of '06.

At Ostend, that very fashionable watering-place, parasols fluttered in a sea-wind. So did ladies' hats under high-piled hair. Their bathing-dresses were scandalously daring, some said, and play was high at the gambling-casino. But under royal patronage, with a bulky bearded man marching in radiance along the *Digue de Mer,* none of this mattered. Garth, on his way home from a professional visit to Vienna, dropped into the casino one night he was long to remember.

"Dr. Garth," said a medical friend of his, "may I present you to Lady Calder?"

And that did it.

Whenever he tried to analyze his feelings about Betty Calder, though this occurred seldom, he recalled two curious facts. It appeared that her late husband, Sir Horace Calder, had been a colonial governor and one of the stuffier bigwigs. She had learned some degree of poise because most desperately she needed it. And yet Betty, twenty-eight years old, seemed less mature than Marion Bostwick at twenty.

It was true that Marion was half a head taller, with the statuesque bearing Betty lacked. Betty preferred solitude, whereas Marion would have died without company. Betty was intensely imaginative, a quality Marion perhaps lacked.

From the moment he first saw her, taking coffee with Dr. and Mrs. Henderson in the Lounge at the casino, and she glanced up and they caught each other's eyes, he guessed many things he would not have spoken aloud. Betty coloured easily, as she did then. Hers was the shyness of intense femininity. Despite her love of outdoor exercise, a strong sense of propriety or even prudery had made her refuse (almost with horror) to go sea-bathing at Ostend in front of all those people.

It was different this summer, of course, when she rented the beach-cottage near Fairfield. In that remote place, with nobody about, she wore the most modern bathing-dress of 1907. Betty had a beautiful figure. It set off her brown eyes and glossy brown hair, spray-stung along the beach. The sum-total was a kind of passionate innocence, and in his heart Garth approved. He couldn't control jealousy; he wanted her all to himself.

Betty, Betty, Betty!

Still, if it explained why Betty seemed so much younger and gentler than Marion Bostwick, it did nothing to explain the second curious fact. It didn't explain why he had never introduced her to Vince and Marion, or even so much as mentioned Betty's existence.

To Garth, now in a motor-taxicab chugging up Regent Street, it began to fret like a major question.

He loved Betty. He was proud of her. His intentions, as he would have replied to a quizzical lift of Vince's eyebrows, were strictly honourable. For what subconscious reason, then, didn't he want Vince and Marion to meet her?

"You've already answered that," declared one of the voices in his own brain. "You want to keep her all to yourself. You're blind-jealous, even of a young idiot like your own nephew."

"Oh, no," the other satiric voice retorted, "that won't do at all. There's some reason to be jealous of Hal. But there's no earthly reason to be jealous of Vince and Marion. Why haven't you ever spoken about Betty?"

Just under a week ago, on Saturday the 8th of June, a new theatrical hit opened at Daly's. Such first-nights were not uncommon; the biggest success of the previous year, Gerald Du Maurier in *Raffles, the Amateur Cracksman*, had opened on a Saturday. For the new piece, a musical comedy called *The Merry Widow*, some friend of Vince's held a theatre-party that occupied four boxes.

Garth accompanied them, wishing Betty were there. A froth of skirts and froth of music, with half its audience humming "The Merry Widow Waltz" or "I'm Going to Maxim's," lifted his spirits almost to the extent of humming too. Afterwards, during supper at Romano's, Marion Bostwick slipped into the chair beside his.

Marion wore a low-cut white gown with silver sequins and an hour-glass waist. The light of crystal chandeliers sparkled on her bare shoulders and her Gibson-girl coiffure. For some time the blue eyes had been turning towards him as though in speculation.

"David," she said suddenly, "have you had any new patients recently?"

It was so unexpected that Garth laughed; he couldn't help himself, while Marion looked haughty.

"Really, now! Have I said anything so very amusing?"

"Not at all, except that it's a new conversational approach to a doctor. Trade is quite brisk, I suppose. It's gratifying to hear of your concern."

"I'm not in the least concerned, thank you. I was merely trying to show an intelligent interest in your work. However, if you don't want me to—!" And Marion lifted one shoulder, and her tone changed. "By the way, David."

"Yes?"

"I'm afraid our motor-car has broken down again. It's Vince's fault, of course. Just because he's an older man he doesn't have to be *so* stupid. But old men often are."

"Old?" exclaimed Garth, who was again thinking of Betty. "Vince isn't old, you know. He's the same age as I am."

"Oh, well, you know what I mean! Anyway, in your case it's becoming. It makes you look so very wise, with those suave airs and that hatchet-face of yours."

"I can't help my face, Marion. I only wish to heaven I could."

"David, I do so wish you wouldn't keep trying to put me in the wrong. Our car has broken down and I loathe public cabs: that's all there is to it. Could you please possibly take us home to Hyde Park Gardens? Oh, and you might care for some refreshment afterwards?"

"With pleasure. Marion, is anything troubling you?"

"Troubling me?" Up went her voice. "I don't think I understand."

"Never mind, then."

Garth employed no chauffeur-engineer. He drove them himself in the big five-seater 20-horsepower Panhard, painted bright green with brass trimmings. Since all the servants had gone to bed, Vince acted as barman and opened a bottle of champagne as they stood round the table in the dining-room.

The dining-room, its walls panelled in black wood to simulate an obviously mock-baronial hall with heraldic shields, was lighted by electric wall-candles in pink shades. Summer ferns banked the fireplace. Vincent Bostwick, tall and thin in evening-clothes with a very high collar, had just lifted his glass to propose a toast when Marion spoke.

"David," she said, "why don't you get married?"

Vince set down the glass. Not for the first time Garth wondered why he had never told them about Betty, and now he was wondering if they had heard anything. Evidently they hadn't, to judge by Vince's laugh.

"Sooner or later, old boy," he said lazily, "every woman gets round to that remark. But you're wasting your time with David, my dear. He's one of nature's bachelors. In any case, I might remind you, he's got his work."

"Yes," cried Marion, "and that's half the trouble. That poor fellow there," her commiserating gesture indicated that Garth might be all of twelve years old, "is so devoted to work that it's positively morbid. He never goes out; we had almost to drag him to the theatre. And he doesn't seem to be interested in anything else except murder."

"Murder?" repeated the astonished Vince.

"Oh, well, you know what I mean! I mean those stories with the detectives in them, the ones David is always reading. Sherlock Holmes, and L. T. Meade, and Robert Eustace, and those silly books by somebody who writes under the name of 'Phantom.' "

"Your mind, my dear," said Vince, "is like a railway yard with trains shunting past in every direction. I know what you mean, yes. But if that's being interested in murder as a practical proposition, then I'm interested in it too."

"Yes, darling. I've often fancied you were. Please don't evade the point." Marion swung round. "And forgive my ignorance, David, but just what is this famous work of yours that you're *so* busy with? What *is* neurology?"

"In general, Marion, it's the treatment of nervous illnesses. Some of them, admittedly, are organic—"

Marion looked impatient.

"That's not much good to me, I'm afraid. 'Organic?' "

"It means they derive from some physical cause: epilepsy, to take one example. For years we've been more or less governed by the system of Dr. Weir Mitchell, who says all such illnesses are organic. If there's no physical disturbance, then there's nothing wrong with the patient that a good rest won't cure."

"That's true, isn't it?"

"Not necessarily. There's a professor of neurology at the University of Vienna who has been preaching a very different approach. His theories have roused the bitterest kind of opposition; and in some respects, if you want my opinion, he makes it too simple. But sooner or later he may change the attitude of the whole profession."

"Really, David? Who's the man at Vienna?"

"His name is Freud. Dr. Sigmund Freud."

"And what does he say?"

Somewhere upstairs a clock chimed the hour. It was very late; Garth ought to have dropped the subject. But he didn't; he went on to tell them.

"Here, now, half a minute!" Vince began in a tone of protest.

But Marion did not seem either shocked or angry, as people usually were or pretended to be. On the contrary, she suddenly laughed. Cradling her arms, all restlessness, she stalked away from the table and then swept back again in a whirl of white skirts and lace.

"What fun! Really, now, the things they do think of! What you're actually saying, David, is that everybody in the world is leading a kind of double life."

"I hadn't thought about the matter in quite that way. To a certain limited extent, though, I suppose it's true."

"Now look here!" Vince again interrupted.

"Darling, please do be quiet. It's fascinating. David dear, answer me just one question. Suppose it happened to be *me?* Suppose somebody came to your office, and told you things about me, and said I was abnormal and unnatural and ought to be locked up in a madhouse to keep me from committing a murder? What would you say then?"

It was as though someone had flung a stone through the window.

"Good God, Marion," said Vince, "why do you keep harping on murder? And what's all this rot about madhouses? You're not serious, I take it?"

Again Marion laughed, this time mocking them.

"No, stupid, of course I'm not serious. You and David pretend to be such men of the world, reading those ridiculous stories, that I couldn't help teasing you a little." She swept out her arm. "And now, if you don't mind, I'm rather tired. Let's forget it, shall we?"

That was the night of Saturday, June 8. On the following Monday afternoon, while David Garth sat in his Harley Street consulting-room during an interval between patients, the speaking-tube whistled at him from the inside wall.

"Excuse me, sir," said the voice of young Michael Fielding, the medical student who 'devilled' for him, "but there's a gentleman out in the hall here. He says he's got to see you, and he says it's very urgent."

"I can't see him now, Michael. You ought to know that. My engagement-book——"

"I know it, sir! But he doesn't want to see you *now*. He wants to make an appointment for nine o'clock on Friday evening. And he'd like to know if he can see you here, in the consulting-room, rather than your going to his house."

"Michael, what's the matter with you?"

The young man cleared his throat. He was a brilliant

student, with much charm despite his too-eager bony countenance and too-eager ways. He almost gulped in reply.

"I know, sir, you don't usually make arrangements like that. But this might be a bit different, I thought. His card says, 'Colonel John Selby. Royal Bengal Artillery, retired.'"

Garth stood motionless by the speaking tube.

He could hear no traffic-noises from outside. Rain splashed the rooftops on a dusky, oppressive afternoon; rain made a hollow drumming sound in the courtyard behind the house; rain streaked and clouded the window-panes as thoughts streaked and clouded the brain.

"That's Mrs. Bostwick's former guardian, isn't it, sir? Anyway, the card's got an address at Hampstead. Anyway, I thought I'd heard the name. Anyway . . . Doctor! Are you still there?"

"Yes. I'm still here."

"I hope I haven't done anything wrong, sir? I'm very sorry if I have."

"You've done nothing wrong, Michael, and I beg your pardon," Garth told him seriously. "Make the appointment. Tell Colonel Selby I shall be happy to see him here at nine o'clock on Friday."

And, now that dusk was deepening to night on the arranged Friday, and a taxicab carried him clanking through those prim, professional squares which lie mummified in red brick between Oxford Street and the southern side of Regent's Park, he faced the realization of another fact.

It was not that he didn't want Vince and Marion to meet Betty Calder. He had been thinking of this problem the wrong way round. In his heart, Garth realized, he never wanted Betty to meet Marion Bostwick.

He could be glad, now, Betty was safely down in Kent. At the end of this evening, whatever he learned, he would take the last train back to Fairfield; he would pick up his motor-car at the inn of the Stag and Glove, where he was spending the week-end; he would drive out to her cottage for a brief, decorous good-night before returning to the inn, after which he could meet her again on Saturday and Sunday. She need know no more of Marion than Marion knew of her.

He didn't want Betty to be contaminated.

Then immediately: "You damned hypocrite," he said to himself. And he all but laughed aloud.

Contaminated?

This would never do. In another moment he would be thinking of evil and depravity and other such terms beloved by moralists. You must forget all that; you must approach your own affairs as impersonally, scientifically, as you approach anybody else's. Besides, except for a few cloudy impressions, and one message from Colonel Selby which might not even concern Marion Bostwick, he had no real reason to suppose there was anything wrong.

The cab turned into Harley Street towards his door. Abruptly, seeing what else was ahead, Garth sat up straight.

"Stop here!" he called to the driver. "Here, just ahead! That will do."

He paid off the cab and heard it thump away. Six men rented consulting-rooms in the house where his office was, and shared the big waiting-room on the ground floor; two of them, Garth and an elderly surgeon who was also a bachelor, lived there as well. Outside at the kerb stood his own motor-car.

At first he thought he must be mistaken; that car should have been at Fairfield many miles away. But it was the green Panhard: empty, splashed with the dust of a long journey, and so hot that he could hear the grease sizzling underneath.

Fishing a key-ring out of his pocket, Garth hurried up the steps. He unlocked the front door and stood staring at the woman who faced him from the middle of the foyer.

"This is quite a surprise, Betty," he said.

2

"There's nothing wrong, is there?" asked Betty Calder. "We drove."

" 'We'?"

"Hal and I."

Hal Ormiston, his nephew. Hal Ormiston, that languid and very superior young man, who made no secret of contempt for a slowcoach uncle. Hal Ormiston, who laughed and got his own way.

"Or, to be exact, Hal did the driving. He wouldn't let *me*, though I wanted to. We did fifty-two miles without a single breakdown, and must have got here almost as soon as your train. Hal was at the cottage, you see——" Betty broke off. "You don't mind, do you?"

"No, I don't mind. But I didn't know my esteemed nephew was visiting you."

"Good heavens, he wasn't visiting me! He went down to the Stag and Glove to visit you."

("He wanted to borrow money, no doubt? And helped himself to the car, of course, when he found I wasn't there?")

Though Garth did not say these words aloud, he did not need to speak them. He had an angrily uncomfortable notion that Betty could read his mind about other matters too.

They stood in a hall of white-painted woodwork, with a black-and-white tiled floor. Potted palms made a kind of jungle, but there were no other furnishings except a hatstand and a telephone table beside the stairs. Though the gasolier had been fitted for electricity, only one bulb was burning in yellow-pale filaments through clear glass. The hall seemed even higher and duskier; noise went up in echoes when Garth closed the front door.

Betty started a little.

She wore a tailored jacket and skirt, and a stiff-bosomed blouse with a watch pinned to it. Without being at all a beauty, she was one of those eager-gentle, modest, well-rounded girls who radiate innocence. Intensely luminous brown eyes looked up at him in an expression between uncertainty and the hurt of a woman misunderstood. Betty remained as cool and cologne-scented as though she had not driven fifty-odd miles through summer heat; her dust-coat and motoring veil, her hat and mica mask, lay piled with a handbag on the table.

"Please," she said. "Please don't!"

"Don't what?"

"Don't think what you're thinking."

"Have I said anything?"

"No. You never say anything. Often I wish you would! You mustn't blame poor Hal. He did take the car, yes; it was because I asked him to."

"How so?"

"Oh, all right," Betty cried. Her footsteps rang on the tessellated floor as she ran to the table. "It's this," she continued, taking a black leather case from under the dust-coat. "It's your brief-case. You forgot it and left it at the cottage this afternoon. I was afraid you might need it for your appointment, so I thought I'd bring it to you."

There was nothing in the brief-case except some typewritten sheets which—here Garth shut up his mind. However, that made no difference. There are times when fatuous man stands appalled at the trouble a woman will take for him.

"You came all this distance just to bring . . . ?"

"Oh, my dear, does that matter?"

"Yes. It matters to me. Betty, the extent of my apologies—!"

"There's no credit in doing what I want to do. And I don't mind your being jealous; I love it, really; but only when I'm expecting it and know how to laugh at it."

"Well, you deserve an explanation. My esteemed nephew, that young swine—"

"Please! If you don't like Hal—"

"No, I don't like him. He has all the assurance of youth at making middle-age feel uncomfortable. I don't like him, so I go on lending him money. Hal, I was about to say, was only the excuse for that disgraceful outburst a minute ago. The real cause is the man who'll be here at nine o'clock; Betty, I wish you were miles away. Where is Hal, incidentally? How did you get into the house?"

"Hal went on to the Criterion Bar. A rather nice young man let me in when I knocked; he said he was your assistant."

"Michael? But there's no reason for him to have come!"

It was as though someone had been listening.

On the right of the hall, at the front, was the big waiting-room with its door closed. Towards the rear of the same wall, beyond the staircase, was Garth's consulting-room. At the back was a room the doctors in this house called the little library, its door ajar. Instantly Michael Fielding, with his usual air of brashness weakened by timidity, opened that last door. All four buttons of his mustard-coloured jacket were fastened as though girded up.

"Maybe that's true, sir," he announced, "but it's just as well I did come. The patient's here already."

"Already? Am I late?"

"No, sir; Colonel Selby was miles too early. He's in the waiting-room. I hope you won't keep him there long, Doctor. If you want my opinion, he's a badly frightened man."

The words rang in echoes. Garth glanced towards the closed door at the front.

"Mr. Fielding," he said formally, "I believe you have met Lady Calder? Yes." Picking up Betty's possessions from the table, coat and hat and veil and mica mask and handbag, he thrust them at Michael. "Take these, if you will. Lady Calder, I think, will prefer to wait in the little library. Then show Colonel Selby into the consulting-room."

"You don't need this, do you?" asked Betty, holding out the brief-case. "It wasn't important after all."

"It's very important, Lady Calder; I thank you." Garth took the brief-case, put it down on the telephone-table, and forgot it. "The little library, Mr. Fielding!"

His tone added, *"Don't argue."* A few minutes later, when he waited in courteous gravity behind his desk, the situation became worse than he had feared.

Into the consulting-room marched a thickset elderly man, iron grey and balding, with a straight back and a voice that seemed to hide behind his teeth.

"We met once before, Doctor," he said, stiffly extending his hand. "Hampstead. Two years ago. Good of you to see me."

"Not at all."

"Ah, but it was! I mean," and Colonel Selby made a repressed gesture, "coming here in the middle of the night. Like a damned thief or something. But I hadn't got much choice. The fact is—"

"Sit down, won't you?"

"Thanks. The fact is—"

Colonel Selby breathed hard. His frock coat with the silk facings, his white waistcoat and broad black cravat set off by a pearl stickpin, all exuded a defiant correctness like the standard of his behaviour. But clenched fists did not help him.

Above the desk was a chandelier holding four electric bulbs in shades like glass flowers. As Colonel Selby lowered himself into a chair of black padded leather facing Garth, the light caught a corner of his eyelid; he shied, and there was a bright glitter of sweat on his forehead.

"Look here." He tried again. "I had to come to you. *Had* to, you being a friend of young Bostwick. In one way that makes it easier. In another way it's worse. Look here: what we say is confidential?"

"Of course. I hope I needn't assure you of that."

"It'll go no further, so help you God?"

"It'll go no further, so help me God."

"Doctor, what do they do to mad people?"

The old house was very quiet. This consulting-room, with its green-painted walls and vague antiseptic smell, had a bright, bleak look of unreality. Across the room towards Garth's left, the ledge of a white marble mantelpiece held a bronze clock flanked by a framed photograph of Betty Calder at one side and a framed photograph of his parents at the other. Fern-and-flower designs had been painted on the mirror above the mantelpiece.

Colonel Selby, whose gaze never wavered from Garth's because the latter kept it there, bent forward with his hands gripping the arms of the chair.

"Straight! What do they do to mad people?"

"That depends on your definition of the word 'mad.' It's a very misleading term. Not all people are 'mad' in the old Bedlamite sense, you know. Many of them only think they are; they've been frightened by a word; they can be helped."

"You mean that?"

"We may be able to prove it. To whose case are you referring? Your own?"

"Me?" After a pause, staring back at him, Colonel Selby let out a gasp. "God's thundering guns! You don't think I'm talking about myself?"

Garth waited.

"Let's say it's a hypothetical case. No! Let's say it's somebody I know. Mind you, this whole business is my own fault. Always tried to be decent, and hoped I was. Still! There's no denying it's my fault. If Blanche ever suspected—"

"Blanche?"

"Mrs. Montague. Friend. Housekeeper. Religious principles."

"Yes, I think I met the lady. Go on, please."

A big hand hovered above the chair-arm.

"I wish I'd come here before, Doctor. You're easy to talk to. I don't mind admitting I've been through a bad patch in the past couple of years. Funny thing: the last straw was tonight, sitting in that waiting-room of yours. Especially with the kind of books you keep there for people to look at."

"Books?"

"Yes. The one where a witch or a devil-spirit takes possession of a woman's body. Or they think it does; it's a story about a mystery; daresay there's a natural explanation at the end. But I saw a bit of that in India. *I* don't think it's funny; *I* don't laugh."

Garth spoke sharply.

"Colonel Selby, there must be some mistake. I shouldn't be likely to put a book of that kind in the waiting-room."

"Well, it's there now. Book with a red cover, by somebody called 'Phantom,' open at the illustration at the front. The illustration's of a woman—well! mostly undressed, you know, bending over a chap who's asleep. I don't suppose it was put there for my benefit, but I didn't like it."

"I tell you, my dear sir, you must be mistaken!"

"And I tell *you* . . . !"

Out in the hall, making them both jump, began the strident ringing of the telephone.

The spell was broken, the thread of confidences snapped off. Colonel Selby, white-faced, dragged his gaze away from Garth's, craning round to look towards the fireplace. Again his hands tightened round the chair-arms.

Many footsteps seemed to be stirring in the hall. The ringing of the telephone ceased. Ordinarily, with so thick a door between, you could have heard no distinct voice from there. It was only that Michael Fielding, like so many people who used the telephone nowadays, felt compelled to shout at it.

"Mrs. Bostwick?" he was saying. "Yes, the doctor's here. But I'm afraid I can't disturb him. No, I can't. If it's as urgent as all that, Mrs. Bostwick, can't you leave a message?"

Another voice had joined that of Michael, who made shushing noises, after which both were obscured in a shattering din as somebody started up the engine of a car out in the street. Garth turned back to his visitor.

"You see, Colonel Selby—"

But Colonel Selby had risen to his feet.

"Sorry," he blurted out.

"I beg your pardon?"

"Afraid I can't go through with this. Afraid I've wasted your time. Damned shame, but there it is. You'll excuse me, Doctor?"

The car-engine was still exploding like a lively Bonfire Night. Colonel Selby's mood, Garth sensed, had changed from any he felt before that moment. Suddenly he lifted both hands, pressed them hard over his eyes, and dropped them as though in an appeal Garth was powerless to answer.

"You'll excuse me, Doctor? You won't try to stop me?"

"Stop you? No; hardly. At the same time, if I can be of any service, I hope you'll think this matter over."

"Thanks. I will. Here's my card. Send your account round,

eh? Wouldn't have troubled you for the world, except . . . My hat and stick: in the waiting-room. May I?"

"Colonel Selby, there are reasons why I ask you to reconsider!"

"Doctor, I can't reconsider. What's done is done now."

Suppressed violence and all, he bowed with a good deal of dignity. Garth bowed in reply. At the same moment, a thing unprecedented, Michael Fielding threw open the door of the consulting-room without being summoned and without waiting to knock.

"Sir," he began, "there's a Scotland Yard man here who won't go away and won't take no for an answer. But that's not all."

"Mr. Fielding," Garth interrupted with cold savagery, "will you be good enough to escort Colonel Selby to the door?"

"I can't help it, sir! There's just been a telephone-message we can't ignore."

"*Mr. Fielding.*" Garth counted to three. "Will you be good enough to escort Colonel Selby to the door? His hat and stick are in the waiting-room. Will you do this?"

"Yes, sir."

The explosions of the car-engine thickened to a roar, altered their tempo, and rolled away down Harley Street. A hollow of silence filled the consulting-room when Michael and Colonel Selby had gone. Garth stood behind his desk, staring down at the blotter without seeing it.

Then someone coughed. Garth looked up. Inspector George Alfred Twigg, non-committal under the curly-brimmed bowler hat, was watching him from the doorway.

"Ah, Doctor! Seems like we're fated to meet this evening."

"If you have been following me, it was more or less inevitable that we should. I hope you weren't waiting too long outside?"

"Ah! That's as may be. Mind if I come in?"

"A consulting-room is usually supposed to be private. But by all means come in. We shall be rid of you the sooner. You must excuse me for a moment, though."

"Oh?"

"For a moment, .I said. I must see to something in the waiting-room." Garth gestured politely towards the black leather chair. "Make yourself comfortable, Inspector."

And he strode out into the hall.

Betty, he supposed, must still be in the little library; its door was closed. The big front door stood partly open to a haze of gaslamps in the street. Going to the waiting-room, Garth threw open that door and looked round from the threshold.

Two lace-curtained windows fronted the street. Colonel Selby had been given time to smoke at least one cigar here; its stub was ground out in a china dish on the centre table, and the scent hung in close air. A dreary room, full of past emotions from those who waited, it had a lamp of mosaic glass burning on the table above scattered magazines. A novel, called *By Whose Hand?* and recently published at six shillings, lay open at its frontispiece.

Though Garth could not see Colonel Selby or Michael Fielding in the street, he heard Colonel Selby say some indistinct words. He heard Michael with a cab-whistle repeatedly blowing the one blast that was the signal to summon a four-wheeler.

"Mrs. Blanche Montague," Garth was thinking.

One blast for a four-wheeler, two for a hansom, three for a motor taxicab. As the single shrill note continued, he did not go near the open book on the waiting-room table. He had seen it before. Instead he was reconstructing memories of the night when he and Vincent Bostwick, also in a four-wheeler, drove up the steep streets of Hampstead to the house at Nag's Corner.

They took the route by way of Swiss Cottage and Fitzjohn's Avenue, the latter hill a hard pull for a cab even when there was no mud. In Church Row they turned to the right, past St. John's Churchyard, up a narrow and even steeper track like a country lane.

Colonel Selby's house was surrounded by a high stone wall pierced with two iron-grilled gates. Though he was not wealthy, Vince said, you might judge he had some private means beyond his retirement half-pay. Mrs. Montague, a dumpy figure with grey-streaked black hair, sat in one corner. Marion laughed. Three persons had committed suicide in the house.

"Stop this!" Garth said to himself.

Turning round, he hurried back to the consulting-room and stopped with something of a shock at his heart.

Inspector Twigg sat serenely in the big chair. Twigg's hat lay beside him on the floor. He was holding the black briefcase, stamped above its clasp with the gilt letters *D.G.*, which Garth had left on the telephone-table in the hall. Twigg held it up and tapped it.

"This thing is locked."

"That's right."

"This thing is locked. Mind opening it up for me?"

"Yes. I do mind." With an effort Garth controlled himself. "You know, Inspector, I've seldom found your equal for sheer unadulterated cheek. It's a new experience to meet you. By Jove, it's almost a pleasure! Have you got a search-warrant?"

"Not yet I haven't."

"Then the case stays locked."

A red bar showed across Twigg's forehead. His ruminating gaze moved across to one corner of the consulting-room, where a screen hid a wash-basin as well as Garth's cloak and top-hat. In sudden wrath the eyes returned and fastened on Garth's evening-clothes.

"You gentlemen are all alike. You think the world's yours. You think you can do what you like and how you like and *as* you like. Maybe, before long, you'll wish you'd been a bit more helpful when you were given the chance."

"Are we getting back to this question of someone who's been leading a double life?"

"By jing, we are!"

"What do you want here? Out with it!"

"Now there's no call to lose your temper, sir," urged Inspector Twigg, raising his hand in a massive gesture like a bishop. "There's not the least little call in the world. But I'll tell you. It's about a friend of yours who's got very peculiar tastes. Some people might claim, maybe, the lady's just a wee bit touched in the head—"

"The lady?"

"That's what I said. And that's what Mr. Cullingford Abbot claims, though I'm a chapel-goer and I've always had a different word for it. Still, that's not the point. It's no business of ours how the lady carries on, or what kind of a reputation she's got, just as long as she keeps away from the law. But she won't, Doctor. She hasn't. I'm just warning you."

"Oh? Of what? If there has been some nonsensical charge against Mrs. Bostwick—"

"Mrs. Bostwick?" echoed the other.

Twigg rose to his feet, slowly, looming large under the bleak light.

"Now who said anything about Mrs. Bostwick?" he asked. "Who mentioned Mrs. Bostwick? I'm not talking about Mrs. Bostwick, in case you hadn't guessed it. I'm talking about your good friend Lady Calder."

3

"Inspector, what's the joke?"

"There's no joke. Except maybe (just excuse me for saying this, will you?), except maybe the fool you've been making of yourself when you thought nobody noticed. This Lady Calder, now: do you know who she is?"

"She is the widow of a man named Sir Horace Calder, who was Governor of Jamaica between 1900 and 1905. He died in '05."

"Oh, ah!" Twigg opened his eyes wide. "She's that, right enough. We'll give her credit for brains. Do you know what else she is?"

"*What* else she is?"

"You've got ears, sir. I'm using the English language. You met her at Ostend, now didn't you?"

"I did."

"Last summer, that was?"

"If it's any of your business, yes."

"She'd gone there after spending six months in Paris. What had she been doing in Paris?"

"I can't tell you."

"*I* can," said Twigg. He threw the brief-case on the desk, where its silvered catch flashed and dazzled. "Before she married old Sir Horace, she was one of four good-looking sisters born out Hoxton way and brought up as dancers for the stage. The Moulin Rouge in Paris is quite a place. But the old gentleman left her well off. So there must be a reason why she went back there last year, when she didn't need to for a display we'll not discuss. I don't know the reason; I don't care. About what she is, I can tell you short and sweet. She's a blackmailer and a professional prostitute."

"Is that what you say? Then you'd better retract it."

" 'Retract?' 'Retract?' " Twigg mimicked heavily. "That's a fine word, that is! That's a fine fancy word for a gentleman who knows all about people's minds, and thinks he sees dewy-eyed innocence, and then finds he's been had for a mug."

"God damn your soul," said Garth—and took a sudden step forward.

"I wouldn't try any games, Doctor. Maybe you can put me out of here; maybe you can't. But you'll see trouble if you try that with a police-officer. And it'll look fine in the newspapers, won't it, for a grand Harley Street specialist like you?"

Garth stopped.

So, in a sense, did Inspector Twigg. It was that maddening word "retract" which made the little eyes grow congested in the big face. Now, evidently conscious he had gone too far, he altered his tone and spoke cajolingly.

"I wish you'd get it out of your head, sir, that we're trying to trap you or do you down. We're not. That's straight. If you'd come along to the Yard when I asked you to, you could have heard all this from Mr. Abbot. He's the Commissioner's secretary. He's your friend."

"I'm fully aware of that, thank you."

"Well! He could have broken it gentle-like." Then Twigg stared. "God's truth, Doctor, you haven't asked this woman to marry you?"

Garth said nothing.

"Yes, I believe you have! Now you're wondering if she's serious. Oh, she'll be serious enough as far as you're concerned! The lady's pushing thirty, as I understand it. If she wants to catch somebody near enough her own age, she won't get many more offers. This is a last chance. But you're not having any more of it, I hope?"

"This concern for my welfare is very touching. What exactly, is Lady Calder supposed to have done?"

"God's truth, do you believe one word I've been telling you?"

"No, I do not."

"There's a telephone in the passage," said Twigg, stabbing out his forefinger, "and Mr. Abbot's still at the Yard. Talk to him! Ask him! If you won't believe me, will you believe him?"

Garth felt a trifle light-headed.

"We can do better than that, I think. We'll put the matter up to Lady Calder herself. Stay where you are, Inspector."

Anger, no doubt, is a sign of weakness or uncertainty; it is an emotional luxury which ought not to be indulged. And he must be very careful with George Alfred Twigg, Garth reflected. Twigg's serene and fishy superiority towered above your wits, less outmatching them than ignoring them. Yet there were times when giving way to one's anger was the only way to keep any kind of mental balance.

Though Twigg said something behind him, Garth paid no attention. He went to the little library, rapped his knuckles on the door, and opened it.

That room was empty.

The street-door remained ajar, creaking in a faint draught.

Footsteps sounded on the pavement outside. Michael Fielding, rather out of breath, bounded up the front steps and let the front door close behind him with a hollow slam.

"Sorry to take so long," he said. "We had to walk as far as Devonshire Place before we could find a cab for Colonel Selby." Then Michael woke up. "If you're looking for Lady Calder, Doctor, she's gone."

"Gone?"

"In the motor-car. I thought you knew. That car of yours makes as much noise as a couple of Maxim-guns."

"Why did Lady Calder go?"

"Doctor, that's not important! I've been trying to tell you about the message from Mrs. Bostwick. It seems—"

"Mr. Fielding, *will* you be good enough to explain what happened here?"

Through the dusky hall, past ornamental palms, Michael approached with the look of a young man now growing as puzzled as he had been ruffled.

"Well, sir, it was a minute or two before Colonel Selby left. It did seem a bit odd, now you mention it; but I had too many things to think about the same time. Lady Calder and I were sitting in the little library, there," he gestured towards it, "when that police-officer knocked at the front door. He said he was from Scotland Yard and the rest of it. I told him you were engaged, but he brushed past into the waiting-room without so much as a by-your-leave."

"Yes?"

"The next thing I knew, Lady Calder ran straight out to the car. She threw her motoring-wraps into the tonneau, and took the starting-handle out of that box beside the front. I thought, 'Here, hullo! She can't drive a motor-car, can she? And she's not strong enough to turn over a starting-handle, surely? It'll break her wrist if she tries.' "

"Lady Calder," Garth retorted, "is not especially strong. But she's sturdy enough, as you seem to have observed. After all, she belongs to the Royal Life-Saving Society."

"Sir?"

"The Royal Life-Saving Society. Bayley Street, Bedford Square. There are ways to rescue a person in danger of drowning, and carry the victim out of the water for artificial respiration."

"Sir, what are you talking about?"

It would not be true to say that waters were closing over David Garth's own head. Yet he retained all too vivid a memory of just such an exercise on the beach near Fairfield, and of Betty's face and body outlined against hard-packed white sand.

"I am telling you, Mr. Fielding, this lady did not run away."

"Deuce take it, who says she did? I thought she might need help, that's all. I was going out to lend a hand when the telephone rang. It was Mrs. Bostwick, very upset about an attempted murder—"

"Mr. Fielding, come with me."

In the little library, as in the consulting-room, four electric bulbs glowed in shades like glass flowers. Morris chairs and smoking-stands gave the room an air of shabby comfort. Round the walls, at irregular heights, ran glass-fronted bookcases with enamelled designs on their doors and more than medical works on the shelves.

First, above Michael's shoulder as the young man faced him, Garth saw the reflection of his own face in the glass door of a bookcase. Next, conspicuous among heavy darkish volumes, he saw another red-bound novel by the author who chose to be called "Phantom."

"Now, Michael, suppose we hear about this telephone conversation. I am to have dinner with Mr. and Mrs. Bostwick later tonight. Mrs. Bostwick was speaking from Hyde Park Gardens, I imagine?"

"No, sir. From Hampstead."

"From Colonel Selby's house?"

"So I understood, anyway. She said she'd got to speak to you, and said, 'That woman will be the death of me.'"

"What woman?"

"That's the part I'm not clear about. None of it was easy. As soon as I said, 'Mrs. Bostwick?' or, 'Is that you, Mrs. Bostwick?' after she identified herself, this Scotland Yard detective was out of the waiting-room like a shot and standing beside me. He kept saying, 'Yes, my lad? What does Mrs. Bostwick want?' I couldn't shush him or make him go away, so it wasn't easy to hear."

"Michael, just how does Inspector Twigg come to know anything of Marion Bostwick?"

"Sir, I don't know! Why don't you ask him?"

"Yes; I propose to. But not until I have a little more information. . . . Wait one moment, now!"

So pervasive was the presence of Detective-Inspector Twigg that Garth half expected to find him standing by the telephone out in the hall. He was not there, though he could be heard whistling between his teeth in the waiting-room. Garth snatched up the telephone, mouthpiece and earpiece at opposite ends of a single instrument hanging from its hook, with a metal ridge along the barrel which must be pressed down before the other person could hear you speak.

Scotland Yard! Cullingford Abbot!

The building called New Scotland Yard was still fairly new, as time went. Its architect had designed it to look like a donjon-keep: massive, built of red and white brick with a conical tower at each corner, and a flying bridge across the courtyard to an annexe on the south. It had been over-crowded since the Metropolitan Police moved their head-quarters from Old Scotland Yard up the road. It was a constant headache of expense.

And yet nothing had changed so much, during these past seventeen years, as the public's attitude towards the Criminal Investigation Department.

When they first occupied the new building, Garth well remembered, both Criminal Investigation Department and Uniformed Branch still faced uproar from their recent failure to find Jack the Ripper. This failure was not greatly the police's fault; reforms of efficiency had already begun. But it seemed as distant as the dark ages. Such reforms were felt only when from the Indian Civil Police they imported Mr. Edward Henry, now Sir Edward Henry, as Metropolitan Commissioner.

Detractors ceased to jeer. In 1905, with the conviction of the Muswell Hill murderers, the system of identification by fingerprints was admitted as evidence for the first time in a British court. Police and public were coming of age.

If most of the triumph must be given to Sir Edward Henry, Cullingford Abbot could claim a great deal of credit too. They called Abbot the Commissioner's "secretary" because no official term existed. Abbot was a colleague; at times he directed the C.I.D.

Edward Henry was a professional civil servant, Cullingford Abbot a well-to-do dilettante with a mission. Edward Henry was brusque but reticent; Abbot, single eyeglass raised and greying moustache a-bristle, became a public figure who dined most evenings in the large blue-and-gilt room at the Café Royal. Abbot could be brusque, but he could also be under-standing. His private hobby was a study of the occult and the supernatural, and yet he worshipped mechanical progress.

"Pray remember," he had told Garth less than a fortnight ago, "that good police-work is simply good organization plus new ideas. This game of yours: what d'ye call it? Psychanal-ysis?"

"Psychanalysis is one term, yes."

"Well! We forced the judges to accept fingerprints. We'll soon force 'em to admit a bullet fired from a rifled barrel can be identified just as infallibly. One day we may be using psych-analysis too."

And so Garth, now making a telephone call to Cullingford Abbot at Scotland Yard, hoped for much in the way of good sense. Then his hopes were swept away.

"Mistake?" repeated Abbot's brisk, benevolently cynical voice. "Oh, no. Inspector Twigg's not an impostor and there's no mistake. I'm afraid there's no mistake, either, about the lady down at Fairfield."

"Betty Calder?"

"That's the gel."

"Seriously, now, can you expect me to credit all that nonsense? Or give one sound reason why it should be so?"

"My dear Garth," Abbot said impatiently, "I can't help what you credit or don't credit. It *is* so. As for reasons, they're older than your psychanalysis. You're forgetting the men concerned."

"What men?"

"When a countryman of ours wants to get away from home and kick up his heels, especially a married man, he takes the boat-train straight to Paris. That's true, isn't it? It happens to a good many people?"

"Yes. It happens to you too."

"Oh, undoubtedly." There was a snap in Abbot's voice. "But I'm not the man concerned in the latest affair of blackmail."

"Who is the man, then?"

"Do you want me to tell you on the telephone?"

"Yes."

"It's a friend of yours named Bostwick. Vincent Bostwick." ("Dear God!")

Garth glanced back over his shoulder. From his position at the telephone-table he could see straight into the little library and slantwise into the consulting-room. Michael Fielding stood facing out from the bookcases; Twigg was now at the consulting-room door. Both had congealed motionless, though Twigg continued to whistle between his teeth, as if both could hear that thin voice over the wire.

"Garth! Confound it! Are you there?"

"I'm still here."

"Let me read you a little of the woman's record," continued Abbot. "Maiden name(interesting term, eh?) Elizabeth Stukeley. Before old Calder married her, in his seventy-third year and also his dotage, she had been a dancer for three seasons at the Moulin Rouge. They've always liked English beauties there. Ever see her without her clothes?"

"I have not yet," Garth said politely, "had that pleasure."

"My reference," Abbot retorted with equal suavity, "was to seeing her in a bathing-costume. I'm told you've done that once or twice. But take the reference as it strikes your mind. Ever notice her legs? They're a dancer's legs. Now, then.

"While she was a dancer at the Moulin Rouge, three men had particular trouble with her after they'd returned to England. I can't reveal their names, but names don't matter. One was a stockbroker, one was M.P. from a good Conservative district, and one was head of a private banking firm. In each case your friend Betty followed him, and wrote to him or called on him. If he avoided her, she finally called on the man's wife. We don't know what happened in two cases; it was hushed up. However, the banker shot himself."

There was a silence.

Inspector Twigg went on whistling tunelessly.

"He shot himself during the autumn of '02, I see," observed Abbot. "H'm! Miss Betty escaped scot-free; the dead man's relatives acknowledged there had been blackmail, but refused to press charges. The following summer she married Sir Horace Calder and disappeared to Jamaica until Calder's death two years later. Last summer, before she met you at Ostend, she was back at the Moulin Rouge."

Again Cullingford Abbot paused. It was easy to picture him: vigorous, insatiably alert, his monocle gripped in his left eye, bending over papers.

"Look here, Garth. Calder is believed to have left her well off. But I wonder! That beach-cottage is a very modest place, I take it?"

"What else should it be?"

"True. At the same time, her home in London seems to be a not very impressive semi-detached house at Putney Hill. There's another fact that may be of more than academic interest. Last summer, also in Paris, we think she joined a Satanist group."

"A what?"

"A Satanist group. Rather lewd rites in adoration of Old Scratch. There's always one in Paris for a few fanatics and a larger group of bored sensation-seekers."

"Abbot, for God's sake! It's not being maintained, I hope, that Betty has developed supernatural powers?"

"No. Hardly. But you were asking for reasons. If she needs money, it explains why she's gone back to the Moulin Rouge for a little blackmail. If she's joined a Satanist group, it explains why she enjoys appearing in the near-nude. Lots of women, even respectable ones, would take pleasure in that if only they dared. Don't let it upset you, my dear fellow."

"It's not upsetting me," said Garth.

"Really? I thought—"

"Never mind. A minute ago you claimed Vince Bostwick

was—was somehow involved with Betty. Is there any actual evidence of that?"

"Mr. Bostwick, they tell me, was in Paris last summer."

"So were thousands of tourists. I said evidence. Did he ever meet her? Did she 'follow him' to London, as you say she followed the others? Did she ever write to him or try to see him?"

"No," Abbot answered almost with admiration, "there's no evidence whatever."

"Well?"

"I'm afraid there doesn't need to be. She's got no change out of Bostwick, that's apparent." Then Abbot's tone changed. "But the old, old game is being played in the old, old way. Confound it, Garth! Three times in the past fortnight she's called on *Mrs.* Bostwick at Hyde Park Gardens."

"How do you know she has?"

"Because Inspector Twigg has made it his business to keep an eye on her."

"Twigg again, eh?"

"If I were you, my dear fellow, I shouldn't underrate him. He's not always easy to get on with, but he's a capable officer. He never lets go. If you put his back up you'll make a bad enemy."

"Well, well, well!" observed Inspector Twigg, himself intervening at this point. "Well, well, well!"

It was impossible to tell whether Twigg had even gained an impression of Abbot's words on the telephone. Rising on his toes in the doorway of the consulting-room, he lowered himself with satisfaction. The light behind him shone on a bald skull plastered with a few strands of brownish hair. Then briskly, he strode towards Garth.

"Abbot," Garth said to the telephone, "I will say good-bye now."

"Stop! Wait! You haven't told me—"

"I will say good-bye now," Garth repeated. He rang off.

"That's just as well, Doctor," Twigg said heartily. "So we'll just hear," and he jerked his thumb towards Michael Fielding in the little library, "we'll just hear what the *young* gentleman has to say. About Mrs. Bostwick's message on the telephone."

"Mr. Fielding," and Garth raised his voice, "you will tell this man nothing. Is that clear? You will tell this man nothing."

He spoke through stiff jaws. He could feel if not see that his own face was white. Twigg stopped short.

"I want no more trouble here, Doctor."

"Nor do I. Mrs. Bostwick is my patient," it was the first lie he had told, "and any communication from her is privileged.

You have no further business in this house, Mr. Twigg. Both of us will be happy to excuse you."

"Now I warn you, sir—!"

"Yes?" Garth waited. "That's the second time you have used those words and the dozenth time you have implied them. You warn me of what?"

"Of landing in bad trouble. Mrs. Bostwick's at Hampstead. I've only to go out there—"

"On the contrary, Mr. Twigg, I am warning *you*. Let me repeat that Mrs. Bostwick is my patient. If you attempt to see her without my permission, either tonight or at any time, you are the one who will land in trouble and very well you know it. There's the door: now get out."

"I won't be told . . . !"

Both of them had powerful voices, the Inspector's hoarse and Garth's clear-edged. Echoes slipped round the white arch of the hall and bounded back in clamour. For perhaps ten seconds Twigg looked at him in noisy breathing. Then Twigg nodded. Returning to the consulting-room to fetch his hat, he marched out over the black-and-white tiles: carefully, as though on tiptoe. At the front door he hesitated, half turning again. He did not speak, but his glance at Garth was more ominous than any word.

The door closed after him.

Wryness, a release of taut nerves, went up through Garth's throat. That wryness ended almost in a smile.

"All right, Michael. What *did* Mrs. Bostwick say?"

"Look here, sir, was that wise? Chucking him out, I mean?"

"I don't know. I am beginning not to care. No, that's untrue; I do care! As you were saying, about Mrs. Bostwick?"

Michael strode out of the little library.

"She wants you to go out there just as soon as you possibly can. She begs it, sir. She's in earnest."

"So I gathered. What seems to be the trouble?"

"While Mrs. Bostwick was alone in the house with her aunt, some woman got in and tried to kill Mrs. Montague. Tried to strangle her. Very nearly did."

"If they want a doctor—"

"They don't. Not in that particular way. Mrs. Bostwick called their own doctor at Hampstead. But she does rather desperately want to consult you about a private matter. This woman that got into the house, and then somehow disappeared through the cellar—"

"Who was the woman?"

"Mrs. Bostwick didn't say," Michael answered after a pause. His tongue crept out to moisten his lips. "Considering what's been half hinted and half looked out of the corners of eyes here tonight, I should hate like the devil to guess."

Garth made no comment.

Brushing past the young man, whose Adam's apple rose and fell above a tall collar, he went into the consulting-room. He went to the mantelpiece, on whose ledge the silver-framed photograph of Betty Calder stood to the left of the clock against a background of ferns and flowers painted on a looking-glass.

There was another photograph of Betty, a smaller Kodak snapshot, inside the notecase in his inside breast pocket. He touched the pocket. Neither photograph could show the colour of the hair and eyes as a vivid brown, or the colour of the half-parted lips as pink. But the face in the silver frame seemed alive, with a strength and passion of innocence, and looked back at him.

"Sir," Michael burst out, "what is going on?"

Again Garth touched his coat over the inside breast pocket. He drew the watch out of the pocket of his white waistcoat, pressed the stem to open its case, calculated times, then shut up the watch and replaced it.

"Sir, I just asked . . . !"

"Yes," Garth said. "I heard you." He turned round. "Would you mind trying for another cab, please? Whatever may be going on, I mean to prove it is not what they think."

4

Marion Bostwick sauntered back and forth in the drawing-room.

She was stately and unhurried. She seemed to be pondering. The hem of her bell-shaped skirt brushed the carpet as she moved.

David Garth, descending the stairs, could look down sideways past the bannisters towards the lighted door of the drawing-room. He stopped for a minute or two, deciding what he ought to say. Then he went on.

Of this house on the heights, itself so tall and narrow as to seem topheavy, he had an impression slightly different from that of his first visit. You still felt uneasiness, a disquiet of atmosphere, a wish to glance back over your shoulder without knowing why. Yet the house seemed a little less dark and cavernous than he remembered. In the drawing-room stood golden-oak chairs, gaunt without upholstery, a high gloss on their carving. The polished golden-oak table had drawers with bright brass loop-handles. There was a mounted tiger's head on the wall above the mantelpiece.

Again Marion passed the door, pressing a lace handkerchief to her upper lip. She wore a semi-formal gown, tight across hips and bust, of some satiny blue material rather darker than the colour of her pale-blue eyes. She started when she heard his footsteps, peering round above the handkerchief.

"Yes, David?"

"They were smallish hands," he said.

"I beg your pardon?"

"The hands that strangled Mrs. Montague. Smallish, but very strong. They caught her from behind; the marks of the fingernails show in her neck. She is lucky to be alive."

"Oh!" Marion's eyes widened. "Oh. Yes, I know. Poor Aunt Blanche! How did you find her?"

"Sleeping."

"I mean, what was her condition when you examined her?"

"I only looked at her superficially. I didn't examine her. She is not my patient."

"You men and your stupid ethics!" Then Marion checked her impatient gesture. "You know, David, I rather wish you hadn't come."

"You sent for me."

"So I did, dear. But even I," said Marion, lifting one shoul-

31

der and turning out her wrist, "even *I* can have the vapours
like any other person. Fortunately it's not so serious after
all."

"It's quite serious enough, Marion. You'd better tell me
what happened."

"How do you mean?"

"As I understand it, I was to have dinner with you and
Vince at Hyde Park Gardens. What are you doing here?"

"Oh, that? Yes, I do owe you an explanation. Though I'm
the one who was put upon and I don't like it and I won't have
it! David, Aunt Blanche sent for *me.*"

Marion's eyes had acquired a certain fixity. Drawing a deep
breath, she sat down very straight in one of the massive chairs
and motioned him towards another.

"David, she telephoned. That's extraordinary. Aunt Blanche
hates the telephone and won't touch it. But this time she was
obliged to use it. She'd sent all the servants out of the house,
she said; packed them off at a moment's notice, and told them
not to come back until late tonight. Some woman was going
to call on her, she said mysteriously, and she didn't care to be
alone in the house. Could I come immediately and keep her
company. Now, really!"

"Yes?"

Garth, who had remained standing, inclined his head. The
light of two lamps shed a deathly pallor on the high gloss of
furniture. Benares brass glimmered in corners.

"Uncle Sel spends every Wednesday and Friday evening at
his club; he wouldn't be here in any case. And Vince was out,
as he usually is, so I couldn't send *him.* Still, it was hardly
eight o'clock. You had said you couldn't be at Hyde Park
Gardens before ten o'clock at the earliest. I thought I really
ought to humour this ridiculous whim of Aunt Blanche's; at
least I could return in good time.

"David, it wasn't a ridiculous whim.

"First I was stupid enough to take a motor taxicab. And the
driver was foolish enough to try that enormous long hill up
Fitzjohn's Avenue. The motor gave a jump and went dead before we were two-thirds of the way up. Then it seemed that
the brakes weren't going to hold, as they don't half the time;
we began to slip backwards; I could almost feel the car
rolling all the way down out of control. That's what would
have happened if the driver hadn't managed to wrench it over
and stop with the left back wheel against the kerb.

"I daresay that's not important, except that I was nervous.
I walked the rest of the way, and through the gate in the wall
out there, and up to the front door. The front door was partway open. It was still daylight, but Aunt Blanche kept all the

blinds drawn on the ground floor. When I stepped inside it was dark. That was when I heard Aunt Blanche's voice crying out.

"She was talking to someone on the upstairs landing. I could just see the two of them behind the balustrade along the landing up at the back of the hall. Aunt Blanche was repeating one word, over and over and over. David, the word was *whore*. That's what she kept shouting: 'Whore, whore, whore.' "

Marion paused.

All the flush and colour rushed back into her face. But the expression of the eyes remained fixed. Briefly, for one flash, the poise and stateliness dissolved; an adolescent peered out through those eyes.

Garth sat down in the carved chair opposite. He moved slowly. He sat there listening, his elbow on the chair-arm and his chin in his hand, without looking up.

"David, I never heard Aunt Blanche use that word before. All of a sudden she stopped, and didn't say anything at all. There was an odd kind of noise. I ought to have gone straight up the front stairs. But I didn't; I ran through the house and up the back stairs. By the time I got there, on the front landing near Aunt Blanche's room—well, you were right. That woman had her by the throat.

"Aunt Blanche was face down on the straw matting. The other woman was bending over with her back to me. Then *I* shouted something, and she looked round. There's a coloured-glass window at one end of the landing. She was about as far away from me as I am from you. I jumped at her and raised my arms like this. And she ran straight down the front stairs.

"The front door was wide open; I thought she was making for that, when she groped round and ran back like a blind person. I shouldn't have understood, except that I fell over Aunt Blanche. If you're near the floor on the landing up there, you can look out through the balustrades to the front gate. There was a policeman out at the gate, looking in.

"The policeman went on. It was a warm night, and not dark; he must have thought the open gate and door were all right. The woman didn't see him go. There's only one other way out of a house like this: down the enclosed cellar-stairs from a door under the main stairs, and through the cellar to a basement-entrance at the side of the house. She made for it.

"This is the silliest part, now. All I could think was, 'We've got her, we've got her.' When she ran down into the cellar, I followed as far as the door to the cellar stairs. It's got a big heavy bolt on this side. I shot the bolt, and held it in place and completely forgot there weren't any servants down there waiting. All she had to do was open the basement door from inside, and go out by the side gate without being seen.

"I was still holding the bolt when I heard the basement door open and slam. It was so quiet I thought I heard her running to the gate, though I may have imagined that. Then I was alone, and it was beginning to get dark, and Aunt Blanche was lying up there without moving."

Again Marion paused.

"I see," observed Garth.

"David dear," Marion said in a totally different voice, "how very tiresome this must be for you! And how dreadfully tiresome I must seem too!"

It was as though no storm of weeping had ever existed. Marion rose up. She had dropped the lace handkerchief; the palms of her hands were pressed together. Five feet eight in height, statuesque again, she sauntered across towards the fireplace.

"It was all very dreadful about Aunt Blanche," she added, turning with her back to the mantelpiece, "and nobody feels it more deeply than I do. But it might have been very much worse, you know."

"No doubt." Garth followed her with his eyes. "When you discovered this intruder had disappeared, Marion, what did you do?"

"Really—!"

"What did you do? Did you communicate with the police?"

"No, I did not. Whatever would have been the good? Besides, think of the talk! Think what people might say!"

"You didn't report an attempted murder because it might cause talk?"

"My poor darling David, that's how the world is. I learned it when I was fourteen years old, thanks very much, and I've never forgotten. When Aunt Blanche recovers, and she's able to talk to me or you or anyone else, I'm sure she'll be the first to agree."

"Possibly she will. But you haven't told me what you did?"

"I telephoned to Dr. Fortescue, of course. He was here within two or three minutes, and between us we got the poor, silly old woman into bed."

"Did you tell him the story you have just told me?"

"I didn't tell him anything, dear."

"You understand, I hope, that Dr. Fortescue will have to report this affair to the police? If, in fact, he hasn't already done so?"

"No, David, I'm afraid I don't understand anything of the

kind. Dr. Fortescue won't say a word. He'll stand by us. People always stand by us."

"I see. A certain woman, whoever she was, brutally attacked and nearly killed Mrs. Montague on the upstairs landing. Aren't you at all concerned, Marion? Don't you want to see her punished?"

"Oh, I want to see her punished." The pale-blue eyes slid sideways. "I don't think anyone will ever, ever know," Marion breathed, "how much I want to see her punished and make her suffer! But I'll manage in my own way, if you don't mind."

"Did you recognize this woman?"

" 'Recognize' her?"

"Had you ever seen her before?"

"Great heavens, no. How absurd!"

"Do you know who she is?"

"No."

"Can you think of a reason why anyone should want to kill Mrs. Montague?"

"Really, David, I make no pretensions to being a mind-reader. Why ever do you ask?"

"If you never saw her before, and don't know who she is or what motive she may have had, it may be a trifle difficult to find her unless the police do. For instance, could you describe her?"

"She looked . . well! I won't use that word again; it's repulsive and disgusting. But she looked to be just what poor Aunt Blanche said she was."

"We were speaking of her appearance, Marion, not her character. Can you describe that appearance?"

"Quite easily. She was about thirty, probably older. Shorter than I am: oh, four or five inches. Brown hair and eyes. Not very pretty, but I daresay tolerable enough for that profession."

"How was she dressed?"

"Her clothes were quite good. Tailored jacket and skirt of Navy-blue serge: from Redfern's, I should think. Stiff-pleated white blouse with lace at the neck. Small gold watch: Garrard or Lambert, it might be. Sailor straw hat with a blue-and-white band."

"By the way, Marion, at what time did you see her? Can you remember that too?"

"Oh, near enough! It was . . . *David.*"

She broke off.

Both of them had been speaking in studiously moderate tones, Garth with apparent disinterest and Marion addressing the wall between the two front windows. A pallor of lamplight shone on the sleek red hair piled above Marion's ears, and on golden-oak furniture, and in the glass eyes of the tiger's head high over the mantelpiece. The unpleasant atmosphere in this house (and Garth suddenly believed he knew its source) had so infected them both that Marion went rigid when they heard a footstep in the foyer.

"David," Marion repeated.

Garth sprang up, went out into the foyer, and almost collided with Vincent Bostwick.

"My dear old boy," drawled the equally startled Vince, who was wearing a grey summer suit and carrying a bowler hat, "are you stalking your prey or something?"

"I wish I could say I weren't."

They looked at each other.

"There was rather a curious note from Marion," Vince said in a louder voice, "when I got home."

"Marion's here, Vince. She's in there."

"Yes, old boy, but doesn't anybody ever answer the door? I must have knocked for five minutes."

"I'm afraid we didn't hear you. We were talking."

"Dash it, somebody might have heard me! I even went round and down those steps to the basement door at the side. There's a night-light in the kitchen; you can see it through the glass panel. But nobody answered; the place was locked up like a fortress. Back I came to the front door, on this Walpurgis night, and blow me to Bedminster if the ruddy front door hadn't been unfastened and on the latch after all. Greetings, old chap. I took the unusual course of just walking in."

"Vince, this isn't funny. All the servants are out. There's nobody here except—"

Garth stopped suddenly.

Perhaps Vince didn't think it funny either, though his air of amiability never wavered. In the long face, its planes and hollows sunburnt or windburnt, little amusement-wrinkles deepened. His crisp hair, parted in the middle, had begun to turn dry at the temples. Through Garth's mind a dozen images of Vince Bostwick, so deceptively different from the idler's look he showed the world, all ended in an image of Vince with Betty Calder.

Forget that! Forget it!

"Vince, are you sure?"

"Eh? Sure of what?"

"That the basement door is locked on the inside?"

"If we're going to be precise," retorted Vince, "I'm not sure the key is turned in the lock, no. But that door has a couple of good fool-the-burglar bolts, one at the top and one at the bottom. I'm pretty sure *they're* fastened. Does it make any odds?"

"Yes. There's been an accident. Go in and see Marion."

"What kind of accident?"

"Go in and see Marion."

Vince went.

Small night-noises creaked and crackled in the foyer. Its walls were panelled to head-height in dark oak; above it stretched roughish material like dull-red burlap. On the newel-post of the stairs a bronze figure of Diana, not very convincingly holding up one electric bulb, illumined stair-carpet, stair-rods, and the balustrade of the upper landing that faced the front door.

Garth glanced round.

He went to the back of the staircase. The entrance of the enclosed steps leading to the cellar, as Marion had said, was cut off by a door still heavily bolted. Garth drew the bolt, pressed an electric switch just inside, and went down into a cavern.

If the atmosphere of any house has grown oppressive enough for suicide, it may have been infected by too much emotion that has found outlet. "I can't stick this place," we have heard people say; "let's clear out." And if such feelings have been repressed, repressed and denied because they are thought to be abnormal or unnatural, the caged prisoner may become even more dangerous.

Garth explored that cellar. He moved through kitchen, servants' hall, pantry, larder, and laundry, turning on lights and watching blackbeetles scurry away. He looked into coal-bin as well as wine-cellar. Every semi-underground window had a locked catch and was sealed up with grime.

It was true that in the kitchen, the first as well as the last room he studied, the key had been turned to an open position in the lock of its big outside door. It was also true that both small tight bolts, top and bottom, remained fastened in their sockets. He needed a wrench of the wrist to open them.

An old-fashioned rush-light burned blue on the coal cooking range built into the flue of the chimney, bringing memories of his own boyhood. Its reflection glimmered in the glass panel of the door. Garth may have been in that cellar ten minutes; his footsteps rang on the wooden stairs as he hastened back. In the drawing-room, alone, Marion Bostwick sat back smiling at him.

"Marion, where is Vince?"

"He went up to see Aunt Blanche." Marion lowered her eyes. "I *said* the doctor had given her morphine."

"Did you tell him what happened?"

"Of course I did. Can't you feel the air shaking, sort of? He's upset, poor old boy. Good heavens, not that I blame him! David, weren't you asking me something just before Vince got here?"

"I was."

"About the time I saw that woman?"

"Yes."

"You won't pin me down in the matter of a minute or two?"

"No." .

Marion walked her fingers along the arm of the golden-oak chair. They slid out, sinuously questing, to touch his sleeve just above the left wrist. No doubt she did not mean to use her sensual allure, which was strong, but it flowed up from the expression of eyes and mouth when Marion lifted her head.

"I was very late, as I told you, from that wretched accident with the motor taxicab. I walked the rest of the distance. When I came in by the front door, it must have been about ten minutes to nine."

"Are you sure of that?"

"Yes. Quite sure. Oh, David, stop!"

She did not explain what she meant by "stop." Garth ignored it.

"You gave quite a good description of this woman, Marion. Would you recognize a photograph of her?"

"I beg your pardon?"

Reaching into his inside breast pocket, he extracted the note-case and took out a glossy-paper Kodak snapshot about the size of a postcard. It showed Betty Calder on the beach near her cottage, facing the morning sun, and behind her the bathing-pavilion built on its low stilts above the tide.

"Is that the woman you saw?"

"David, where did you get this?"

"Is that the woman you saw? Look at it, please. Is that the woman you saw?"

"Yes. Yes, it is! She doesn't wear stockings with a bathing-costume, does she? You don't know her, do you?"

"Yes, I know her quite well. Her name is Calder. She is the widow of a former Governor of Jamaica, and we are to be married some time this year."

"Oh, my God," Marion whispered after a pause. *"Oh, my God."* Her hands flew to her cheeks.

For all his assurance, for all his quiet speech, Garth's heart gave a painful bound and seemed to be choking him. What peered out of Marion's eyes was horror, commiseration, real affection.

"It doesn't matter what you've already said," he insisted, "provided you say it only to me. Or to Vince, if it comes to that. Don't go on saying it, that's all. You haven't been telling the truth, now have you?"

"But I have been telling the truth! I have! Every word!"

If he had not known better, he could have sworn Marion believed this. Garth controlled his voice.

"Marion, listen. At ten minutes to nine this evening, Betty Calder was at my house in Harley Street. She must have been talking to an assistant of mine named Michael Fielding. I myself can testify she was there at just nine o'clock; I was exactly on time for a professional appointment with—" He checked himself.

"With whom?"

"It doesn't matter. Let me stress the important fact. The house is so far from here that a matter of a few minutes, or ten minutes or even twenty minutes, makes no difference at all. Betty Calder couldn't possibly have been at Hampstead either before or after the time you say she was.

"That's point number one; it's irrefutable. The second point is equally strong. A while ago you told me this 'mysterious woman' ran out of the house by the basement door and slammed it when she left."

"And I still say so! It's true!"

"Marion, did you go down into the cellar at any time?"

"No! No, of course not!"

"Did anyone else go down there? Dr. Fortescue, for instance?"

"No; why ever should they?"

"Well, I did. The basement door was still secured with two tight, stiff bolts until I opened them a few minutes ago. A combination of Messrs. Maskelyne and Devant themselves couldn't have gone out by that way and left the door fastened on the inside. Even if you were mistaken about hearing the door open and close, your 'mysterious woman' couldn't have got out through a window; they're locked too. She couldn't have returned by way of the foyer; you yourself bolted the door to the cellar-stairs and left it bolted. And she's not there now."

"My poor David," cried Marion; who seemed less angry than badly upset on his behalf, "you're very much in love with this creature, aren't you?"

"Confound it, Marion—!"

"Well, aren't you?"

"Let's say I'm fond of her, yes. But forget that; don't run your own head into a noose. If the police learn of this affair, will they swallow any such childish story as yours?"

"Whereas, if they don't learn of it, I daresay your own high and mighty sense of professional ethics will compel you to tell them?"

"Damn my sense of professional ethics," Garth horrified himself by saying. "You and Vince have been closer to me than any person I ever knew except Betty. I'll protect you if it becomes necessary. I think you knew that when you brought me here to try me with your version of what happened. But leave Betty out of it. It's bad enough to hear her called a cheat and a whore. You'll not outrage common sense by saying she can be in two places at once or melt through solid walls."

Marion jumped up from the chair.

"Every word I told you," said Marion, articulating slowly through stiff jaws, "was the strict, sober, literal truth. And I hope to die if it's not. Make him believe me," she cried to the ceiling, and kicked her heels backwards like a child in a tantrum. "Dear God in heaven, make him believe me!"

A new voice, interrupting with a flurried "Hoy!" of protest, caught them in mid-flight as though a bucket of cold water had been flung over both.

Vince Bostwick, for once in his life rather pale, strode into the drawing-room over the bright-coloured Indian mats. He was smoking a cigarette, which, as he saw Marion's cold eye, he hastily crushed out in a brass bowl on a side table. Otherwise Vince appeared anything but mild.

"My dear old boy," he said, looking Garth up and down, "I never heard you carry on like that. I didn't know you could."

"Didn't you?" Marion cried, lifting her upper lip. "Didn't you really, now?"

"No. And a word in *your* ear, my pet. Did you persuade old Dr. Fortescue not to tell the police about your Aunt Blanche? Did you even ask him not to?"

"My poor Vince, it wasn't necessary. I hinted. He'll do what I ask."

"If you think so, my dear, you'd better look out of the front window."

Marion did not move.

"Uniforms," added Vince. "From what I remember of this district, one of 'em is the inspector from the police-station on Rosslyn Hill. Any comment, David?"

"A question, anyway," replied Garth, also turning to Marion. "You said you didn't tell Dr. Fortescue 'anything' about this business. What does that mean?"

"Well, I had to say *something*, hadn't I? I couldn't simply ignore it, could I? I said Aunt Blanche had been attacked by a woman who got away by the basement door, just as she really did. But I said she was probably a sneak-thief, and I didn't get a good enough look at her to be sure of her afterwards."

A sharp rapping at the front door, deferential but authoritative, echoed with hollow summons through the foyer.

"Then you better think of what you'll tell these chaps," said Vince.

Vince went out to answer the door, squaring his shoulders before he touched the knob. Garth followed him.

Outside at attention stood a bulky figure with a military air and a large grey moustache, wearing the flat uniform-cap of an inspector. The helmet of a constable rose behind him. Vince was always at his best with minor officials, who worshipped him.

"Oh, hullo," he said with welcoming lightness. "Er—Inspector Rogers, isn't it?"

"Sir!" said the Inspector, stiffening and saluting. "Colonel Selby at home, sir?"

"Colonel Selby is at the Oriental Club this evening, I'm afraid."

"Just between ourselves, sir, it wasn't the Colonel I wanted to see. You're Mr. Bostwick, aren't you? The Colonel's son-in-law?"

"Not exactly son-in-law, but that's near enough. Yes?"

Inspector Rogers's face grew even greater and more uncomfortable. He saluted again.

"Bad business, this, sir, about the poor lady who was hurt. Still! We've got a witness, sir, who believes she may be able to help if she can have ten minutes' conversation with Mrs. Bostwick."

"Witness?"

"Yes, sir. If you'll look out towards the gate, you'll see her sitting in the Panhard motor-car. Her name is Lady Calder."

5

"Lady Calder," Vince repeated.

He looked round at Garth.

"Yes, old boy," Vince's far-from-languid glance added, as plainly as though he had spoken, "I was listening to your last conversation with Marion."

From the top-floor windows of this house, Vince had once remarked, it was possible on a clear day to see out over one edge of the Heath as far as St. Paul's in the distance. Even if any such view had been possible now, Garth would not have looked at it.

An untidy front garden, with rhododendrons and a monkey-puzzle tree, stretched out to the high stone wall fronting Nag's Corner Road. Past a door in the wall, where the iron-grilled gate stood open, he could see the light of a street-lamp glimmering on the green paint and brasswork of the motor-car.

Garth's first thought was: "Inspector Rogers. How does Vince remember these names? How does he remember *all* their names, gratifying every man-jack of them?" Afterwards he could think only of Betty.

"Lady Calder," repeated Vince. "Thank you, Inspector. Ask Lady Calder to come in, won't you?"

"Very good, sir!"

In the foyer, which had known so much emotion, there was a similar sort of explosion. Marion Bostwick, skirts rustling, swept with imperious dignity out of the drawing-room and marched towards the rear of the foyer.

Drawing-room and dining-room were in the right-hand wall. At the end of the foyer, facing front, was a smaller room; and this, as Garth saw when Marion turned on a light inside, was the sort known as a man's den.

Betty Calder walked up the path from the gate.

She was pale under the straw hat with the blue-and-white band. It seemed that the shrinking, reticent Betty had gone past embarrassment, even past humiliation. Perhaps not quite past either; she hesitated when she saw Garth, and spots of colour appeared in her cheeks. But determination carried her on.

Inspector Rogers, the sort of police officer whom Garth liked and trusted as much as he disliked and distrusted

Inspector Twigg's kind, made sympathetic noises beside her.

"Now, my lady," he was saying, "this is Mr. Bostwick here. That's Mrs. Bostwick, back in the Colonel's study. This gentleman—?"

"I am acquainted with Dr. Garth," said Betty.

"Another doctor? Ah, I see! That's good."

Betty's waxen pallor did not change. It seemed all but inhuman. The bronze figure of Diana on the newel-post held a lamp that clearly illumined both women: Marion just inside the den, Betty facing her and slowly approaching.

Garth, falling into step beside Betty, said, "Gently!" and touched her elbow. Betty's whole body was trembling; her elbows were pressed against her sides, her arms back and fingers crisped like claws.

The emotional atmosphere shot up several degrees. With a sudden angry gesture Marion moved forward and stopped just as suddenly on the threshold of the den: not in fear, you sensed, but in wonder at what she saw. Betty stopped too. Then nothing stirred in the foyer of dark oak panelling and red burlap walls above.

Betty's soft voice rose up.

"Inspector," she cleared her throat, "will you please, please do what you half promised you would? Let me be alone with Mr. and Mrs. Bostwick for ten minutes? Yes, and with Dr. Garth too! Afterwards it doesn't matter what happens."

"Inspector—" Vince began quickly.

"Be quiet," said Garth.

"Well, now, my lady," fumed Inspector Rogers, "I don't know as I ought to do that. Still! You're a rare plucked 'un, unless I'm very much mistaken, so I'll risk it. Ten minutes, mind! Me and the constable will wait outside."

"You won't wait outside," said Vince. "There's whisky in the dining-room there. Help yourself. And the constable too."

"Well, sir . . ."

Marion, shoulders still back in regal dignity, retreated farther into the den. Betty followed, with Garth and Vince after her.

Three more big-game heads, a panther and a black buck and a snow-leopard, looked down from a dark wallpaper twined with flecks of dull gold. The room was redolent of cigars and of its brown-leather chairs. Framed photographs decorated the walls, mainly of shooting or of pig-sticking groups. There were no books except some bound copies of *The Field* on top of a glass cabinet enclosing a rifle-rack. Though the chandelier had been fitted for electricity, a green-shaded brass gas-lamp—Colonel Selby preferred old-fashioned ways—stood on his neat desk. Another tiger's head, this time with skin attached, lay on the floor.

Garth closed the door. He was still holding the Kodak snapshot, which he returned to his notecase. And Betty still refused to meet his eye.

"Look at me," she said to Marion. "Look at me again!"

"I am doing so, thanks very much."

"You didn't really see me in this house tonight, did you? You saw someone who looked rather like me, and was dressed exactly like me. I can't bear any more of her. I've tried, and I've tried very hard to be respectable too. But I can't bear any more of her."

"Her?" Marion cried. "Are you calling yourself so much of an innocent?"

"No, I am not innocent. I am almost what she is, except that I'm not a criminal. A good many times, when she was drunk, I appeared in her place on the bill. The worst of it is that in my heart I didn't really mind doing that; I even enjoyed it, until—"

She paused.

"But that's finished," Betty said. "If she tries just one more trick, so help me God, I mean to kill her and take the consequences. I'm not the person you saw, am I?"

"Do you know," exclaimed Marion, whom these statements seemed to fascinate as much as they startled and mollified, "I'm beginning to think you're not."

"*Betty*," Garth said gently.

"Don't touch me," Betty cried in her turn, and twitched her shoulder away. "You won't even want to touch me, after tonight. You don't understand."

"Betty, don't be a fool. Marion saw one of your sisters, I imagine, if in fact she saw anybody at all."

Vince Bostwick, who had been opening a silver cigarette-case, shut it up with a click. Betty faltered, the brown eyes turning towards Garth at last.

"How did you know that?"

"It's not a very complicated supposition, considering what Twigg said. Sit down there," he indicated a brown-leather sofa at right angles to the empty fireplace, "and let's understand the more obscure features."

"But—!"

"You too, Marion. The other end of the sofa."

"Oh, just as you please," sang Marion, with an elaborate kind of shrug. "I can't understand a word of all this, but just as you please."

"Come off it, Marion. You're not altogether ignorant of the blackmailing dancer from the Moulin Rouge."

"I have not the remotest idea . . . !"

"Sit down there, both of you. We're in a damned awkward situation, and we haven't much time to meet it." Garth waited. "That's better. Betty, when Inspector Twigg turned up in Harley Street tonight and said he wanted to see me about someone leading a double life, you felt panic and you ran away. That's understandable; no one could blame you. But what brought you first to the Hampstead police and then here? Where did you learn about Marion and Vince? I don't recall ever having mentioned them."

"Those things were accidents. I had better tell you about Glynis."

"Your sister?"

"Yes."

It would have been too much to expect those two women of all women to sit side by side like patient Griseldas, though Marion was the easier because she was frankly curious and did not seem at all ill-disposed towards Betty.

But Betty was no longer so much sustained by that desperate determination. For the first time, clearly, she felt this as a social occasion. She began to reflect on what she had been saying in the hearing of strangers. Betty rose up. Hesitant, with a quick little apologetic gesture of her gloved hand, she ran over and then turned to face them with her back to the wall. She was not at all beautiful but vitally pretty, the prim Navy-blue serge and white blouse emphasizing her femininity.

"I—"

"You have three sisters." Garth held her gaze. " 'Born out Hoxton way,' Twigg said, presumably meaning born in poor circumstances, and trained as dancers."

"Yes! Glynis is the only one who matters. Glynis is a year older than I am. She wouldn't even look very much like me if she hadn't deliberately begun to dress like me ever since I married Horace Calder. That's a part of Glynis's sense of humour, if you want to call it that. It's caused all the trouble. Glynis always said I was a—"

"A what?"

"A prude," Betty cried out. "I always hated the life we were brought up in. I *hated* it. I don't deny that. As long as seven years ago Glynis got her first engagement as a dancer at the Moulin Rouge. A year later she wrote me in England; she said she was making an enormous wonderful salary at the Moulin Rouge (of course, the money wasn't from there); and, since

I wasn't very successful (that was true), she had a use for me if I cared to join her in Paris.

"The 'use' was to act as a kind of hanger-on, and do her turn for her when she couldn't appear. I knew all about her men, naturally. This isn't a pretty story. But I swear I never knew nearly every affair ended in blackmail or attempted blackmail.

"In the autumn of 1902 Glynis returned to England for a short time. A banker named Mr. Dalrymple put a bullet through his head, and Glynis lost her nerve and said her name was Elizabeth Stukeley when the police questioned her. Though you may not believe me, I never learned this either until much, much later.

"Glynis can be awfully likeable when she wants to be. She only began to change towards me in the following year. Sir Horace Calder, the Governor of Jamaica (that's the office they call Captain-General) saw me in Paris and asked me to marry him. I couldn't believe he was serious, but he was. Well, I accepted him. He was almost seventy-three years old, and I accepted him. I told you this wasn't a pretty story. Glynis laughed and laughed, but she nearly went out of her mind."

Betty did not speak hysterically or even loudly, but only with that odd expression of stolidity she could sometimes wear.

"I accepted him," she said. "Would you have accepted him, Mrs. Bostwick?"

Whereupon Marion laughed. It was a ringing laugh that made Garth's nerves crawl.

"Well, Mrs.—but it's *Lady* Calder, isn't it?" Marion answered, before he could intervene, "I really don't know. I might have done, but I doubt it. That's *rather* old, you know. And I prefer them to be young. Oh, most certainly young!"

Vince Bostwick took a cigarette out of the silver case, broke the cigarette in two pieces, and flung them on the floor.

"Steady!" Garth said. "Betty, the time is running out. You were saying?"

"I think the suicide had frightened Glynis a little. While I was in Jamaica, she went to live at Trouville—"

"Trouville?"

"In Normandy."

"I know where it is, Betty. Yes?"

"Glynis stayed there until a year ago. My—my husband was dead. The management at the Moulin Rouge had changed; the people are always changing too. She went back; she said her name was Lady Calder now, and she wanted work again. The French love titles, but that wouldn't have helped her if she hadn't been a really good provocative dancer (do you understand, David?) of the sort they wanted. And I was in Paris last summer, and yet I *still* learned nothing at all until . . ."

"Until when?"

"Until less than a fortnight ago. Glynis turned up at the cottage and told me everything."

Betty turned fully to face him.

"They had given her the sack for drinking. She wanted money, and I gave her money. I would have given her the earth. I could have proved I had never been a blackmailer or a—or the other thing, though Glynis laughed and swore I couldn't. But what would have been the good of that? I *had* danced at that place. A fortnight ago I thought I would have died rather than let you learn of it. That's all there is."

"No, Betty, it's not all there is. Vince and Marion here, where did you learn they even existed?"

"Do you think I'm not interested in anything that concerns you? I can't help being interested! They're your closest friends. Hal Ormiston said so."

"My nephew again, eh? He told you?"

"Yes. He said he was quite well acquainted with Mrs. Bostwick."

The four bulbs in the chandelier shed a light as bright and bleak as that in Garth's consulting-room. Betty stood shivering against the wall. Marion sat bolt upright on the leather sofa.

"Since he *is* David's nephew," Marion proclaimed, "it may scarcely be accounted surprising that Vince and I should be acquainted with him."

"Scarcely," Garth said without looking at her. "When you left Harley Street in the motor-car tonight, Betty, where did you go first?"

"To number 38b Hyde Park Gardens. Hal said that was their address."

"Why did you go to the Bostwicks'?"

"Dr. Garth, please do stop! I—I had my reasons."

"They are what I am trying to establish. Betty, the good Glynis was blackmailing you. Has she been blackmailing anyone else?"

"I . . . don't . . . know."

"Marion," continued Garth, who himself was now the one with an air of pleading, "considering what common sense can't help telling us, do you still say that before this evening you never set eyes on the Glynis Stukeley who sometimes calls herself Elizabeth Stukeley?"

"I most certainly do say so!"

"Did *you* ever meet her, Vince?"

"No, old boy," Vince answered coolly. "Any reason for asking that?"

"Only that the Scotland Yard people think you did."

"Are you joking, old boy?"

"No, I am not. I wish I could convince both you and Marion, each of you in a different way, that it's as serious as it can be." Garth's head ached. The black wallpaper, with its spots or flecks of dull gold, seemed to be moving round him like the vision of Betty's intent, beloved, concerned face.

"In any event, Betty," he added, getting a grip on his wits again, "and forgetting the reason why you went to Hyde Park Gardens . . ."

"One of the reasons," Betty said, "was that I thought you might be going there yourself when you left Harley Street. You had told me you would be having very late dinner with 'some friends.' Almost as soon as I had got the engine of the car working, I heard young Mr. Fielding shouting at the telephone. He was speaking to Mrs. Bostwick; he seemed to be distressed. I never knew Mrs. Bostwick wasn't at home."

"And you also thought, 'Is Glynis up to her games again?' "

Betty did not comment on this.

"At Hyde Park Gardens," she was addressing Marion now, "I spoke to the butler and pretended to be a friend of yours. Will you forgive me, Mrs. Bostwick?"

"That altogether depends," retorted Marion, "on what you told him."

"Nothing at all! I only said I was a friend of yours, and asked if I could speak to you!"

"Really?" inquired Marion.

"All people aren't trying to hurt you, Mrs. Bostwick. Do believe me: all people in the world aren't trying to hurt you!"

"Really," Marion repeated.

"Just one moment, old girl," Vince interrupted with an abrupt change in his whole demeanour. All the strong, easy charm flowed back to him. "Let me speak to the lady!"

Though Betty made a despairing gesture as she turned back towards Garth, Vince caught her gaze and wouldn't let it go. Tall and lean, impeccable in grey with a gardenia in his buttonhole, he was no longer Vince the bluff sportsman or Vince the idler who apologetically read too many books. He had become Vince the wise counsellor, ready to press Betty's fingers in sympathy.

"My wife means well, Lady Calder. And old David, of course, is the cleverest chap I know. But sometimes he's a bit too much of a pious St. Anthony and a Spirit of Conscience—"

("And now I am a pious St. Anthony, am I? If only you knew!")

Vince could not have heard unspoken words.

"—David's a bit too much of that, I mean, to observe what's under his nose. That butler (he's a devil of a stuffed shirt, between ourselves) told you Marion had been called away on an urgent summons to her former guardians, Colonel Selby and Mrs. Montague, at Hampstead. You'd said you were a friend of Marion's so you couldn't very well admit you didn't know where they lived. Is that it?"

"Yes! That's it exactly!" Betty gave him a grateful look. "Thank you for understanding."

("God's teeth, does it require Aristotle or Sherlock Holmes or Prince Ahriman from the 'Phantom' stories to make so brilliant a deduction?")

Here Vince did take Betty's hands.

More fires were being lighted under the bared snarl of the big-game heads round the walls.

"What'd you do next, Lady Calder?"

"I—I hailed a hansom and drove round and round trying to find a post-office or a shop that was open so that I could look at a London Directory. Nothing was open. Then I thought they might have a telephone of their own. There was one telephone in an Underground Station; there usually is; but the Exchange said they hadn't got any such name."

"They've got a telephone here, my dear."

"Mr. Bostwick, I swear . . . !"

"Good old Aunt Blanche hates the devilish instrument and keeps it a secret. That's all. Next?"

"Well! I just told the cabby to drive to Hampstead. We were a good way up—Rosslyn Hill, I think—when I saw the blue lamps of a police-station on the other side of the road. They'd know *there*, I thought; they'll be certain to know where the house is; but have I the colossal cheek to walk straight into a police-station and ask them?

"Of course I shouldn't have had the courage, though I left the cab and crossed the road, if it hadn't been decided for me. That officer, Inspector Rogers, was standing on the steps of the station. A tired-looking elderly man with a black medical bag was talking to him, and telling him what happened here. They paid no attention to me; they never even saw me."

Betty wrenched away from Vince.

"David," she added, "you never met Glynis. You didn't see her or hear her at the beach less than a fortnight ago. Saying—"

"Yes? Saying what?"

"Glynis said, 'Everything you have is mine, ducky. Your money and your house in London and your jewels and your clothes too. I'll use this cottage when I like, and swim from the pavilion when I like; and if you're not very careful, ducky, I'll take 'em all over.'

"I said. 'You'll keep away from my friends,' I said, 'or I'll kill you or I'll have you put in prison.' And Glynis said, 'You won't kill me, ducky, because you wouldn't dare. You won't put me in prison, because you haven't the evidence. Anyway, you wouldn't. Your own sister, ducky? *Your own sister?*'"

Marion Bostwick drew back with a little cry.

For an instant Betty's mimicry of voice and expression had been almost frightening, as of a woman years older in experience.

"Well, Glynis is going to learn different," Betty resumed. "I made up my mind when I heard Dr. Fortescue talking to Inspector Rogers. It's true, the doctor said, it was too dark for Mrs. Bostwick to see much of this so-called 'woman sneak-thief' who got away through a basement door. But Mrs. Bostwick did tell the woman's height, and the colour of her eyes and hair, and that she was wearing Navy-blue serge with a straw hat.

"I knew it was Glynis, right enough. I knew she attacked this Mrs. Montague, just as she once attacked a woman at the Moulin Rouge. And nowadays there are such things as fingerprints, aren't there? *She'll* take over, will she?

"So I walked up to the Inspector and said, 'I can tell you who the woman was.' He said, not taking me very seriously, 'Well, now, miss, I hope it wasn't you?' I said, 'No, I was somewhere else and I can prove it. But if you'll take me to Colonel Selby's house—now!—I'll tell you her name and where she lodges in London.'

"All of a sudden I could see him wondering if I *was* the woman. I said, 'Take me there! Take me! Let me speak to Mrs. Bostwick.' I didn't expect to find you here, David my dear. But I'm glad you are. There's bad blood in me, as there is in her. Now it's all straight. I'll go out and tell them where to find Glynis. And I don't want you ever to see me again."

Betty stopped, her eyes brimming over.

"I'm sorry," she added. "I don't want you to look at me even now."

And she ran for the door.

"I really think—" began Marion.

"Betty," Garth said in a voice he very seldom used, "stay where you are."

It was Vince who seized her arm, gripping it and turning her round. Marion leaped up from the sofa.

"Unless you have stopped playing detective, Vince," said Garth, "would you mind asking the question the police are bound to ask? The question we've somehow got to meet or land in trouble? If Marion is telling the truth . . ."

"*If* I am telling the truth?"

"Yes. I'm not convinced you are. But if Marion is telling the truth, and we all agree on it, how did Glynis Stukeley or any other person leave this house through a door double-bolted on the inside?"

Vince released Betty's arm.

"Yes, old boy, I see what you mean. It'd be a fine question, I agree, to throw at us in a puzzle. But it's only academic, isn't it?"

"Academic? Rogers won't stay out there drinking whisky in the dining-room. He'll go straight down to the cellar. You know what he'll find."

The thin little amusement-wrinkles deepened round Vince's mouth and eyes and then vanished in an instant.

"Quite," he agreed, "I know. I overheard you telling Marion you'd drawn both bolts yourself. Consequently, if the blue-bottles won't accept honest people's words, they'll find the door both unlocked and unbolted just as Marion said it was."

"Ah, I see," Garth said after a pause. "We support what is convenient, then, because otherwise it might lead to uncomfortable conclusions."

"Well, what else can we do?"

"You might be right. Sure you're not acquainted with Glynis Stukeley, Vince?"

"Never saw her in my life, old boy."

"Still, you've seen Betty. I am supporting *her.*"

"It's not necessary," Betty cried, "for anybody to support me. May I be allowed to see the Inspector now? And then please, *please,* may I never have to see any of you again?"

She spoke in an unnatural voice, hot with shame and humiliation, face averted. And so, because Garth was touched to the heart, he must half yell at her.

"I told you once before, Betty, not to be a fool. Those things don't matter."

"Don't they? To you?"

"No! When you go back to Fairfield tonight, I'll go with you. If Glynis should happen to be there, we'll see her together."

"Oh, no, we won't! I mean—"

Betty shut her eyes, and opened them again.

"I mean," she said, "it's nice of you to pretend. I love you for pretending. But it does matter. It will matter. It can't help mattering. If you believe you can meet me again without wondering what I am and what's in my mind, then make it tomorrow, late tomorrow, when you've had time to think it over. But you won't. It *is* over, David, and I wish to God it had never started. Tell this man not to touch me, please. I'm going to see the Inspector."

And Garth made a sign to Vince, who stood aside.

But he should not have let her go. Certainly he should not have let her return to Fairfield alone. Whatever was diabolic in this, it burst over David Garth towards six o'clock on the following afternoon.

PART II

THE IMPOSSIBLE

Like *"s'il vous plait"* in Paris, *"if you please,"* or *"please,"* is generally used in ordering refreshments at a café or restaurant, or in making any request. The English forms of politeness are, however, by no means so minute or ceremonious as the French.

—BAEDEKER'S *London and Its Environs* FOR 1908

6

Fairfield-on-sea, even late during a Saturday afternoon in June, could hardly be described as a place of gaiety.

No pier marred Fairfield's dignity. No banjos twanged on its sands, no blackface minstrels sang, no wandering preacher began to explain what was wrong with the world and went into a fit when he explained it. Though many of the inhabitants were elderly or invalid, still more were merely prosperous and sedate.

It was true that a few bathing-machines—those curious eighteenth-century survivals, Garth reflected, like narrow out-houses on wheels—could be rolled towards the tide so that stately bathers could undress inside and take a dip without any necessity for appearing on the beach in bathing-costume. But the tide was out now, showing a vast surface of shiny grey mud under a grey overcast sky.

It was also true that they had built up a sea-front parade with tall lamp-standards of ornamental ironwork. There was a formal garden with mummified benches, and a gilt bandstand from which, on occasion, you might hear the strains of Gilbert and Sullivan. But at this time, towards six o'clock of a warm day, most people were still snugly indoors after tea.

Except for one or two dogs who grew nervous and could not be prevented from barking, Fairfield lay in a hollow of silence.

"Now I wonder!" David Garth thought.

Some distance away along the coast to the north was a larger, noisier watering-place which bore the regrettable name of Bunch. Occasionally, a matter to be ignored by Fairfielders, some veer in the wind would carry strains not unconnected with giddy-go-rounds and coconut-shies. Of the two towns Garth himself might have preferred Bunch. But you might not have guessed this to see him walking southwards along the parade now. In that direction lay the open country where Betty's house loomed above the coast; and, still farther south, a third seaside-town named Ravensport.

Garth had discarded his professional silk hat and frock coat for country tweeds and a Trilby. He still looked formidable and black-browed because he was thinking of last night, and of certain wild words spoken shortly before Betty Calder had left the house at Hampstead.

Betty was still there, being questioned by Inspector Rogers in the den, when Vince Bostwick made an explosive suggestion to Garth.

"Old boy, forget your repetition of 'impossible,'" Vince had said pettishly. "Are you still talking about trying to explain a door double-bolted on the inside?"

"Yes. Strangely enough, I am."

"Well, you know," said Vince, "I think *I* can explain it."

A remark like this, made at the wrong time, brought Marion near a scream.

Since Inspector Rogers was using the den to question Betty, the other three had gathered in the drawing-room. Marion paced back and forth, fanning herself and once or twice smoothing down her gown across the hips.

"The fact is," said Vince, whose eye seemed to have turned inward, "I was thinking of this writing-chap. 'Phantom.' Very clever, whoever he is. Now, 'Phantom'—"

"If you men don't stop going on about stories," said Marion, "I think I shall go quite, quite out of my mind. Stories! Stories! Stories!" Her voice went up the scale at each repetition of the word. "Your ridiculous stories have nothing whatsoever to do with all this."

"That's not so certain, my pet," replied Vince. "If you're telling the truth, as David says, *somebody* played a trick with the bolted door."

"Oh? Who did?"

"Suppose I did it myself?"

Marion drew in her breath, staring. Every object in the room, from bright Indian mats to golden-oak furniture, seemed to have acquired a hard lustre. Vince extended a long finger and pointed at Garth.

"When I knocked at the front door," he went on, "you and Marion were too absorbed to hear me. That front door was unlocked. Very well! Suppose the basement door was also both unlocked and unbolted, as Marion says? Suppose

I had already slipped into the house, by whichever entrance you please? Suppose I wanted to prove my dear wife a liar and land her in difficulties with the police? Suppose I bolted the door myself, and then slipped upstairs and made a noise out in the foyer as though I'd only just arrived from the front?"

"That's not fair," Marion cried out. "It's not *fair*."

Retreating rather blunderingly, she groped for the arms of a chair and sat down.

"You're having your revenge now, Vince, aren't you?" she accused him. "The night we saw that musical play, *The Merry Widow*, I—I teased and joked you a little about something else. Now you're getting back at me." Her expression changed. "You didn't really do that, did you?"

"No, dash it all, of course I didn't! It's not a thing even for me to joke about."

Vince's expression changed too. He went over and dropped his hand on Marion's shoulder.

"I'm still in love with you, you overgrown child, though it goes against the grain to admit I am." Worry sharpened the long features. "*I* didn't do that, no, but somebody else may have. Somebody may be waiting to spring a trap, and let the bobbies know this house was locked up after all."

"But the police won't learn that! Inspector What's-his-name believes everything we say!"

"H'm. Maybe. You never can think two moves ahead, my pet."

"But, Vince—!"

"What do you say, David? Isn't that the reasonable solution?"

"Well," Garth told him, "it's a remotely possible solution. When I first thought of it . . ."

"You'd already thought of it? About me?"

"Yes, about you. It's fairly obvious."

"Now that's a nice thing to tell me, I must say," exclaimed the outraged Vince, with all his banter struck away. "You mean you think I did that?"

"No. I don't think you did it; I don't think anybody else did it. This house is like a sounding-board; every floor creaks and cracks; the wooden stairs to the cellar are even worse. Marion and I were alone here. Even if we were preoccupied, I can't imagine that happening without my hearing anything at all. There are several other reasons, but let them go. I could almost swear it's not the true explanation."

And, as they were to discover under grim circumstances, Garth was quite right. For the moment, bedevilled, he could see only the look on the other's face.

"But, good God Almighty—!"

"What's the matter, Vince? You're the one who has been so casual and bland about all this. What's the matter now?"

"I've been thinking, that's all. Unless it happened in that way, it couldn't have happened in any way. It's a ruddy impossibility!"

"Ah. If you're finally convinced of that, Vince, we can go forward a little. Somebody may very well be laying a trap for us. If so, we must be prepared to meet it."

"How?"

At the back of the foyer, in something of a rush as though at the end of a strained interview, the door of the den opened. The lamp of the bronze Diana quivered on the newel-post. But Betty was walking slowly, with greater despair in the set of her shoulders. Inspector Rogers escorted her towards the front door.

"Yes, my lady, that's all for the moment. It won't *be* all, I'm afraid. It's a pity this woman's your sister." Here Betty made a sharp gesture as the Inspector spoke. "Still, if she's the one our people want to talk to (as you might say) for other causes, it can't be helped and maybe it's just as well."

"Will they arrest her?"

"That's not for me to say, my lady. Until Mrs. Bostwick makes an identification, yes or no, there's no proof she assaulted the poor lady upstairs. I've got her address here," Rogers tapped the notebook in the breast pocket of his tunic, "and I'll pass it along to Scotland Yard." Then he added, "No offence being meant, there's still one thing I'm bound to ask."

His tone hardly changed at all. He remained aloof but fatherly, chin drawn in and large grey moustache towering above her. But Betty stopped short in the middle of the foyer. Catching sight of Garth at the doorway of the drawing-room, she flushed and turned away so that she faced Inspector Rogers.

"Yes?" Betty asked.

"There wouldn't be any special reason, my lady, why you're going back to this country cottage tonight?"

"But I—I live at the cottage during the summer! I've been there since the middle of May."

"You wouldn't be meeting this sister of yours, maybe?"

"No, certainly not," Betty cried in obvious astonishment. "Glynis is in London; I just gave you that Kensington address."

"What I mean to say: you wouldn't apprehend no danger from this sister, would you? Or maybe try to do something foolish in return?"

Garth suddenly took a step out towards them. Inspector

Rogers's eyes held him back. Though Rogers addressed Betty, his words were plainly meant for the other man.

"Now, now, my lady, I've promised you we needn't trouble Dr. Garth or his motor-car to drive you to Charing Cross. The constable's gone to fetch a cab; he'll be back in a brace of shakes. What I mean to say—"

"Then say it, please."

"There's been threats, you tell me. From your sister. To take away your money or your property or what not. She talks about the cottage and about a 'pavilion.' Meaning no intrusion, my lady, but what *is* this pavilion? Something like Brighton Pavilion, maybe?"

"Good heavens, no! You might call it a permanent and elaborate kind of bathing-machine, a hut as big as a small cottage in itself, with two rooms for keeping the sexes apart."

"Beg pardon, my lady?"

And Betty began to laugh, as Marion had laughed earlier in the evening.

"For keeping the sexes apart, all very modestly." The laughter, not without a touch of hysteria, throbbed and rang until Betty swallowed hard. "I'm awfully sorry, Mr. Rogers. It's not at all comical. The people who built the cottage also had supports driven into the sand and built the pavilion ten or a dozen years ago."

"Oh?"

"Nobody uses the pavilion nowadays for changing in. If I have visitors, they change in the cottage. But we do use the pavilion for bathing from, and for watching the sea from the little veranda, and sometimes for making tea; and we run up a flag if it's occupied."

"Do you have many visitors, my lady?"

"No. Didn't I tell you I'm an outcast? Only Dr. Garth and —and Mr. Hal Ormiston." Betty broke off. "Why? Does it matter?"

"Maybe not. I hope you'll take a well-meant tip, though. Just you keep your head, my lady, when *you* go for a bathe."

"What do you mean by that?"

Pontifical footsteps marched up the path outside, the front door opened.

"Cab's here, Inspector," reported the constable.

Every word, every inflection remained vivid in David Garth's memory. The scene was still with him as he strode along the seafront parade at Fairfield late on that following afternoon, with a damp wind flapping at his hat under a dark overcast sky.

He had so concentrated on memories that he almost walked into the steps of the Royal Albert Aquarium, whose dressed stone and ornamental ironwork closed off the southern end of the parade. The sea lay on his right. To return to a path parallel with it, he must go left past the aquarium into Balaclava Road, then right again into Sebastopol Avenue, until all macadamized surfaces out of Fairfield ended in an unpaved road along the bank of the coast.

Thus, in a hollow some five miles long between these Kentish cliffs, the flattish beach curved between Bunch on the north and Ravensport on the extreme south. The latter town, once a small powerful seaport, had fallen on sleep since the Middle Ages; it retained only a few picturesque survivals and two of the best pubs in England.

On the outskirts of Fairfield, Garth passed the inn of the Stag and Glove. His rooms there were still booked; but he had left his car in London and come down by train; he did not pause at the inn. Ten minutes' quick walking, now, would bring him to Betty's cottage in open country.

And then—?

"There is one question," he decided, "so obvious that everybody last night forgot to ask it. At the same time, in a matter of blackmail, it may become the most important question of all."

The clock at St. Jude's Church, above a grim terrace of villas behind him in Fairfield, rang the quarter-hour to six. But he had no opportunity to ask Betty that important question. When slightly less than ten minutes brought him to a turn in the road and he could see Betty's house, other matters drove it from his mind.

To call the place a cottage, admittedly, was the usual misnomer of long habit. A substantial stone house, rather long and low-built, with a red tile roof, stretched beside the road behind a low wall and a rather high evergreen hedge. The beach, which you could see from either north or south of the grounds but not from in front of the house, lay behind it under a slope of scrub grass. To the right of the grounds a cycle-track—Betty was a willing if not very efficient cyclist—made a faint trail from the road down across scrub grass towards the beach.

And in front of the cottage, haunting Garth, stood his own motor-car.

He stopped and looked at it.

The car was pointed towards Fairfield. Its engine, running at half-throttle, made a thump and clank against death-quiet air. Though some manufacturers had begun to design cars with windscreens and a suggested form of canopy against dust, the Panhard had neither. Dust lay thick even over the leather cushions of the tonneau, in which somebody had thrown down a linen coat, a pair of gauntlets, and a cap with sinister-looking mica eyepieces.

"Hello, Nunkie," said a self-assured voice. "Good afternoon, Nunkie. Though it's not a very good afternoon, is it?"

The engine kept throbbing.

Mr. Henry Ormiston, a slight and fair-complexioned young man with nose held rather high as though to balance a chin held forward, strolled down the unpaved path from Betty's cottage to the wooden gate between the evergreens. He wore a straw boater on the back of his head, and peg-top white flannel trousers; his hands were thrust into the pockets of a red-and-white striped jacket.

"You seemed to be pondering, Nunkie. Were you?"

"Frankly, I still am. I am wondering whether the English language contains a more objectionable word than 'nunkie,' either used as a diminutive for 'uncle' or in fact used in any other way."

"I'm afraid there are a lot of things you think are objectionable, Nunkie."

"Then you are spared a self-evident illustration. What are you doing here?"

"My dear Nunkie," Hal said gently, "it's no good trying to act superior or coming the high and mighty doctor at my expense. It never impresses me and it won't help you, so don't try it on. Besides, you know, that's pretty poor repartee."

" 'What are you doing here?' I asked."

"So you did." Hal, completely unruffled, smiled and waited. "When I called at Harley Street, quite early this morning, your housekeeper said you'd already gone out in something of a dither. She didn't know where you'd gone, or told me she didn't. But she said you planned to be here about this time."

"That, I suppose, was why you took the car again?"

"Naturally. By the way, I had to buy petrol; and there are two more tins in the tonneau now. Shall we say a modest tenner?"

"Are you sure ten pounds will be enough?"

"No, but I can make do with it for the moment. Your sarcasm's not lost on me, Nunkie. It's subtle, of course, but it's not lost on me."

No sign of life stirred in the stone house. Garth's nerves had begun to crawl with apprehension and with his desire to see Betty. He would give any sum to get Hal away from here, at once, with no delaying action being fought; quite clearly, Hal knew this; and it was a mistake to reach towards the pocket that held his notecase.

"Now I wonder," Hal said instantly, eyes narrowing, "why

you've become so generous all of a sudden. I'm always wondering things like that, and I also wonder if your dear, dead sister's son can persuade you to part with a larger donation. Incidentally, did you ever meet a fine upstanding officer named George Alfred Twigg?"

"Did *he* turn up in Harley Street too, by any chance?"

"He might have. I don't know what you've done to him, Nunkie, but I don't think he likes you at all. I'm not sure he likes Betty, either."

"Where is Betty?"

"Yes, I imagined you'd be wanting to know that. I imagined—"

Hal Ormiston then did a curious thing. Standing inside the gate, he removed his straw boater and held it horizontally above flat fair hair. At first it was as though he were shedding a benediction on himself, and next as though some further advantage to himself had occurred to him, and next as though he grew uncertain. Hal's imperturbability, Garth knew, came mainly from inexperience. There might be some flaw in the superciliousness of that raised nose and outthrust jaw.

But the effect, against a lonely landscape, was sufficiently weird.

"I'm quite fond of that little charmer," he declared. "She's got money, too. I should take her away from you, Nunkie, if she didn't have much the same attitude as another woman who—"

Garth would wait no longer. He threw open the gate and started up the path towards the cottage. But Hal, replacing the hat, was ahead of him. Together they reached a big front door, with the brass figure of a goblin as door-knocker, standing open on a very broad, low-ceilinged hall which stretched through the house to broad glass doors at the rear.

Through those doors showed pallid daylight.

"It's no good shouting," said Hal. "I've already tried that. She's not here."

"Where is she?"

Hal hesitated, in a hall that smelled of old wood and stone. He went to the glass doors; he opened them towards beach and sea.

"She went for a bathe," Hal answered, "and she hasn't come back. I hope nothing's happened to her."

7

"The tide is out now," Garth said. "Are you telling me Betty went to swim with the tide completely out?"

Hal looked almost human, except that one corner of his mouth lifted.

"Don't try your tricks, my respected ancient. She went out there two hours ago, and the tide had been ebbing for less than an hour. It won't be full high-tide again until about nine o'clock tonight."

Garth spoke more loudly.

"Well, that's all right," he said. "Betty usually goes for a swim about that time: four o'clock, just before tea. She often has tea at the pavilion afterwards."

"I know that, Nunkie. Now why are you telling me? But she doesn't usually take as long as this, does she?"

"I'm only telling you—!"

They both glanced out to sea, where damp smoky-looking clouds curled along the horizon.

Just outside the glass doors, a stretch of dirt and hummocky scrub grass extended some three or four yards before sloping gently to the beach. And they could see the beach spread out in front of them like a map of the world. Its sand above high-water mark was white, its sand below high-water mark was damp and hard-packed, a dingy grey; farther out, well beyond the pavilion, it became only a floor of mud.

The sea lay there as a living presence, breathing back salt air and an iodine tang across mud-flats. But you thought less of the sea than of sea-monsters. The pavilion, on its blackish wooden piles, stood more than thirty feet below high-water-mark on a beach sloping so gently that it hardly seemed to slope at all. Beyond the pavilion the grey surface stretched perhaps forty or fifty feet more. There was no footprint anywhere in the sand.

This latter fact, at the moment, did not impress Garth or strike him as important. Anyone who walked into the water two hours ago would have had all footprints washed out by the ebbing tide. And yet Garth found his collar strangling him and the salt air difficult to breathe.

"Hal, how do you know Betty went out there?"

"I saw her go."

"You saw her from here?"

"It'll be better for you, my respected ancient, if you don't keep putting words into my mouth. No! I was driving your car along the road up there," Hal made a gesture behind him and towards the left, "in the direction of Ravensport. I saw her walk down the beach and wade out towards the pavilion. She was wearing her usual bathing-costume, and one of those big puffy hard-rubber caps."

"Did you speak to her?"

"All that distance away?" Hal's lip lifted again. "It's not likely, is it? I gave her a hail, and she raised her arm to wave back. And it won't be wise to tell me I'm lying, either. There's another witness who saw her. There's a witness I just happened to be driving to Ravensport."

"Oh? Who was the witness?"

"That friend of yours from Scotland Yard. Cullingford Abbot."

Garth spun round. "Now what was Abbot doing here? Why were you driving him to Ravensport?"

"Ah! That's the question, don't you think? As for what he was doing here, I'm sorry to tell you that's none of your business. And, anyway, I don't know. He's a close-mouthed swine, like all these police people." Hal's face darkened. "I dropped him in Ravensport; I spent an agreeable couple of hours at a pub called the Red Warden; I came back here in the hope of finding you, not two minutes before you turned up. Have you got all that?"

Garth turned back towards the sea.

"Betty!" he shouted.

There was no reply.

"*Betty!*"

Again his voice rang out over that lonely beach; and again there was silence except for the clanking, thudding engine of the motor-car at the front gate.

"When you returned here from Ravensport, and found Betty wasn't in the house, why didn't you go out to the pavilion?"

"And get my shoes mucked up with sand and mud? Come, now, my venerable ancient! Do you see any green in my eye? It's no business of mine if—"

"Stop there just one second, Nunkie," Hal added in swift coolness, as Garth started out over the grass. "Before I can let you fly to your beloved, I must remind you of something else. You won't mind if I take the car, I'm sure. But there's a little matter of ten pounds to be settled between us."

They looked at each other. Taking the notecase out of his pocket, Garth extracted two five-pound notes, folded them into a small wad, and flicked them into the grass at the young man's feet. It was as though his own shout rang back at him from the sands. Hal's voice went high and thin.

"You're an arrogant bastard, Dr. David Garth. Maybe, before we're all many hours older, you'll wish you hadn't done that."

Garth paid no attention; he was running.

He left shallow, sharp footprints as he ran. Behind him the throbbing of the car-engine sputtered, giving a spurt of noise and then a metallic jump. Glancing over his shoulder, he was in time to see the green car chug up and round the rise of the road north towards Fairfield. Garth slipped on the greasy surface, but kept himself from falling.

Three wooden steps led up to the pavilion's floor-level, and to a doorway covered by a vertical red-and-white-striped canvas sunblind, new a year ago, which could be raised or lowered by strings just inside. It was half lowered now, and he did not trouble to try raising it farther. Instead he dodged underneath and stood up again.

Another wall, parallel with the landwards outer wall of the pavilion, made a cramped and darkish little entry. In this wall facing him were two identical little wooden doors, both partway open as usual, that led to the two rooms of the pavilion. Projecting out from the wall between these doors hung an ancient canvas curtain, like a screen.

"Betty!" Garth called again.

But the stamp of silence had returned.

He ran into the left-hand room, pushing open a door that scraped the floorboards. The little room was empty. From each room another door, its upper panel opaque glass, led out to the little veranda towards the sea.

A faint gleam of daylight showed him a chair or two in this room, a tiny looking-glass on the wall, half a dozen hooks for clothes. Garth stood breathing a miasmatic stuffiness, that smell of rotting wood salt-crusted, of sand and sea-air and heat imprisoned throughout a day, which stifles our lungs on any pier.

The last tenants of the cottage once used this pavilion for "bathing parties." A large framed photograph, taken about 1897 and left behind on the wall of Betty's sitting-room, still showed two small rowboats—one containing three over-dressed ladies, the other containing three overdressed gentlemen—drawn up on the beach at high-tide. After the photographer had uncapped his lens they would have impelled themselves out over shallow water, using oars as punt-poles, so as to reach the pavilion without getting wet.

These people were gone now. They were ghosts. Garth

counted slowly to ten. Then he opened the half-glazed door and went out on the little veranda.

This was empty too. But a high-backed wooden rocking-chair stood a little way along to his right, not far from the other door to the second room. On the floor of the veranda beside that chair stood a cup and saucer containing the dregs of tea which did not date back to 1897.

"Betty!"

A breeze stirred heavily across mud-flats. Long-damp wood seemed to absorb sound as it had absorbed water. Garth could not even hear his own footsteps when he went to that other door. And then, as though at the end of an eternity, he found her.

It was a few seconds before he could go inside the room. His knees felt shaky, and he held to the knob of the door he had just flung open.

She lay face down on the floor in that other room. The pallid daylight fell faintly on her dark-brown bathing-costume, and on her bare thighs and legs, and on the canvas shoes she always wore to swim. Her head in the bathing-cap was towards a table against one wall, a table on which stood a tea-caddy, and cups and saucers, and an unlighted spirit-lamp. He could not see her face, which was just as well. She had been strangled.

Through his mind ran words Betty had read aloud to him, less than a week ago, from a so-called fashion-hint in a magazine.

" 'A discarded heavy wool-mohair skirt,' " she had quoted, " 'can be made over into an excellent new bathing-costume.' " And she had added, "Ugh!"

He was held there momentarily by that scene of frozen violence, as no doctor should have been. But this, he told himself, was different. "A discarded heavy wool-mohair skirt can be made over into an excellent new bathing-costume. A discarded heavy wool-mohair skirt can be made over into an excellent new bathing-costume. A discarded heavy wool-mohair skirt, can be—"

He went to that lifeless body, gently touching her as he moved her face up. He looked at the swollen, cyanosed face; he touched the white-sash-cord embedded in her throat and knotted hard at the back of the neck. And he stood up very quickly.

The woman was not Betty.

But this alone failed to move him so much. This alone did not make him get up so quickly, and look quickly round the dim, stuffy, evil little room. The woman's body was almost at life temperature. A little blood on the edges of the nostrils had scarcely dried. Whoever the woman was (and he now believed he could guess well enough), she had been dead for not much more than fifteen or twenty minutes.

Fifteen or twenty minutes.

He took out his watch and opened it. Incredibly, the hands stood at no later than just six o'clock.

Garth replaced the watch. Afterwards he stood motionless, and only his eyes roved.

The open door to the veranda was just opposite the partly open door out to the little entry on the beach side. This had once been a bathing-pavilion for privacy; there were no windows. The table with the tea-things stood against the wall to the right as you faced the veranda door. Amid a clutter of china and spoons beside the spirit-lamp was a half-gallon jar in which Betty kept water to brew tea, together with a kettle, an earthenware teapot, and a tin of condensed milk.

Garth looked at the wall opposite. From one of the hooks along this wall hung a long bathing-cape of brown serge with horizontal yellow stripes. It belonged to Betty, he knew, although she very seldom wore it. He went to the cape, explored its inside pockets, and in the second one found a handkerchief with the initials G. S.

Glynis Stukeley.

Her figure much resembled Betty, yes. The face—not considering that bitten tongue and those protruding half-open eyes against discolouring, you couldn't tell about the face. Quickly he returned to Glynis Stukeley's body, and adjusted her face down just as he had found her.

Next he glanced along the table. He reached out to touch the teapot—and then, drawing back as though he had been burnt, his arm swept off a cup which smashed on the floor with a hellish noise and a spray of china-bits like a small bomb.

At the same moment a familiar voice outside the pavilion, calling his name and growing louder as it called, brought him alert to meet what must be met. He hurried out into the entry towards what might be called the "front" door of the pavilion, whose red-and-white canvas sunblind remained half lowered. He yanked the cords down and raised it fully.

The first thing he saw, even before he saw the face of the woman who had hurried out there, was an overturned bicycle.

It lay more than forty feet away, up the grass slope of the cycle track humped to the north of the house.

"Hal—" began Betty's panting voice.

"What about Hal?"

"I passed him in the road. He looked—"

Betty stopped. She was wearing a different straw hat, a dark skirt, and a dove-grey silk blouse without a jacket but with a high lace collar. Life assumed reality again; life caught up its pace as it caught up these two people, and flung them along with a rapidity that would not now cease until the last word of murder was said.

"Betty, did your sister come down to see you?"

"Yes. She's still here."

"Where?"

"At the house, I suppose. She must have come back from bathing. Over two hours ago we had the most awful, screaming fishwife row; I called her things that would have shocked the life out of your friends. So I ran, or pedalled, rather. But your note said you'd be here at six o'clock, so I couldn't—"

"My note? What note?"

Betty's breathing had slowed down, though her flush remained high. She was staring at him with dilated eyes and an unnatural look as though inspiration were about to fly to the heart of truth. About to say something, she changed her mind and thrust out her left hand palm upwards.

A smallish sheet of paper, folded several times lengthways, showed in the open palm of the grey kid glove. Garth tied the cords of the sunblind round its rusty hook, holding the blind high.

"When we first met," she cried, "you wrote me two or three notes on a typewriter. I kept them, even if they were on a typewriter. That's your typewriter, isn't it?" And then, "Why are you asking all this? Have you seen Glynis? Has Hal met her?"

"Betty, I don't want to alarm you. . . ."

She was standing on the damp sand a little way out from the three steps that led up to the pavilion's door, and holding herself with unnatural rigidity as she looked up at him.

"I don't want to alarm you. . . ."

"Then answer me something. Please, please answer me something! Will you do that?"

"If I can."

"Has something happened," said Betty, *"that I'm afraid may have happened?"*

"Yes."

For a second he thought she was going to give way. It was almost as though the colour went out of Betty's eyes. He descended the steps, put his arm round her waist, and held her tightly while she trembled.

Anyone who saw them standing there might have thought them alone in the world as they were alone on the beach; and, in a certain sense, this was so. Betty's left arm, with the note thrust into the palm of the glove, had dropped to her side. For a moment he did not touch the note.

"Betty, listen to me. Your sister is dead. She is in one of those two rooms in the pavilion, the right-hand one as you face the sea. What happened to her is what almost happened to Mrs. Montague last night. Can you bear to hear this?"

"I'm all right. *I hated her*."

"Yes. That's what we must guard against. We shall be no good to each other if we don't face facts. You understand that?"

"Oh, David, I'm sorry," she cried out at him. "Oh, God, darling, I'm most awfully sorry!"

"For what? There's nothing to be sorry about, my dear. You didn't do this, I take it?"

"No! No! I wanted to, but I knew I couldn't. What I meant was—"

"I know what you meant. It doesn't matter."

Betty flung her arms round him. Then, with a spasmodic effort, she straightened her shoulders. He was still speaking slowly, gently, so that she seized strength and almost caught his mood.

"This is being even more foolish," she said after a pause, "than I usually am. Please ask me anything you like."

"Very well. This quarrel with your sister: when did it happen? When did you last see Glynis alive?"

"It was over two hours ago," replied Betty, with a composure that may have been feigned but was nevertheless strong and compelling. "I can't remember the exact time," her hand flew to her breast, "and I'm not wearing my watch. It may have been ten minutes to four. Anyway, it happened in her bedroom."

"In 'her' bedroom?"

"Yes." Betty looked back steadily. "Glynis turned up this morning bright and early from Fairfield railway-station. She brought a valise, and said she thought she would be staying for a day or two. She also laughed and said, 'But don't think that gives you your opportunity, ducky. No, no, no! I left a letter in London to be opened in case anything nasty happens to me.' "

Garth spoke with some violence. "This sister of yours would appear to have been a good deal of a pathological case."

"Of a what-kind-of-case?"

"Never mind. She is not laughing now."

"Don't say that!"

"I beg your pardon. You were telling me?"

"Fortunately," Betty went on in a rush. "Mrs. Hanshew

wasn't here." A picture of that eminently respectable house-keeper rose in Garth's mind like a picture of Mrs. Grundy. "You see, Mrs. Hanshew's daughter has been ill over at Bunch. Yesterday evening, before Hal and I started for London in that wretched car, I gave her permission to visit her daughter and not return until Monday. In my own way, David, I'm quite as cheap and vulgar as Glynis is. I simply couldn't endure the thought of anyone knowing Glynis was here. She'd kept her visits secret before this, and now she'd begun them openly. Then, when I got your note in the afternoon post—"

"Ah, yes. That note of mine. May I see it?"

Betty stared at him.

"But I thought you'd forgiven me," she cried. "You—you *did* write this?"

"Yes, to be sure I wrote it. All the same, may I see it?"

Betty snatched the paper out of her glove, unfolded it, and handed it over. It was no time to tell her he had never seen the note before, and knew nothing about it.

The murky sky threw changing shadows across a sheet of his own professional stationery, the smaller kind of notepaper on which accounts were sent out. *My dear,* ran the typed words. *I shall be with you at six o'clock on Saturday. Yours unalterably.* There was no date. As a signature it bore only a capital "D," written in ink.

But it had not been typed on the official machine used by Michael Fielding to send out his accounts. Instead some-one had written it on the personal, private typewriter he kept in his living-quarters at Harley Street for a double life of his own which now seemed so comic and so grotesque.

"Betty, did you keep the envelope of this?"

"Yes, of course I kept it." There was almost reproach in Betty's cry. "I can tell you now it. was postmarked London, West, at 12:30 A. M. I can show you the envelope. But what difference does that make? If you sent it . . ."

"My dear, I have already told you I sent it. I was thinking of something else."

He was thinking, in fact, of certain expressions on a young face in Harley Street last night; and of a red-bound novel carefully left open in the waiting-room. But he did not say as much.

"Gently, now! Here." And he handed back the note. "You were telling me about your sister, and what happened at the cottage this afternoon. Yes?"

Wind ruffled Betty's hair.

"Well, I'd given Glynis the large bedroom on the ground floor at the back." She made an uncertain gesture towards the house. "When I got that note I brooded and brooded, and finally I ran back to her room. She had found one of my bathing-costumes, and she was putting it on. I said, 'You're not going out on that beach; you're not going to disgrace everything I've ever tried to be.' Glynis said, 'What's the matter, ducky; don't you want your young man to meet me?' I said, 'I don't want anybody even to *see* you here; you sha'n't do it.' And Glynis said, 'If you're not very careful, ducks, I'll wear much less than a bathing-costume. You've done it often enough, I'll be bound.' That was where the screaming started. And I just ran away."

"Did you tell her about the note from me?"

"Oh, God, no!"

"Well, Betty, she did use the bathing-costume. Two witnesses saw her walk down the beach and into the water. The witnesses say it was you."

"But I didn't do any such . . ."

"Gently. I know you didn't. And we may be able to establish that." Garth shut his eyes, visualized other matters, and looked at Betty again. "You left here with your bicycle at some time before four o'clock. Where did you go? To Fairfield?"

"In the direction of Fairfield, but not into the town. I was in the country west of it. Sometimes I rode, but mainly I just walked and pushed the bike. I was so horribly upset that I even forgot your note."

"Did you meet anyone you knew?"

"That's always the question they ask in the stories, isn't it?"

"Did you?"

"I don't know." Her brown eyes, shy and nervous and intensely imaginative, wandered past him towards the pavilion. "There were so very few people; incredibly few people. Probably that was because it looked like rain, and yet the whole country-side seemed as lonely as though it were haunted."

" 'Haunted?' " Garth repeated.

"Yes, that sounds silly; but I think you understand what I mean. It's the same kind of feeling you can get, especially towards twilight, in one or two of those mediaeval buildings at Ravensport. Anyway, I was having tea at some country place with a sign outside that said, 'Bed and Breakfast,' and 'Fresh Eggs' underneath, when I saw the clock and remembered your note. And I raced back here so hard I feel sticky and horrible all over. Just this side of Fairfield I passed Hal Ormiston, driving your car in the opposite direction and looking very angry."

"Did Hal see you?"

"Yes, of course. He must have done. We were only a dozen feet apart and he wasn't going very fast, though he didn't seem to be paying much attention. Is—is that important?"

"Several things my nephew says, for once in his life, may be of the most vital importance. Don't shrink back Betty! I want you to understand this situation exactly as it is."

"Yes? I'm all right! *Yes?*"

Garth extended a hand behind him.

"Your sister was strangled to death in that pavilion," he said. "She was murdered there, in my opinion, about twenty minutes to six o'clock. There's always a lot of conflict in the medical evidence about a disputed time of death; we needn't insist on that, or try to fix the time by such rules. But there *is* evidence to show that somebody, somebody who isn't in the pavilion now, must have been there within the past twenty-odd minutes."

"Somebody?"

"I mean the murderer. In the room where she died the earthenware teapot is about a third full, and that tea is still scalding hot."

"Darling, I don't understand you. I swear to God I don't! Couldn't—couldn't Glynis have made tea for herself?"

"Oh, yes. It doesn't matter who made the tea or who drank it or who didn't drink it. But at any time that woman could possibly have been killed, at any time within any medical limits, the tide was almost as far out as it is at this minute. Now look round you. Look back up the beach. Look out towards the sea. Look down under the piles of the pavilion."

The inshore breeze, further ruffling Betty's hair, smoothed at her skirt as well. She glanced quickly over her shoulder, looking round her, and then just as quickly back again.

"There are your footprints," Garth continued, "coming out here from the grass slope where you left the bicycle. There are my footprints," he moved his arm to point, "coming out here from the back of the cottage. There's not another mark anywhere. You see that?"

"David, I—"

"You see that, my dear?"

"Yes!"

"The murderer had to leave the pavilion after he killed Glynis. He's not there now. And in some fashion, explain it how you like, he or she or some damnable witch of the low-tide managed to leave here without a single footprint in all that wet sand."

Neither of them spoke for a moment or two.

One sound they heard, carried by the breeze, was little more than a ripple or whisper from far away in the hollow of the sea. But the tide had turned; its lap at the edges would presently become the soft, shaky thunder of the tide rolling in.

The other noise struck at them from the opposite side. It was the clop and jingle of an open carriage: a dilapidated carriage, such as you usually found at railways-stations in seaside towns, but driven at a brisk pace along the road from the direction of Ravensport.

"No, Betty!" Garth was looking past the driver of the carriage at its two passengers. "Don't move. I know both those men. We shall have to face this out."

They had not long to wait, once the carriage had disappeared on the other side of the house. The two men in question appeared almost immediately, having walked through that broad central hall, at the open glass doors which faced the pavilion.

They were looking quickly round them. But they did not comment, even to each other, until they had marched straight out across the sands. A single eyeglass glinted, even though there was no sun to make it glint.

"My dear fellow," said the not unsympathetic voice of Cullingford Abbot, "we have heard, rightly or wrongly, that something most unpleasant has happened here. I only hope, for your own sake, that what we've heard is not true."

The other man was entirely non-committal.

"Well, well!" said Detective-Inspector George Alfred Twigg, shaking his head and avoiding Garth's eye. "Who'd ha' thought it, now? Well, well, well!"

8

Along this part of the coast, with varying voices and in different irregular rhythms, clocks had finished striking nine.

At Betty Calder's house the noise could be heard softly, not at all discordant, as dusk deepened into night. Softly too, and in silken undulation, moved the surf at high-tide.

But the atmosphere in Betty's sitting-room, where Cullingford Abbot looked at David Garth, did not quite accord with this.

At the back of the stone house there were two long and low-ceilinged rooms, one at either side of the central hall; each with three windows overlooking the water that stirred whisperingly below scrub grass and beach. The room at the left had been intended as a bedroom for the late Glynis Stukeley. The room at the right was the sitting-room—cluttered, lace-curtained, its padded chairs draped in cretonne—where Betty had spent too much time dreaming over books.

A paraffin lamp in a yellow silk shade hung from the ceiling. If you glanced out of the open windows, here in this sitting-room, you could see a hurricane-lantern burning inside the pavilion. But Garth sat on the window-seat, his back to the sea, and faced Cullingford Abbot, whose back was to the fireplace.

Though their talk remained polite, even after three hours' questioning, exasperation lurked at its edges.

"My dear fellow," said Abbot, his facial muscles gripping the single eyeglass so that one side of the face seemed to go lopsided, "can't you help us any further? Can't you?"

"I have told the truth. Every word. If you don't believe it . . ."

"Oh, I don't say I disbelieve you! Not altogether."

"Thank you."

"Tut! There is no need for sarcasm."

"No sarcasm was intended," Garth told him sincerely. "I appreciate your consideration. I appreciate your allowing Lady Calder and me to have a meal at the Stag and Glove."

"You understand, let's hope, that I was obliged to accompany you?"

"Yes. Of course."

"Very well. Now, then!"

Abbot, short and stocky, wore a frock coat and an elaborate cravat. His grey moustache curled above a firm mouth, and his grey hair was cut short. He could not be called at all dandified; he was too formidable. The gleam on his eye-glass seemed to come rather from the eye behind it than from the light that shone there.

"There are several reasons," he said, "why I want to be fair. We made one mistake in the matter of Lady Calder. I'm honest enough to admit that."

Garth lowered his head.

"She's not the blackmailer we thought she was," Abbot continued. "She didn't drive that banker Dalrymple to put a bullet through his head five years ago. We weren't too much to blame, I might point out. Glynis Stukeley gave her sister's name at the time of the Dalrymple suicide; Glynis Stukeley used her sister's name *and* title when she went back to the Moulin Rouge in '06.

"However! We've been making inquiries since Lady Calder told this story to the Hampstead police last night. We already had a set of the blackmailer's fingerprints, taken (unofficially, let's admit) when Dalrymple died. Fingerprints weren't al-lowed in evidence then; and, anyway, there was no prosecu-tion. The woman dead out in that pavilion is the one we've been after."

"Thank God."

"Amen. But don't you see, my dear Garth—" he spoke persuasively, as a reasonable man, lifting the lapel of his coat to sniff at the gardenia in the buttonhole—"that all this is quite irrelevant?"

"Irrelevant?"

"To the question of whether Lady Calder strangled a sister who was driving her out of her mind. Inspector Rogers, at Hampstead last night, overheard her threaten it. 'If she tries just one more trick, so help me God, I'll kill her and take the consequences.' Weren't you actually there yourself when she said that?"

"Yes."

"And what sort of trick, by Lady Calder's own admission, was this sister playing on her today?" Abbot waited. "Now look here, young fella-me-lad. I've tried to give you every advantage. So far I've taken the questioning entirely on my-self. I don't want to turn you over to Twigg unless it becomes absolutely necessary."

"Then send for Twigg, by all means. It seems a pity not to give him his opportunity."

Some of the cynical benevolence was wiped off Abbot's face. He squared his shoulders, a mannerism copied from Sir Edward Henry.

"Oh, Twigg may get his opportunity. Some people think

it not wise to question a witness too soon. Let him sweat a little first. That's what Twigg believes, I understand. Do you follow me?"

"Yes. I am still telling the truth."

"Confound it, man, can't you help me a little?"

"How?"

"Well, how does it feel when *you're* penned into a corner? Early this afternoon, before I came down to the country, I spoke to Mrs. Bostwick at Hyde Park Gardens."

"Did you enjoy yourself?"

"Quite frankly, I did." Abbot smoothed at the under-side of his moustache. "She's a charming young lady, very. I don't often meet 'em in the way of business. Last night you put that poor woman through one devil of an inquisition. I ought to put you through a worse one—and Twigg's the man to do it—except that I think you're honest. I keep wondering. Why can't you help me?"

"I'm trying to help you!"

"Very well. Here's your chance. Mrs. Bostwick gave you a perfectly straight story, confirmed by all evidence. A woman nearly strangled Mrs. Montague, and escaped afterwards through an unlocked and unbolted cellar-door. Straightforward, eh? Fair enough?"

"I suppose so."

"Yet for some reason, Mrs. Bostwick tells me, you disbelieved every word she said and all but frightened the poor girl out of her wits. Why did you doubt her?"

"Abbot, there are professional reasons why I can't tell you!"

"Oh, no. You shouldn't have told Twigg you were Mrs. Bostwick's medical adviser. She denies it. In fact, she disowns you and says she wants nothing more to do with you."

"I see."

"So that won't wash." The monocle gleamed like a dragon's eye. "And don't say the police suspect Lady Calder of attacking Mrs. Montague. We don't suspect that. We've pretty well established she was attacked by Glynis Stukeley. You've got no reason to shield Glynis Stukeley. Why did you doubt Mrs. Bostwick's story?"

"Abbot, did you ask Mr. Vincent Bostwick the same question?"

"Yes. He couldn't understand either. Why did you doubt Marion Bostwick?"

Garth looked at the floor.

He put his hands on his knees. He started to get up, but thought better of it. He looked up at the yellow silk shade of the lamp, and at the open bookshelves round the walls.

Behind his head, beyond lace curtains and open windows, the long surf swayed and rippled at the edge of the beach. Farther out, where an occasional low wave struck under the piles of the pavilion, reflections from the light inside it trembled against dark water.

And still the inscrutable Abbot watched him.

"Look here, I'll be quite frank with you," Abbot said abruptly. "You're a clever chap, Garth. I don't underestimate you. And I won't ask you, not now anyway, to change one bit of your testimony about what happened out there at the pavilion—"

"Abbot, for the last time . . . !"

"I won't ask that, I say," the other struck in, "if you're equally frank with me about other matters. Is it agreed?"

Abbot stalked out to the middle of the room. Behind him the ledge of the mantelpiece was cluttered in Betty Calder's happy, untidy fashion with silver-framed photographs. One of them, Garth saw, was a snapshot of a woman who must be Glynis herself, pictured with Betty when both of them were much younger. Betty's presence haunted all her possessions, even when she waited terrified and half-sick in an upstairs room.

"Is it agreed?"

"Yes, it's agreed. If I'm accused of intimidating Marion Bostwick—"

"That's what you did, wasn't it?"

"I don't know. When I think of Betty there," and he pointed to the mantelpiece, and Abbot craned round to look, and suddenly it was as though cold fingers gripped Garth's throat, "I wonder how many times we hurt patients instead of helping them. The most detestable thing in this world is a kind of calm know-it-all bullying that shakes its head fishily and warns people of the direst consequences if they don't do as they're told. That's why I can't get on with Inspector Twigg. He reminds me too much of a nephew of mine. Abbot, you remind me of somebody too."

"What the hell are you talking about? My personal appearance—"

"I didn't refer so much to your personal appearance, any more than Twigg looks in the least like Hal Ormiston. If we're talking about personal appearance, I should say you look more like a certain Mr. Frank Harris."

For the first time, without intending to do so, he had stung Abbot badly.

"Frank Harris? That bounder who used to hold forth at the Café Royal, and boast about his power over women?"

"Forgive me. I was trying—"

"Quite so. You were trying to divert me again. Don't go on trying it; I need information. For instance! When I wanted a word with Mrs. Montague, they told me on the telephone she's not at Hampstead."

"They've taken her to a nursing-home, you mean?"

"No, young fella-me-lad, I don't mean that. I mean Mrs. Blanche Montague is in Fairfield at this very minute."

"In Fairfield? That's impossible!"

"Why? Is it medically impossible, after the attempted strangling?"

"No, it's not medically impossible."

"Well, then?"

"Abbot, I didn't examine the lady. But there was much bruising and possibly worse damage as well. In a case of that sort, you always risk oedema of the larynx."

"What does that mean, in plain language?"

"If the patient gets excited and raises her voice, or even drinks hot tea instead of something cold, her vocal chords may swell so much that it needs an operation to save her life. I wonder her doctor allowed her to get up."

"According to Marion Bostwick," Abbot retorted, "her doctor didn't allow it. And she was raising her voice, right enough. Mrs. Montague has relatives in Fairfield; she's the sort, they tell me, who would have relatives in Fairfield. She kept on screaming to be taken away from Hampstead until Colonel Selby agreed to bring her here. Colonel Selby's at the Imperial Hotel; she's with her relatives, guarded behind another doctor's order not to be questioned. I came especially from London to Fairfield so that I could question her, and drew blank.

"Failing that, I went on to Ravensport (your nephew very kindly drove me) to join Twigg for a word with the Ravensport police, who until recently have been keeping an eye on Lady Calder. This morning, by my own order from London and therefore my fault, they'd stopped keeping an eye on her. That scarcely seemed important (eh?) until an anonymous telephone-call at near six o'clock warned 'em there was trouble at Lady Calder's."

"An anonymous telephone-call," repeated Garth. "I see."

"Do you, young fella-me-lad?" Abbot asked with extraordinary intensity. "But let's return to Mrs. Blanche Montague. What does that woman know? What did she *say* to Glynis Stukeley, if it was Glynis Stukeley, that made the Stukeley herself go berserk? We thought, at first, your friend Vincent Bostwick was being blackmailed—"

"But you don't think so now?"

"No, we don't. As I had to admit last night, on the telephone, there wasn't a shred of real evidence to connect Vincent Bostwick with the danger from the Moulin Rouge. And this morning, as I mentioned a moment ago, our people in London made inquiries at Glynis Stukeley's lodgings. She hasn't been seen with Vincent Bostwick or with any other man, except . . ."

·"Yes?"

"Except," and Abbot turned the eyeglass full on him, "except a young man in your employ named Michael Fielding. Suppose you tell me everything you know about young Fielding."

There was a pause. The surf dragged and rustled.

Garth should not have lost his temper. He should have held it back, held it back, held it back. . . .

"Michael Fielding," he replied, "is studying at Bart's Hospital on a pittance of a legacy from a clergyman uncle, helped out by what I pay him. He is brilliant, unsure of himself, impressionable, and perhaps not very stable. But he's not a murderer; neither is Betty Calder. Abbot, why can't you leave Betty out of this?"

"Tut, now! It's overwhelmingly probable she strangled that blackmailing harlot, just as Twigg says she did."

"You really believe that?"

"Yes; I'm afraid I do. If one sister is capable of a murderous attack, so is the other. There's the same blood between 'em. Why should I forget that? Because of her beautiful eyes?"

"No," said Garth. "Becaues you and your God-damned Twigg have been wrong every step of the way. You were wrong about Betty being a blackmailer; wrong about Vince Bostwick being the victim. You'll never in this world prove Betty was concerned in that murder, and I challenge you to try."

Abbot looked at him.

"Indeed," he remarked, very deliberately taking the gardenia out of his buttonhole and very deliberately hurling it into the empty fireplace. "Very well, then. Go your own way. I've finished trying to help you."

Instantly the door to the hall opened, and Inspector Twigg was in the room.

"Oh, ah! Did you call me, sir?"

A draught whipped between door and open windows. It belled out the curtains, it set the silk-shaded lamp swinging, it clapped shut the door with a crash that seemed to echo in the thunder of the surf below the pavilion.

"Did you call me, sir?"

"No, but I was about to. Take charge of the questioning. Conduct it in any way you please."

"Oh, ah!" said Twigg. "Oh, ah! I don't mind admitting, sir, that suits me right down to the ground."

"And it suits me too," said Garth, who had jumped to his feet.

"But a word of warning to you, Inspector," added Abbot, iron-fair and tightly inscrutable again. "You will conduct it according to some instructions for police-officers known as the Judge's Rules. At all times you will remember those rules."

"*I* can remember 'em, sir, *I* can remember 'em! Just so long as Dr. Garth here has got it through his head he's in quite a serious position: he may be headed for prison if not worse; and he can't order people about at his own sweet will."

"Stick to your questioning, Mr. Twigg," snapped Garth. "Try not to begin bluffing before you've said ten words to the witness."

"Bluffing, am I?"

"*Stop this*," said Abbot.

The bursting quality of the silence clamped over them like a lid. Nobody moved for perhaps ten seconds. Then Garth sat down again on the window-seat, leaning back with an outward assumption of casualness. Twigg, his bowler hat on the back of his head, took only a little longer before his look smoothed itself out to the agreeable.

"Well, now, sir," he said heartily, "that suits me too."

"Go ahead, then," said Abbot.

"Mind you, though!" added Twigg, as if suddenly remembering something and carefully defining his terms. "It might be, Mr. Abbot, I've had to disobey some of your orders already."

"Oh? How so?"

"Well, sir, it's Lady Calder. She tried to run away. I had to question her in private before you wanted me to, and maybe speak a bit sharp to her. Bless you, sir, all women get a bit hysterical at one time or another!"

"*Sit down, Garth*," snarled Abbot. But his large grey moustache showed implacably against a congested face. "Inspector, if you have gone one step beyond—"

"Oh, I've kept to the Judge's Rules! You ask the lady herself if I haven't. And I didn't have much choice, as you might say. We've got a witness outside, Sergeant Baines and I have, that makes it look pretty bad for the lady without another word being said."

"Who is the witness?"

Twigg did not reply.

He walked over towards Garth, who again had sat down. Dragging out a large padded chair, Twigg pulled it sideways and himself sat down on the arm so that he towered above the man on the window-seat. He took out a notebook and the stub of a pencil.

"Now, then, Doctor," he began.

9

"Inspector," David Garth asked some three-quarters of an hour later, "how much longer do we need go on with this?"

"Plenty of time, sir. Plenty of time!"

"May I point out that we have been over the same old ground at least half a dozen times?"

"That's right, Doctor. And we may have to go over it half a dozen times more. Eh?"

"Do you mind if I get up and walk about?"

"Not a bit, sir! You do just that. Now, then: about the last question I was asking . . ."

It had begun to shake Garth's nerve, and he knew it. This did not come from mere repetition, which would not have troubled him. But he could not meet Twigg's slippery maneuvering, or once strike back with any vital reply. Time after time Twigg would take him almost up to ground he had been expecting, and then lead him away before he could use his answers.

Cullingford Abbot sat watching the exchange with a look between impassivity and cynical admiration. His eyeglass turned back and forth from Twigg to Garth like that of a man at a tennis-match; a thin cheroot was in his mouth, and smoke drifted up towards the light.

"I hope you're following me, Doctor?"

"I am following you, Mr. Twigg. Go on!"

Abruptly Garth rose up from the window-seat, glancing out of the nearest window.

The sound of that surf was not in the least loud; it only seemed loud to his heightened senses. The drag of water was so gentle that two uniformed policemen, now launching a tiny boat into the tide, could easily push it to the pavilion with oars for poles. The boat swayed and swung as they tied it to a hook by the door.

Long before dark they had taken plaster casts of the foot-prints. Long before dark they had seemed to be taking endless photographs inside the pavilion, using a tripod camera and magnesium flash-powder. What were they doing now?

Garth, with a frustration beyond any he would have im-agined, walked towards some low bookshelves at the other side of the fireplace. The bright-coloured prints above all these bookshelves were mostly reproductions of paintings by Mr. Maxfield Parrish, showing supple nudes against purple dawn or dusk; no very high standard of taste, he supposed, but why shouldn't Betty choose them? Again he kept wondering where Betty was now, and what she had been telling Twigg.

Then her name struck at him and he turned round.

"I beg your pardon? What did you say about Lady Calder?"

"We're coming to her, Doctor. What time was it, again, you claim you got here this afternoon?"

"It was a little before five minutes to six. Possibly six or seven minutes to the hour. I can't be more definite than that."

"And Lady Calder was expecting you?"

"Yes."

"Oh, ah. But she wasn't here?"

"No. I have already explained why she wasn't here."

"So you have, Doctor. No call to get excited!" Twigg looked at his notebook. "You met your nephew, you say, and he told you Lady Calder had gone out for a bathe?"

"He told me that, yes. But it was not Lady Calder. It was her sister. The witnesses, including Mr. Abbot there, were too far away to distinguish between the two. If you doubt that—"

"Doubt it? Now what makes you think we doubt it? I tell you straight, Doctor, I'm downright pleased to hear you say so. When you sign your statement, I'll make good and sure you testify to that."

"One moment," said Cullingford Abbot, taking the cheroot out of his mouth.

"Now, sir, if *you* go interrupting . . . !"

"One moment, I said!"

Twigg's colour had come up, but he restrained himself.

"*I* can testify to it," Abbot told him. "I saw her. And there's no doubt, from tests taken at the pavilion, that woman was Glynis Stukeley. But don't ask Dr. Garth to testify *he* saw her at four o'clock; you'll wreck your case. Now get on with it."

"Thanking you very kindly for the correction, sir, and I will." Twigg looked back at Garth. "At the time you went out to that pavilion, Doctor, were there anybody's footprints in the sand except yours?"

"No, there were not."

"Oh, ah. You can swear to *that*, can you?"

"Yes, I can."

"You want me to get on with this, Doctor, and Mr. Abbot wants me to get on with it. So we'll do just that. You've been telling me how you discovered the Stukeley woman's body. How you turned her over to identify her, and turned her back again. How it was you as smashed the cup we found smashed there. How you touched the teapot, and it was still very hot. . . ."

"I do say that, yes. You must have touched the teapot to discover it for yourself. Surely you did that, Mr. Twigg?"

"I'm asking the questions, Doctor; you're answering 'em. Just you try to remember it. So we'll take something else."

Garth's senses were strung suddenly to cold alertness. A new note had come into Twigg's voice; he made tasting noises with his tongue.

"On a hook against the wall, you say, you found a lady's bathing-cape, brown serge, yellow stripes across it. In one pocket there was a handkerchief labelled G. S., and you put the handkerchief back in the pocket. Right?"

"Yes. The bathing-cape is there now."

"Oh, ah. It's there now. Did you take that cape out to the pavilion, Doctor? Or did Lady Calder take it there?"

"Neither of us. The cape was hanging from the hook when I arrived."

"Would it interest you to hear, Doctor, that the dead woman wasn't wearing or carrying any such cape when she went out for a bathe?"

Again nobody moved. Garth could hear his own watch ticking.

"Well, Doctor? We've got two witnesses to that, I'd have you know. Mr. Abbot is one of 'em."

Still Garth did not speak. Cullingford Abbot, a stamp of ugliness on his face, nodded briefly and looked Garth in the eyes.

"Dammit, man," he snapped, again removing the cigar, "I can't help the fact if it's so, can I? The damned woman had no cape. There it is."

Twigg's almost invisible eyebrows went up.

"Got that, Doctor? Only your footprints and Lady Calder's, as you've kept on telling me, went out on the sand to the steps of that pavilion. Not another mark anywhere! If Glynis Stukeley didn't wear the cape or take it herself, how did it get there?"

Again silence.

"I can only say . . ."

"Better not say anything, Doctor, unless you can give me an answer. And that's only the starter." Twigg, shifting himself on the arm of the padded chair where he had inched round to face Garth, turned over another page in the notebook.

"About that business of the tea being hot," Twigg continued, "you're making a mighty lot of it, now; a good deal more'n a humble copper can tell you it's worth. Maybe the tea was hot. Maybe it wasn't. Mr. Abbot and me, as soon as we nabbed you and Lady Calder outside the pavilion, had to hustle you back here so you wouldn't mess about with things any longer. By the time I got a chance to look at the tea, it might have been brewed last January. It'll make no odds to a jury either way. Got that?"

"Perfectly. Lady Calder and I, it seems, are to pay for your own negligence in looking at evidence."

"I want no more trouble with you, me bucko," Twigg said softly. "Got *that?*"

Any outsider who saw David Garth at that moment, his jaws less saturnine and a drop of sweat running down his temple, would have thought him clean finished and nearly at his lowest ebb. And so he was almost finished—almost, but not quite.

"So let's leave what's not important," pursued Twigg, "and take what is important. You want me to believe (ho, lummy!) you two are so innocent the Almighty might make a new Garden of Eden and turn you both loose in it. Let's see about this innocence.

"You say you were so surprised-like to find the tea scalding hot that you knocked a cup off the table. That was when Lady Calder ran out to the pavilion. And she was calling your name. Is that so?"

"Yes!"

"Doctor, how did she know you were there?"

"I've told you a half a dozen times Lady Calder was expecting me!"

"All right. Let's suppose she was. But that pavilion's got no windows. There were two doors, an outer door with a sun-blind half drawn and a wooden door only partly ajar, between you and anybody on the outside. She couldn't have seen you. How did she know you were there?

"And don't tell me," Twigg added, holding up his hand as the other attempted to speak, "don't tell me, for sweet little green apples' sake, she could take one look at some footprints in the sand and recognize they were yours. Ho, now! You expect a jury to believe she wasn't inside that pavilion, strangling her sister either with your help or without it?"

"Yes," retorted Garth, taking a step forward. "Because it happens to be true."

"She was gallivanting round the country on a bike for nearly two hours? And never went near the place, let alone inside it, until she turned up at shortly past six o'clock?"

"Yes! That's true too!"

"It is, eh? Let's see."

Twig put the notebook back in his pocket. He surged up from the arm of the chair, a bulky man with pale eyes in a red face. With great deliberation he went to the door of the hall and opened it.

"Come in, Mr. Ormiston," he said.

Cullingford Abbot craned round from his chair, cheroot poised at the edge of his teeth. Hal Ormiston, now wearing a dust-coat over jacket and flannels and with his straw boater discarded, marched into the sitting-room as though brought there by the consciousness of heroic purpose. Twigg slammed the door just as the draught whirled.

Garth turned away. Hal didn't. It may be that apprehension lurked somewhere in his soul, but his nose was up and his chin out. Nor could anyone have failed to be reassured by the heartiness of Twigg's greeting.

"Oh, ah! I won't delay you long, sir," said Twigg, touching one finger to the brim of his bowler hat. "And maybe it's a pity (for you, I mean) your car broke down in Fairfield and you had to come back here. But it's not a pity for the law. Before you say what happened with that car, though, maybe you'll tell us about a woman you saw on the beach when you were taking Mr. Abbot to Ravensport?"

"Glad to, Inspector," said Hal.

"Well, sir?"

"The woman wasn't old Bet. I thought there was something funny at the time, so help me! The walk was a bit different and so was the swing of her, if you see what I mean. But there wasn't enough different really to notice, or I'd have noticed it."

Twigg turned a bland jowl towards Abbot and Garth.

"I'm not going to prompt you, Mr. Ormiston. No, by jing! I'm sticking to the Judge's Rules. Can you tell us, maybe, what the woman had on? Clothes, like?"

"She was wearing a brown bathing-costume without sleeves and without stockings. She was wearing a puffy cap with a rubber lining. She was wearing canvas shoes with rubber soles. That's all. Anyway, that's all I saw."

"Was she carrying a towel, maybe? Or anything like that?"

"No."

"Not a bathing-cape? Nothing? Ah, just so! And this was about four o'clock, wasn't it? Good! Tell me, sir: is that your uncle standing over there?"

"That's old Nunkie. I told him to pull up his socks if he didn't want to land in a mess, and it's no fault of mine if he has."

"Just so, Mr. Ormiston. Did you see Dr. Garth hereabouts at any time this afternoon?"

"You bet I did."

"What time would that 'a' been, maybe?"

"I met him outside the cottage here," answered Hal, fashioning the syllables with great care, "at ten minutes to six o'clock. He was in one hell of a dither about something, Nunkie was."

"Did you see him go out to the pavilion?"

"Don't put words into my mouth, Old Sausage," Hal corrected with great swiftness. "Don't *you* do that either. I don't like it. I saw him *start* out there, if you like. That's all I did see. He paid me some money he owed me, and I left."

"What time was that, sir?"

"Not much later than ten minutes to six. Hardly a minute later, if you ask me."

"I do ask you, sir, and I'm greatly appreciating it. Were there any footprints or marks in the sand before Dr. Garth went there?"

"How should I know? I didn't see any."

"Sir, did you see Lady Calder then?"

"You mean old Bet? No. I didn't see her then. And I didn't see her at any other time." Cullingford Abbot rose to his feet, flung the half-smoked cheroot into the fireplace as previously he had flung the gardenia, and sat down again. Garth stood motionless, as though poised and waiting. And Twigg, who apparently expected him to spring forward, held up a hypnotic hand.

"I'll just ask you to be sure of that, Mr. Ormiston. We've heard Lady Calder was seen riding a bicycle between here and Fairfield after you left in the motor-car. We've heard you couldn't help seeing her, because you passed her in the road."

Up went Hal's eyebrows.

"If you heard that, Old Sausage, you heard a downright, smacking, out-and-out-lie. I didn't pass anybody, Old Sausage. I didn't pass a living soul."

"Well, well, well," Twigg remarked after a pause. "Well, well, well!"

Hal, chin up and nostrils dilated, was looking steadily at Garth. So was Twigg, who had turned round in a leisurely way.

"That's how it stands, Doctor. You can have the tea hot. You can have the victim dead well inside the time you say. That's all the worse for you. According to Mr. Ormiston, you were going out to the pavilion at not much later than ten minutes to six. Mr. Abbot and I got here at ten minutes past six and found you and Lady Calder standing out there by the steps. In those twenty minutes not a witness saw you; not a witness saw Lady Calder. Both your sets of footprints go out there; nobody's come back. If neither of you two killed the Stukeley woman, who else *could* have killed her?"

Twigg paused, drawing in his breath.

"I've got a bit of an idea, Dr. Garth, you don't think I've got much in the way of brains. Not like the coppers in those fancy stories, anyway. That's as may be. But there's the case against your sweet and holy Lady Calder. Let's see you get her out of it."

"Yes," said Garth, "I think I will."

"What's that?"

"I said I think I will," repeated Garth, with unholy joy to see his enemy step at last on his own ground.

A whole series of creaks and cracks seemed to have afflicted the woodwork of the room. Hal Ormiston was looking away. Garth moved out slowly—his eyes on a level with Twigg's, his hands at his sides.

"Mr. Twigg," he said formally, "I was not allowed in the pavilion after you arrived. Suppose you show me the photographs your men took? Or at least tell me what you found there on the floor?"

"Ho, now! As if I would!"

"Oh, yes, you will," said Cullingford Abbot.

Abbot had jumped to his feet. Twigg turned slowly towards him.

"Mr. Abbot, sir, are you teaching me how to do this? Do you want to nab murderers, or don't you?"

"I am interested in nabbing murderers, yes," Abbot said suavely. "I am also interested in fair play."

"God's truth," yelled Twigg, "and he talks about fair play. This thing is no cricket-match, Mr. Abbot. You amateurs wouldn't think so if you had to work as hard as we do."

"Possibly not." Abbot looked back at Garth. "By the way, my dear fellow," he added, with his large moustache bristling towards Hal Ormiston, "I imagine it was that young daisy who made the anonymous telephone-call to the police-station?"

"Yes." And Garth nodded. "It's the most probable supposition, at least. It's been the most probable supposition all the time."

"Ah! I thought so. Now will you answer Dr. Garth's questions, Inspector Twigg, or shall I answer them for you? Which is it to be?"

"I'll answer any ruddy questions Dr. Garth thinks he can ask. He won't slip out of this one, I'm telling you, not if I have to go over your head to the Commissioner."

"Mr. Twigg," said Garth, "what did you find on the floor?"

"On what floor? Where?"

Any patient who saw David Garth at this particular later moment, eyes glittering in a pale face, might well have thought the specialist in neurology himself required treatment.

"We have heard a great deal," he said, "about footprints outside the pavilion. Let us hear something about footprints inside it. My nephew well and truly remarked he had no wish to get his shoes covered with sand or mud. But anyone who went to the pavilion could not very well have avoided it. Did you find sand-traces of my footprints, Mr. Twigg? Did you find them going through the room on the left, out on the veranda, and round to the room on the right? Just as I said I did?"

"Oh, ah! We found 'em. And we've got photographs. Does that prove you didn't kill Glynis Stukeley?"

"No, it does not."

"Well, then?"

"Mr. Twigg, did you find any footprints left by the dead woman?"

"No, naturally we didn't! She'd been in the water. She'd been for a swim. She hoisted herself back to the veranda when the tide was still up, long before she died. The only footprints *she'd* have made would be prints in salt-water, and they'd have dried on the floor."

"Quite right," said Garth. "The wet state of her bathing-costume just matched an estimate of that time." Then he raised his voice. "Mr. Twigg, did you find any footprints left by Lady Calder?"

Five seconds ticked past.

Cullingford Abbot had taken a pigskin cigar-case from his inside pocket, but he did not open it. Moustache drawn down, head a little forward, he kept the eyeglass fixed on Twigg.

"You found no such footprints," said Garth, "although Lady Calder also walked through the sand. Is that correct?"

"Ho, now! It would 'a' been easy to—"

"Would it?" asked Garth. "Is it reasonable to imagine a pair of murderers erasing one set of tracks and leaving the other? Even supposing we had done so, where are the cleaning materials we used in a hut without water laid on? How could it have been managed without leaving any traces for you to find? You didn't find those traces, Mr. Twigg, because Betty Calder was never inside the pavilion."

Clamping one hand across his forehead, he pressed hard

at both temples. Then he straightened up and spoke with toiling lucidity.

"I will be frank with you, Mr. Twigg, as I don't think you are being frank with me. I can't explain how that murder was committed. It's a little like the murder in a novel called *By Whose Hand?*"

"Ah!" breathed Twigg, who was watching him closely.

"I can't explain how that bathing-robe appeared at the pavilion. There are several things I can't explain."

"Ah!" said Twigg.

"You may arrest me as the murderer, though in the long run I don't think you will. When you have ceased to be as angry with me as I now am with you, for personal reasons alone, I think your own good sense will prevent you. You may arrest me, I say. But you can't touch Betty Calder."

"I can't, eh?" Twigg strode across to the door, held the knob as he threw it open, and raised his voice. "Sergeant Baines!"

"Sir?" called a voice outside.

"Sergeant Baines, where is Lady Calder?"

"Inspector, you locked her in her room upstairs! Inspector, I don't think you ought to 'a' done that."

"Never you mind what I ought to 'a' done! Fetch her here, will you?"

Once more the strong draught, blowing between door and windows as the door was held open, made a chaos across the sitting-room. As curtains streamed out and lamp-shade swung wildly, you might have fancied the pictures themselves flashed their bright colours in rattling frames. Cullingford Abbot strode over beside Twigg.

"Sergeant Baines," he said, "be pleased to forget that order. Twigg, shut the door."

"Sir—"

"Did you hear what I said? Shut the door."

"Now so help me Jinny," breathed Twigg, "but fair's fair and a joke's a joke. Mr. Abbot, are you trying to tell me what Dr. Garth says is conclusive?"

"Tut! It's anything but conclusive. The dog's still got jam on his whiskers, and plenty of it too."

"Is it an apology you want, sir? Maybe I spoke too sharp. All right! Maybe I shouldn't have called you an amateur. All right!"

"Why shouldn't you have called me an amateur? In one sense, at least, I am an amateur. Of horses, of French cooking, of women, and even (God help me) of crime too. But I am very much an official of the Criminal Investigation

Department. There are two reasons why I don't propose to let you go on with this now."

"Oh, ah? Because you gentlemen always stick together?"

"No." And up went Abbot's eyeglass. "The first reason is that he has thrown just enough doubt on your case to make the difference. The second reason, and to me perhaps the better one, is that I believe Dr. Garth."

"And I'm to forget all about it, am I? Is that what you're saying?"

"No, it is not. If I could persuade you and Dr. Garth to shake hands and forget your differences, you might make the best detective team on earth. We're not dealing with a fool, my good Twigg, even if he does get his notions out of books. You are to—"

Abbot stopped abruptly. The other was not even listening.

"Book!" whispered Inspector Twigg. "Now why didn't I think of that before? Books!"

And the whole atmosphere changed for the second time.

Garth felt his heart give a sickening sort of bound; this was the most dangerous ground of all. "Not again!" he was praying to himself. "Not quite so soon. Not again!"

Twigg's big face smoothed itself out to urbanity. He looked round the room, along the row of shelves. Whatever he saw, it appeared to be in one of the shelves just to the left of the fireplace. He lumbered over towards the shelves, stretching out his hand.

"Do you honour me with your attention, Inspector?"

"Sir?"

"In future, Inspector, you will not be quite so quick off the mark. You will leave these people free of your threats until—"

"Ho!" said Twigg. He turned round. "They'll never be free of me, either of 'em, until that innocent little prostitute gets what she deserves. But you're right, Mr. Abbot, not to let me fall in a trap like the doctor wanted. I've just remembered something else. By jing! I've just remembered something else."

10

"They've gone now." Betty said. "They've all gone. But what did he remember?"

In the road outside the cottage, under high incurious stars, the wind blew with a coolness grateful to Garth's aching eyes and muscles. He was emotionally as exhausted as though physically he had finished one stage of a dangerous rock-climb.

But it was only one stage, not the summit.

"Betty," he said, "you can't stay here alone tonight. It's almost unheard of for the Stag and Glove to take in a single woman as a guest, but we'll see if we can get them to put you up. Go and pack a bag, will you?"

"I was only asking—"

"Betty, for God's sake go and pack a bag!"

"You hate me, don't you? I can't blame you. If you also realized . . ."

"Betty, I know you didn't kill her. I think I know who did, and I'm beginning to believe I know how it was done. If the question is whether I hate you, the answer is no. The answer is that I love you far too much. For the rest, let's leave that until I am a little more my so-called reasonable self. Will you go and pack a bag, please?"

Betty nodded.

Her eyes seemed enormous in the dim light. Except that she had changed her flat-heeled cycling shoes when she and Garth and Abbot had gone to dinner much earlier at the Stag and Glove, she still wore the dark skirt and grey blouse of that afternoon. Suddenly she turned and ran up the path to the house.

Garth's watch told him it was now twenty minutes past eleven. If a house containing only paraffin lamps can be said to blaze with light, the cottage did so at this moment. All bogles were held at bay. No witch or goblin crept across the sands to strangle without a trace. Glynis Stukeley's body had been removed.

But Twigg, ever-present and ever-watchful . . .

Shutting away the image, Garth himself went up the path to the house.

Not even several years as the wife of Jamaica's Captain-General had freed Betty from the notion that you had a "best" room for occasions which were mainly uncomfortable ones, and seldom used otherwise. If anything, her experiences added to this belief.

To the left of the central hall, at the front, lay a dining-room in the best artwork style of 1907. To the right, matching the sitting-room at the rear, was a drawing-room congealed to rural effect with plants in those glazed pots called *jardinières*.

Somebody hissed at Garth as he passed the drawing-room. Vincent Bostwick, in frock coat and striped trousers, a silk hat cradled in his left arm and a silver-headed walking-stick in his right hand, stood under a lamp hanging from the ceiling. Its light emphasized the middle parting of Vince's hair and threw into relief a weather-beaten face now somewhat hollow of eye.

Garth, by this time past any sort of surprise, looked at him from the doorway.

"Vince, how did you get here?"

"I walked here," retorted Vince, choosing to take him literally. "It's only a short distance to Fairfield, and less than that to the Stag and Glove. The fact is, old boy, Marion and I are putting up at the Stag and Glove."

"Since when?"

"Don't ask questions! Tell you later. The fact is—"

"Then we're all here? We're all at Fairfield."

"Well, yes," admitted Vince, jabbing out with the ferrule of his tick at a stand holding a *jardinière*. "You might call it a gathering of the legions or whatever is the heraldic term for a muster of vultures." He jabbed again. "I've been dodging bluebottles; and they're not easy to dodge. Have they all gone?"

"The police? I hope so. Do you know what's happened?"

"Yes. I met Hal in the road after Cullingford Abbot slung him out of here."

"It's a relief to hear somebody met him in the road. Have you seen Betty?"

"Not exactly face to face, but that's what I wanted to ask you about. I couldn't help overhearing you two. David, do you think you'd better take your—do you think you'd better take Lady Calder to the Stag and Glove? Wouldn't she be more comfortable at the Palace Hotel? Or the Imperial?"

"No. Marion can chaperone her. That is, if Marion still doesn't 'disown' me."

"If you meant what I think you mean," retorted Vince, looking him in the eyes, "that was a misunderstanding. You haven't got it straight!"

"Everybody," Garth said despairingly, "Goes on telling me

that. Perhaps they're right. Vince, will you do me a favour? Go back to the Stag and Glove; tell Fred Easterbrook (that's the proprietor; the fat man with the barman's curl) I shall bring Lady Calder there in about half an hour. Meanwhile . . ."

"Yes, old boy?"

"A police-officer named Twigg has just had a dazzling inspiration about what he thinks I've been doing. I've got to discover what he thinks or he may have me in a corner again."

"It's not all gas and gaiters, is it?" Vince asked suddenly.

"What isn't?"

"Losing your head and your heart and everything else." Then Vince checked himself, the veins swelling at his temples. "Right," he added, expressionless again. "I'll tell Mr. What's-his-name. See you tomorrow morning."

And he clapped on his hat, stalking past Garth towards the front door.

Twigg! Good old Twigg!

Garth returned to the back sitting-room, where padded chairs and sofa covered in rose-patterned cretonne had become as disordered as people's emotions. Past the window he could see that they had blown out the hurricane-lantern inside the pavilion. There remained only a dark sea now kindled by a late-rising moon.

From the doorway he looked round at the bookshelves and at the paintings of Mr. Maxfield Parrish's chaste female nudes. Betty's liking for these paintings represented less a taste for the sensuous than the liking, as with so many other women, for exotic dream-scenes out of a fairy-tale. Though the new Viennese science regarded with suspicion even a fondness for fairy-tales, it regarded too damned many things with suspicion.

Whereupon, beyond a clutter of silver-framed photographs on the mantelpiece, he found himself staring at a framed photograph on the wall. It was the "bathing-party" picture of 1897, left behind by previous tenants. It showed two rowboats of holiday-makers so posed and poised for the camera that they looked stuffed.

"Betty," he remembered having asked her not long ago, "why do you keep that idiotic scene? You don't know any of the people, do you? It has no sentimental value?"

"No, of course not!" Betty had answered. "I honestly don't know why I keep it, except that it's rather funny. I'll take it down, if you'd rather I did."

But he was glad now she hadn't taken it down.

That afternoon, as he stood over a dead woman, there

had come into his mind a terrifying half-notion of what might have happened at the pavilion. It was only a glimpse. It was only a wild guess. But it leaped at him like a strangler, making him smash a cup.

That same half-notion, inspired by a faded photograph and the memory of a canvas screen set out at right-angles between two doors that were side by side, screamed again with a silent voice in Betty's sitting-room at past eleven o'clock.

Again he put the thought away. Inspector Twigg had been given some sort of glimpse in this room too. Garth walked over to the bookshelves on the left of the fireplace. He was reaching out towards one particular shelf, just as Twigg had done, when the door to the hall opened and closed sharply.

"Mind if I come in?" demanded the voice of Cullingford Abbot. And then, "Forgive me if I startled you. Didn't mean to."

"That's of no consequence. Come in, by all means."

In fact, despite a jump of the nerves, Garth could have welcomed him with joy. About Abbot there was a quality both hearty and heartening; Garth had never felt it so much as tonight. And yet, though Abbot wore his silk hat rakishly, he showed a certain embarrassment. His eyeglass hung on a cord down the white waistcoat. He seized the glass, twitched it into place with a grimace, and then bristled.

"Look here. I'm a copper and I'm proud to be one. I can't expect you to trust me. All I'll say is, Twigg doesn't know I'm here. I brought the carriage back."

"Twigg—" Garth began at very near fury.

"Twigg's an honest man. You may not credit that, but he is. It's only, sometimes, he can be as arrogant and intolerant as you are."

"That's the second time today someone has called me arrogant. Arrogant? Can you tell me why?"

"My dear chap! Yes! I can. You can understand and tolerate and sympathize with nearly every person on this earth. When you stumble on the very rare person you can't tolerate because you can't in the least understand, you blow up. Like Twigg. Or like your nephew. Not that I'd give much shrift to Master Hal, mind! However . . ."

Abbot, short and stocky, almost strutted as again he paced beside the fireplace.

"This case is more fascinatin' than ever. Look here, Lady Calder had nothing whatever to do with the murder, had she?"

"No, she had not. If you're finally convinced of that . . ."

"Oh, *I'm* convinced of it."

"And it's not, I hope, because of her beautiful eyes? As you yourself put it? It is not because you were impressed by her as you were so impressed by Marion Bostwick?"

"Now why in blazes," said Abbot, taken aback as he had taken Garth aback the moment before, "must you go on reminding me of Mrs. Bostwick?"

"Isn't that true? That you were very much impressed?"

"Frankly, yes. And I flatter myself," Abbot said with dignity, "she was not unimpressed by me." He touched his moustache. "But that's beside the point. It's Lady Calder's innocence we're bound to establish. Agreed?"

"Oh, yes."

"I can't get a word out of Twigg. If you told him he was trying to behave like Sherlock Holmes (which he is), and not at all like Lestrade or Gregson (which he couldn't), he'd rave at you and say he had no time for fancy yarns. And yet he was reaching out towards some book over here."

"Correct. He was reaching out towards this."

From the end of the second shelf down Garth took out a paper-covered novel published that same year in the *Daily Mail* Sixpenny Series. He handed it to Abbot.

"*The Mystery of the Yellow Room*," Abbot read aloud, "by Gaston Leroux. Is this book what I think it is?"

"It's a murder mystery, possible the greatest of its kind. At the beginning there is what appears to be a near-murder at a pavilion—"

Abbot's grey head whipped up.

"No, no!" Garth corrected him. "The pavilion is in the grounds of a French chateau; it's not in the least like the hut we have here. But the doors and windows are all found fastened on the inside. Later in the story, its most sensational incident, the murderer disappears before the eyes of four witnesses."

"H'm," said Abbot.

"Now if you'll glance farther along the same shelf," and Garth pointed, "you'll see another book. In cloth this time. Also published this year. *The Thinking Machine*. Author: Jacques Futrelle."

"Another Frenchman?"

"No; Jacques Futrelle is an American. And it's a book of short stories. But the best stories concern impossible or apparently supernatural happenings which are explained naturally at the end."

"H'm," said Abbot.

Bending down, quivering with alertness, he ran his eye along several shelves.

"I like the literature myself," he continued, "but Lady Calder seems to have a particular passion for it."

"Don't jump to the wrong conclusions! Those shelves are full of stories about mysteries, and blood and everything of the sort, because I gave them to her. You might even say I forced them on her."

"Well, my dear fellow, she doesn't seem to have disliked them. Look! There are four or five novels, the ones bound in red, by that chap 'Phantom.' They look as though they'd been read half to death. And, after all, why the devil shouldn't the lady like 'em? I've read some of 'Phantom's' stuff myself. It's as wild as wind, but it's first-class."

Garth straightened up. All the high gods seemed to be laughing at him.

"Thanks very much," he said in his stately way. "*I* am 'Phantom.' *I* wrote those red-bound books. That's the secret of *my* double life, the one I thought you or Twigg had discovered when Twigg approached me last night at Charing Cross Station." He paused. "Now go ahead, I beg, and laugh your head off."

And he braced himself as Abbot also straightened up.

There was, in fact, more than a frosty twinkle behind Abbot's eyeglass, and a beginning of mirth that might explode over the whole face. But Abbot, clearly, had not missed the pouring bitterness of his companion's tone.

"Dammit, man, it's nothing to be ashamed of!"

"No?"

"No, certainly not! Why didn't you use your own name?"

"I hardly thought the British Medical Association would approve. And I still doubt they will approve if they should happen to learn."

"Tut! Aren't there other doctors . . . ?"

"There are. But they gave up medicine when they turned entirely to literary work. They can invest their books with dignity. Above all, they don't profess to cure some people of nervous illnesses while scaring others under the name of 'Phantom.' "

"H'm. Yes. I see." Abbot champed his jaws. "Who knows about this?"

"Nobody, I had hoped. I've worked through a discreet literary agent. Last night, though, I could have sworn Twigg knew or guessed."

"Why?"

Garth gestured round the room.

"By accident, early yesterday evening, I left a brief-case in this house when I took the train to London. The brief-case was locked; it contained nothing except some typewritten pages of a new story about a murder at the top of an inaccessible tower."

"Well?"

"Well, the brief-case happens to be impressive-looking. Betty though it must be full of clinical notes, and followed me to town with it. There it caught Twigg's eye; he was at his most sinister when I refused to open it. And I still wonder if he knows."

"Does Lady Calder know?"

"No; fortunately not."

"H'm. Those books look as dog-eared as though—"

"No, I tell you! One of our deepest urges is to boast in front of the woman we're in love with. I have managed to avoid boasting; possibly," Garth added with restraint, "possibly because there's so very little to boast of."

"Dammit, man! If your conscience bothers you as much as all that, why do you go on writing the stuff? I take it you don't need . . . ?"

"No, I don't need the money. I do it for the same reason you are up to your eyes in police-work when you don't need the job either; because I enjoy it. I can only hope readers enjoy it one-tenth as much as I do."

"You enjoy scaring 'em, you mean?"

"Great Scott, no! That's only the excuse for the story; we don't really meet ghosts in Piccadilly Circus. It's the exercise of one's ingenuity, the setting of the trap and the double-trap, the game you play chapter after chapter against a quick-witted reader."

"Precisely, in short," Abbot inquired with great politeness, "what's been happening to you here tonight?"

"Let's try to forget that, shall we? It is not so very entertaining when fictional situations turn out to be real. I ought to have stopped this at the beginning, when I heard Marion Bostwick's story about a vanishing woman and a haunted door. It's true I didn't see then what I see so clearly now. But I ought to have seen it."

"Will you have the goodness to tell me," said Abbot, suddenly lifting *The Mystery of the Yellow Room* and shaking it in the air, "why we forever go round in a circle to a charming girl like Mrs. Bostwick?"

"Because, in one sense at least, Marion is at the centre of the case. She's at the centre of everything."

Abbot threw the paper-bound book into a chair. Garth, disregarding him for a moment, walked to the nearest window and stared out at the pavilion and the strengthening moon. Then he turned back.

"Abbot, have you forgotten why you came to Fairfield in the first place?"

"No; but—"

"Not so very long ago, in this room, you were much exercised about Mrs. Blanche Montague. 'What does that woman know? What did she say to Glynis Stukeley, if it was Glynis Stukeley, that made Stukeley herself go berserk?'"

Garth gnawed at his under-lip. "Well, if I read matters aright, Marion knows too. She knows as well as anyone. And, fortunately, she's here."

"Here?"

"Marion Bostwick is at the Stag and Glove, where I mean to take Betty tonight. Whether I relish the prospect or not, I must speak to Marion like a Dutch uncle. In case Twigg should be preparing more unpleasant surprises, it can't be delayed much longer."

Abbot expelled his breath.

"Suit yourself, my dear fellow. At the same time . . ."

"Yes?"

"Everybody in London, it seems to me, has read one book by 'Phantom' called *Instruments of Darkness*. And another called *By Whose Hand?* Take care another side of your hobby doesn't become real too! I told you, didn't I, that Glynis Stukeley (only we thought it was her sister) is said to have joined a Satanist group in Paris? Yes?"

Every breath of wind had died. Lace curtains and yellow-shaded lamp hung as motionless as the books on the shelves.

"Abbot, you're not serious?"

"Think not?"

"Even allowing your own hobby to be the occult, surely *you* don't expect to meet ghosts? Or believe that woman was done to death by supernatural means?"

"I spare you," Abbot said impassively, "a hackneyed quotation that begins, 'There are more things—' I merely refer you," and he pointed at the shelves, "to a book of much higher quality than your own. Its scene is a place named Baskerville Hall. And my quotation is, 'The devil's agents may be flesh and blood, may they not?'"

There were quick footsteps outside the door. Betty Calder, wearing a brown tweed skirt and jacket as severe as her usual costumes, and a hat which seemed to be decorated with a white ribbon, threw open the door and spoke before she had seen Abbot.

"Darling, I've packed a bag. And I've been turning out

the lamps. It's all dark except for this room. Oh! I beg your pardon!"

She shied back. Belatedly Abbot removed his own hat and gave her a bow of immense gallantry.

"No, dear lady. No! I most heartily beg yours."

"The police aren't back here, are they? Not again? Not tonight? Forgive me, but I don't think I could bear . . ."

"Pray be easy, madam. This call is entirely unofficial. As I was telling Dr. Garth, I arrived with the carriage from the railway-station at Ravensport. And I shall be spending the night myself at the Palace Hotel in Fairfield. You'll allow me, I hope, to drive you both to the Stag and Glove?"

"That is most kind of you, Mr. Abbot. But I'm not sure . . ."

"It's very kind indeed, Abbot," Garth said quickly. "We shall be happy to accept."

Betty, he could see, was nearing the end of her strength. The brown eyes had gone to him, for confirmation or denial as they usually did, when Abbot asked the question. Though clearly she was relieved when he spoke, several things caught them up at once and carried them again towards a point of panic.

"Yes, to be sure," Betty murmured. "The back door is locked. There's only this."

Buttoning her glove, Betty turned to the left of the door. From a hook beside the door, all but invisible against tan-and-white wallpaper and a white ceiling, a cord ran up past the jamb and across the ceiling on staples to a pulley in the middle. You could lower or raise the lamp to light it or to blow it out. Garth was about to assist her when Abbot's voice struck in and held him where he stood.

"Garth, do you mean to help me in this?"

"In what?"

"With the particular witness in question?" Abbot seemed reluctant to mention Marion Bostwick's name. "The lady we were speaking about. If she has been concealing information, and you're already aware of it, why don't you tell me now?"

"Believe me, there are reasons why I can't. And they are professional reasons, though you won't credit that either."

"Who doubts you, confound it? *I* never have! You may remember, I stopped Twigg—"

"Yes. I'm sorry."

"Well, it seems to me I should be there when you question her. Then there's the matter of young Fielding."

"Michael? You may take my word for it, Abbot, Michael had no knowingly or consciously guilty part in any of this!"

"Ah? Then you think he may have had *some* part to play in it?"

"I don't know. I can't tell." Garth's head had begun to ache again. "Tomorrow, if you like, I'll send Michael a telegram and ask him to come down here. No; tomorrow's Sunday; I can't send a telegram."

"You can, I believe, if you go to the Central Post Office in Ravensport. What do you say?"

That was the point at which Betty almost cried out.

She was lowering the lamp. Garth, like a man trying to look in two directions at once, had seen her gaze move towards the chair in which lay the paper-bound copy of *The Mystery of the Yellow Room.* Instantly Betty's gaze flicked away from that chair, and upwards.

The white lamp-cord snaked across the ceiling. He saw realization dawn in Betty's eyes at the same instant it entered his own mind. There was a cord like that in nearly every room here. Although this one had been just over his head all evening, it had never once occurred to him that a short length of such sash-cord had been embedded in the dead throat of Glynis Stukeley.

"Allow me," he said. And he was at Betty's side.

There was no danger that the lamp would run through its pulley and smash in flames on the floor; a knot beside one staple prevented that. But he had seen Betty's arm tremble, and her colour recede.

"Abbot, is the carriage outside?"

"Naturally!" the other said with some impatience.

"Then have the consideration to escort Lady Calder, won't you? I must blow out this lamp. We can't stumble about in the dark."

"As you please. But have you been listening to a word I'm saying? Is it necessary to question the lady tonight? Can't it wait?"

"Yes, I suppose it can wait. Vince and Marion will have gone to bed anyway. And I'm tired; I can't remember being so tired since the Pretoria campaign in the South African War."

Garth would have said almost anything to silence Abbot. Desperately he wanted to have a word in private with Betty. But this, under the circumstances, became impossible.

The lamp was extinguished, the cottage left behind. The clop and jingle of the landau bore them through a moon-washed world to the Stag and Glove. There was small difficulty about accommodation, even in June. Garth already occupied bedroom and private sitting-room in the north wing of a half-timbered house whose black beams and white plaster had seen the end of the fifteenth century. Vince and Marion seemed to have retired to a similar set of chambers in the south wing. Though Betty's room at the rear might be less spacious, it was a good deal more comfortable.

But Cullingford Abbot wouldn't leave them.

Betty, now so cool and composed that she seemed a different woman, chatted interminably. When at length Abbot told his driver to go on to the Palace Hotel, Mr. Fred Easterbrook bounced in like a spirit of respectability to hover near them.

"I am of Fairfield, look," the proprietor's eye seemed to be saying. "No members of the lower orders can get yelling drunk in my bar. If a single lady and a single gentleman want rooms unexpectedly: why, no harm done and I'm sure it's all right. Still—!"

And so, in the raftered inn-parlour with the brass warming-pans round the walls, his eye remained eloquent.

"Ain't there anything else I can get you, sir?"

"Nothing else, thanks."

"Here's your bedroom candle, ready and lighted. Wouldn't you like a hot Scotch and water, sir? Mr. Bostwick had one."

"No refreshment now, I thank you. That will be all."

"It's not a bit of trouble, you know, sir. Past midnight; my wife and the girl are both asleep; but I'm always awake. Wouldn't you like a hot Scotch and water?"

"Mr. Easterbrook—"

"Then here's Lady Calder's bedroom light, sir. By your leave, my lady, and gentleman's too, I'll escort *you* to your room. This way, my lady."

There was no getting round the iron laws of respectability, even in the matter of saying good-night. Garth bowed. He watched them go up the stairs to the landing, and back along a passage towards the rear.

Then he himself marched up the ancient staircase, its oak treads hollowed. He turned left into the north wing, along the solid if uneven floor of a corridor with a bottle-glass window at its far end. He opened the door of his sitting-room—and stepped into the dark.

Garth sensed that presence waiting for him before he had even entered. He closed the door behind him. Holding up the candle in its metal dish, he went over to a chair between the sitting-room windows. Marion Bostwick, wearing slippers and a heavily frilled nightgown, sat bolt upright and looked at him.

11

If Marion had not laughed . . .

Garth felt no relish for what he must say to her. Case-histories are one thing. In no stranger should any bodily or psychic illness move the physician's emotions lest it trouble his judgement. He must not deal with what too closely touches his own life.

But it was a startling laugh, callous and with a touch of brutality. Marion sat bolt upright, hair elaborately dressed and gleaming. The whole room reeked of her personality and of the perfume she wore.

She was in a chair with a ladder back, against a white plaster wall between two latticed windows. The small candle-flame was reflected in her eyes. Stretching up both arms behind her head, elbows out, and seizing the supports of the chair at either side, Maron leaned back with a feline grace and crossed her knees.

"What's the matter, David? Why don't you tell me not to speak so loudly? Why don't you tell me to whisper? Why don't you tell me there are people all about, just dying to make a scandal?"

"That would be true, wouldn't it?"

It was as though Marion's impatience at such a notion ached so deeply that it could be expressed only by a curse or a prayer.

"You needn't worry. Nobody can hear us; these walls are too thick. Nobody saw me slip in here. Or are you think-ing about Vince?"

"I wonder, Marion, if you can guess what I am really thinking."

"Vince is asleep. I poured chloral in his whisky." At once nagging and coaxing, at once storming at him and yet wheedl-ing in unconvincing tenderness, Marion had lowered her voice. But she still seemed to be crying out that all things were unfair. "Don't be stupid, David. I want to be nice to you. I'm *trying* to be nice to you. But you don't make it easy, do you? There are times when I could *kill* some of the men I know!"

"Whereas in actual fact," Garth said, "you only tried to kill one woman."

Marion dropped her arms and sat up straight.

In one corner of the room a deep-voiced grandfather

clock seemed to rustle rather than tick. Garth went back to the door. There was a new bolt, but the latch was of wood. He stood looking down at it.

Even the Stag and Glove, he supposed, was not really old as time went in this island. They had built it more than a century after England's life began to depend on the wool that must be sent in ships and the ships that must be guarded against pirates; and Fulke de Raven, first Deputy Warden of the Cinque Ports, kept watch from his tower above the Narrow Seas.

But these reflections could become dangerous. If you stood motionless in the stream of time, listening to crying voices out of the past, you might presently believe that your feelings or your neighbour's were of puny significance because they had been experienced so often before and would be experienced again when you had gone. Whereas they did matter; they were the only reality; there was no shame in feeling the hurt.

Garth bolted the door, locking himself in with Marion. Near the middle of the room there was a large round table with another ladder-backed chair beside it. He put the candle on the table and sat down opposite her. Though the light now touched her face only dimly, he did not need to see it. Marion's distended nostrils and protuding eyes were in grotesque contrast to the seductiveness of her perfume.

"Vince, I imagine," he said, "has told you what happened late this afternoon?"

"The murder? Dear, dear! How very awkward for you!"

"Yes, it's awkward. Glynis Stukeley was strangled to death in—" here he hesitated—"in a pavilion on the beach at the back of Betty's cottage. All the evidence indicates she must have been strangled either by Betty herself or by me."

"And that's unfortunate too."

"By God, it is! But for whom? I doubt that even Inspector Twigg, a police-officer who hates my guts, really believes I was the one who killed her. It's Betty he's after. And Betty is innocent."

"What makes you think she's innocent?"

"Because I know Betty. What good should I be at my work, what earthly good at all, unless I had some knowledge of the human mind? Or, if you prefer, of the human soul?"

Moonlight silvered the latticed windows. The tall clock, as leisurely and unhurried as time itself, threw out its beats against silence.

"Twigg is one person, Marion. Cullingford Abbot is quite another. He is no more shrewd or imaginative than Twigg, but he has more experience with the kind of people Twigg hates. His very first impulse was to question Mrs. Montague; he'll do it soon; and he may get the truth out of her. Also, after a talk I had with him tonight, he is certain to question you too."

"You told him," Marion whispered. "Whatever filthy things you may have been thinking—how could you? Because— because of this Viennese doctor who says, doesn't he, doesn't he, that the deepest wish in our lives goes back to some kind of sexual feeling?"

"Whatever he says, at least I believe yours does. To a certain kind of sexual feeling, anyway."

"You *rotter*," Marion whispered. Then she sprang to her feet, fighting for breath. "Oh, Christ love us and help us, could there ever be such a rotter as the man I thought was my friend and Vince's friend?"

"Sit down, Marion," Garth said coldly. "You're frightened, that's all. I told him nothing."

"What's that?"

"I told him nothing. I promised to protect you, and I have kept that promise. But there are other people to be considered now."

"You fool! You utter imbecile! Do you dream for one minute I killed that awful creature at your fancy-woman's place this afternoon?"

"Oh, no.'"

"Then what—?"

"I don't say you killed her, though you may have done. Nothing is certain. I was referring to another incident; connected with the murder, possibly even bringing about the murder, but a separate act that has only served to confuse the trail. I meant the attempt to strangle Mrs. Montague on Friday night. Tell me, Marion. You were the woman she really called a whore, now weren't you?"

Tick-tick went the tall clock, a rustle of movement through eternity.

"That part of your story sounded real. When she hastily summoned you at night with the servants all sent away, and an elderly woman went on shouting 'whore' in a darkened house, that rang true. Why should it have upset Glynis Stukeley so much? Why should it have upset her in the least? What else, after all, had she ever pretended to be? But it upset you, Marion, whenever you let yourself remember."

Marion Bostwick, a lithe shape in a heavily frilled white nightgown, flung herself across towards the door. The old floorboards creaked and cracked; the candle-flame trembled.

But she did not run far; perhaps she had not intended to run far. She returned, treading very lightly and quickly, to face him again.

Garth had not moved. He sat with his elbow on the table, right hand shielding his eyes even from dim candlelight.

"I'm sorry, Marion."

"What are you accusing me of? *What?*"

"Do you truly want me to tell you? Everything?"

"Yes!"

"Poor old Vince had never met Glynis Stukeley. But you had. He was not her victim; you were. All our reasoning must begin there. I hope you see to what other conclusion it presently leads."

"Well, I don't!"

"Never mind, then. We won't pursue that. Let us return to actual events at Hampstead early last night."

He dropped his hand and looked up.

"When Mrs. Montague lost her head and cried out specific accusations, you lost your head too. I know you had not meant to kill her. But you almost went too far. And then you were obliged to explain it.

"Glynis Stukeley was not even in the house. I think you saw her somewhere that evening, so that you could describe her clothes, though there I am only guessing, and about other matters, unfortunately, I am not guessing.

"You are not a deeply imaginative girl, Marion. But you have a quick, rather brutal kind of cunning. Always provided your courage holds up, you can seize an advantage and sweep through with it. If you accused Glynis herself of being the attacker, could she outface you? Would anyone believe her blackmail-charges *then?* Surely Mrs. Montague too, from her very horror of scandal, would back you up and support your story once you had given her time to think it over?

"You thought she would. You said she would. It ran through every word you spoke to me at Hampstead last night. Glynis's own sister believed you. You remembered to unlock the cellar door from inside; if you had not forgotten the two bolts, and had drawn them back as well, I might have believed it myself. And if that were all anyone could hold against you . . ."

"All?" Marion interrupted. "All? You call me that word, or as good as call me that word, and still you say it's not all?"

"No, Marion. You know it's not all."

Her quick, shallow breathing had an almost terrifying effect in the dim room. It went on in little gasps, steadily, like the slower beat of the clock.

And Garth also jumped to his feet, now almost as pale as she was.

"I beg you, madame, refrain from saying I preach. You are not 'evil'; let us leave such talk to those who have never been human. You have only the cruelty of the very young, the child who lashes out for what it must have, and fails, and then must call on all the adult world to be protected. If that fails too, you are willing to use any easy weapon at your disposal—seduction, for instance—as you were and are ready to use it with me."

"You *dare!*"

"Stop acting, Marion. I tell you the truth."

"Aunt Blanche . . ."

"Yes. We must not forget her or what she said to you. Like other children, Marion, you can see facts about yourself when you want to see them. If Mrs. Montague had called you a whore and no more than that, you would not have been frightened enough to attack her. There was something else. What was it?"

In a different voice Marion said, "Somebody's listening at the door."

Silence struck at them like a fist.

Both windows were closed. The candle-flame stood steady in windless air. Under these black beams, over the hollows of an ancient floor, it was all but impossible to move without noise. Garth reached the door; he eased back the bolt; very softly he lifted the latch.

Only the moon entered, through a bottle-glass window at the end of the passage.

That window, as he peered out, was on his left past the bedroom door. Towards his right the passage stretched away some fifteen or twenty feet to a steep stair-head and the inn-parlour below. A smell of old wood and stone, of scoured grates and brass-polish, filled the passage like a smell of the past itself. Distantly, through another open window, there was a multitudinous whispering of trees.

Someone might well have crept up to that door, unless this were another trick of the elusive Marion. And yet, as he discovered when he closed the door and turned back, all Marion's pretence had gone. She had dropped sideways into the ladderback, in a convulsion of anguish all the more real because she felt it as so unfair.

"David, what am I to do? Help me! I don't ask much, but I do ask that. Don't stand there like a bump on a log; help me! Oh, dear God, what am I to *do?*"

"I don't know."

"Who was out there? Was it . . . ?"

"Nobody! Nobody was out there! If you don't lower your voice, though, you'll rouse the whole house after all." He waited, hot and cold all over. "Do you appreciate even now, Marion, that you might have committed murder? That you might have killed a woman who has never been anything but kind to you?"

"Oh, what's the good of talking like that? I had to do it, hadn't I?"

Garth looked at her.

"Well, hadn't I? I wish I hadn't, but what else was there to do? You said you weren't going to go on at me!"

"I am not going to go on at you. Do you imagine you're the first person who ever told lies?" Then he caught himself up. "No. No, according to your lights, I suppose you couldn't have acted in any other way. The point is—"

On the large round table there was a wooden box half full of Sullivan cigarettes. He had left them there on Friday, forgetting to fill his case. Taking a cigarette out of the box now, he lifted the candle to light it and was astonished to find his arm shaking uncontrollably until with an effort he steadied both arm and candle-holder. Marion, her eyes smeary with tears, glared up at him sideways as though this lighting of the cigarette were the worst act of treachery he had done.

"Now pay attention," he said. "How could you describe what Glynis Stukeley was wearing on Friday night?"

"Oh, what does it matter?"

"Answer me!"

"I saw her. She was there."

"She was where?"

"She was sitting in the side road past Uncle Sel's house. I saw her when I got there on foot, though I pretended not to see her. She was waiting."

"Well?"

"I think Aunt Blanche asked her to come there at the same time *I* was asked. I think that horrible woman guessed there was danger; I think she smelled danger; I think she was afraid of being caught in some way. So she waited. But I knew she'd never be able to prove she wasn't in the house if I swore she was; they wouldn't believe the cabby, either. I might not be able to get her hanged, but at least I could get her put in prison for life."

"Marion, for God's sake!"

"You want me to tell the truth, don't you? What *do* you want?"

"Then you had seen or met Glynis Stukeley before?"

"Yes! You know I had!"

"Where had you seen her?"

"When I was in Paris with . . . when I was in Paris."

"Was she blackmailing you?"

"She didn't get the chance. But she wanted to."

"Why? What did she know about you? Was it . . . ?"

And then, on the edge of victory, Garth hesitated. Marion's eyes brimmed over.

If there were good reasons why he hesitated, and these reasons had nothing to do with delicacy or consideration now, he cursed himself none the less. Behind the screen of Marion's words lurked another person whose violence had not stopped short as hers had done, and who might not stop again at killing if a certain position in life were threatened.

But Garth hesitated. Marion (always alert, always with antennae to catch the mood of any man) saw it at once. She was on her feet, appealing.

"I know what you're going to ask. I'll die before I tell you. I'm not going to have people say . . . well! what they *will* say if they learn. Knowing what you must know, David, in the name of pity or mercy can you ask me to degrade myself by admitting that? And how long it's been happening with that particular one?"

Garth looked at the cigarette. He dropped it on the floor, grinding his heel on it. He turned away from her, and then back again.

"You can't, David. You know you can't. It'll be bad enough whatever happens. What am I going to *do?*"

"And I tell you again, I don't know! It's not so much your fault, perhaps. There are lies and subterfuges in all our lives, God knows. And Vince loves you; that's the main consideration. If only there were some means of hushing this up while still keeping the police away from Betty . . ."

"Isn't there some means? Isn't there?"

"There may be. I must try to think. It won't be easy. And if any outsider heard and understood the conversation we are having at this minute—"

He broke off, swinging round.

Whatever Marion had heard before, there could be no doubt about what they heard now. The footstep in the passage outside was light and furtive. But a side of a shoe had brushed the skirting-board. Then there was no more sound.

PART III

THE DARKNESS

In England Sunday, as is well known, is observed as a day of rest and public worship. Shops, places of amusement, and the City restaurants are closed the whole day, while other restaurants are open from 1 to 3, and from 6 to 11 P.M. only. Many museums and galleries, however, are now open on Sun. (see p. 82).

—BAEDEKER'S *London and Its Environs* FOR 1908

12

The warmth of that Sunday afternoon, with a blaze of sunshine on water and parade and sea-front gardens, lent to Fairfield a strength of life and colour that might almost have been mistaken for abandon.

It is true that at just past three o'clock, with the tide high though on the ebb, the beach lay deserted. Bathing was not permitted on Sunday. It is true that full church-going costume was *de rigeur* for an afternoon stroll, so that the sun flashed on constantly lifted top-hats and the grave inclination of parasols from the Florence Nightingale Monument at the northern end of the parade to the Royal Albert Aquarium at the southern end.

But it remained a heartening sight.

Its two large hotels, the Palace and the Imperial, raised their turrets and awnings in Victoria Avenue behind and parallel with the sea-front gardens, with names in gilded letters two feet high. Motor-cars quivered along Victoria Avenue, though at a pace so decorous that only a honking of bulb-horns disturbed horses. In the gardens beds of scarlet geraniums and blue lobelias against white alison drew glowing circles and triangles round a rococo band-stand in which heavy brass was being massed, like artillery, for the first number of the usual Sunday afternoon concert.

Sunday, June 16. And we see our protagonist in formal morning-dress.

David Garth, approaching from the south past the side of the aquarium, glanced along the parade and then scanned the gardens. It was as though he were hoping to see someone; and yet, at the same time, avoid seeing someone else.

He went up the sandstone steps of the Royal Albert Aquarium. There he stood with his back to its elaborate ironwork façade, watching the few people who drifted in and out of the doors, and again scanning the gardens. He had consulted his watch only twice when he saw the approach of Cullingford Abbot, fresh gardenia in buttonhole and silk hat again glossy.

"But, my dear fellow," said Abbot, going gingerly up the steps of the aquarium, "why here? Of all places, why here?" He put up his eyeglass to study the façade. "Do you know, it's so aesthetically horrible that I honestly like it?"

Whereupon he got a close look at Garth.

"By the way, speaking of the aesthetically horrible—" he added.

"I had a bad night. I couldn't sleep."

"You look as though you hadn't slept for a month. Bad as all that?"

"Almost. It was one of the reasons why I telephoned you."

All about them passed a joy of blattering voices, even through stately Fairfield. Bicycle-bells rang in afternoon air. At one side of the aquarium's doors a poster in red letters announced the opening of the new Brooklands Motor-Racing Track at Weybridge.

Nearly every public pronouncement, in this year, carried similar news of speed and progress; as when the Cunarder *Mauretania* won the Blue Ribband of the Atlantic with a record that would not be beaten for twenty-two years, and Signor Marconi spanned the same ocean with his ghostly signals. Yet no doubt the real concerns of every person on that promenade today were whittled down, like Garth's, to some urgent private worry.

"Tell me," he went on. "How much power have you got at the Criminal Investigation Department?"

"H'm. All I need, I suppose, if I care to take it."

"Twigg has been put in charge of the Glynis Stukeley affair, I understand?"

"So I understand too." Abbot's expression sharpened. "Why?"

"Come inside," said Garth.

From the bandstand in the gardens came an experimental whump and boom as instruments were tested. A crowd had begun to gather there. The inside of the Royal Albert Aquarium, despite its height, was extraordinarily dark and damp. Water in an aquarium is confined; it is behind glass; it should not, you think, seem to soak the visitor himself to his very bones.

"One of the reasons I chose this place," Garth continued, "is that Twigg isn't likely to look for me here until I can establish some kind of defence."

"Defence?"

"Yes. You've heard what the best form of defence is. Are you in the mood for any kind of bargain or negotiation?"

"That depends. What have you in mind?"

"Specifically, I want you to deal with Twigg. I want you to keep him from questioning Betty or Marion—either of them— for twenty-four hours. And I want you to refrain from questioning them yourself."

They had begun to move round the echoing hall, deserted by those who had left for the band-concert. But they did not so much as look into the glass cases; they were watching each other. They stopped, and Abbot whistled.

"My dear chap! You don't ask very much, do you?"

"I am asking very nearly the earth, let's admit. At the same time . . ."

"Oh, don't let it trouble you." Abbot's moustache went up in a sardonic grimace. "I am no stickler for rules. In effect, though, you are inviting me to come over and join you in the enemy's camp."

"No, I am not! I spoke of a bargain."

"And what do you offer in exchange?"

"I think I can offer you the murderer. Wait!" he added. "Under ordinary circumstances, I know, a remark like that would be sheer nonsense. The amateur who believes he can match himself against the official police belongs in a book and nowhere else. This is the thousandth case, the different case. I might have invented it myself."

"Quite so. Twigg thinks you did."

"I might have invented it for a story, that is."

"Yes. It's almost the same thing."

They continued to pace, past witless-looking fishes, with Garth's harassed and desperate face reflected in the glass beside Abbot's cynically amused one.

"Damme, man, I like your nerve! I mean that sincerely. Stop! I'm only wondering if it's feasible, which I doubt. Twigg thinks you're a wrong 'un; in his own phrase, a cross cove. By this time he's not even sure of me." Abbot hesitated. "Look here, what's been happening since last night?"

"All merry blue blazes has been happening since last night! Do you know what it is to have two frantic women on your hands at the same time?"

"Now that remark, my dear fellow, *is* open to misconstruction."

"Yes. All right." Garth shut his eyes, opened them, and went on pacing. "I seem to have lost my sense of humour as well as any sense of proportion or of truth-telling. The trouble is that an explosion is likely at any minute. Twigg arrived at Ravensport from London quite early this morning. Incidentally, why do the Ravensport police appear so much in this? Why do you all make a headquarters there? Isn't Betty's house within the Fairfield area?"

"Technically, yes. But Fairfield's police are rather too much like Fairfield's inhabitants. Ravensport, mediaeval town or not, is more up-to-date. About Twigg: you were saying?"

"He has discovered something, or rather several things, about which he'll do no more than hint to Betty. One thing has to do with her bicycle—"

"Oh?"

"The other concerns some lengths of white sash-cord which appear to have been left in the bedroom Glynis Stukeley never lived to use. I can't establish the actual facts. If Twigg won't do more than hint to Betty herself, it's unlikely he'll tell me."

Abbot pondered.

"Garth," he said, "suppose I agreed to your fantastic suggestion? Hold on!"

"Yes?"

"I don't think it's at all feasible, mind. Let's allow it is. If I'm not to join in the hunt myself, or have the pleasure of seeing Mrs. Bostwick again soon . . ."

"It needn't prevent you from seeing Marion. That's a part of my plan."

"Well confound it," and Abbot turned a wintry, toothy smile, "you must give me a sporting run for my risk! What is this plan of yours?"

Not too distantly the Fairfield band, as though you could see all its members, sailed together into the opening bars of the Poet and Peasant Overture.

Abbot looked irritated as the music engulfed them. Since they were not far from the entrance, he deliberately walked back and with no by-your-leave to anyone pushed shut the big front doors of the Royal Albert Aquarium. All sounds were muted except a drip of water. He and Garth were alone in a place which seemed damper and gloomier. But hope surged up at last in David Garth.

"This morning after breakfast," he answered, "I went to the Central Post Office at Ravensport. Just as you suggested."

"Ah! To send a telegram to young Fielding?"

"I changed my mind about the telegram. It might not reach Michael in time; it might not reach him at all. There was a possibility he might be at Bart's Hospital this morning. And he was. I spoke to him on the telephone."

"Well?"

"Abbot, I've been very stupid in this affair. If an impressionable young innocent like Michael became involved with the late Glynis—or, to be exact, if she deliberately picked him up—it was no coincidence. Nothing has been coincidence. And if Michael can give us the answers to just two questions, it's the first move towards forcing the murderer into a corner. But I can't wait. Twigg is too close."

"Granting that, you still haven't told me this plan of attack! What is it?"

Garth took out his watch, consulted it, and put it back.

"Michael has taken a train due at Fairfield in just over twenty minutes. Betty is meeting the train. She'll bring him in a cab to the Palace Hotel, your hotel. If I am standing outside the hotel at that time, it means you'll give my scheme a chance; and they'll stop. If I am not outside the hotel, they will meet me at another place."

"Anything else?"

"Yes. Vince and Marion Bostwick meet us too. Abbot," Garth added with desperate sincerity, "I apologize for putting you in a position like this. I apologize for what must seem to be vulgarity and melodrama—"

"My dear fellow," interrupted Abbot, with an explosive little chuckle behind closed teeth, "never apologize for either vulgarity or melodrama of the sort I think you mean. This pleases me. By Jove, it does!"

A dozen feet inside the big doors, they faced each other in different moods. Their voices had a hollow reverberation under iron girders.

"The gathering of such a group, you know," Abbot pursued, "should have stimulating results."

"I am hoping it will."

"Are Mr. and Mrs. Bostwick necessary to this conference?"

"Yes. They won't like it; but then nobody will like it, especially Betty. Let me add a fact which will mean nothing to you at the moment, and yet it ought to be indicated for bitter irony's sake. Marion Bostwick has not the faintest notion who the murderer really is."

"Now why the devil should she have?"

"Forgive me." Garth checked himself. "That should not have been said, and may never have to be said at all."

"Look here, if you fail in this . . . ?"

"If I fail," Garth said, "the police have lost only twenty-four hours. If by any remote chance I succeed, at least three persons will keep some of the things they value most in life. What do you say?"

"Done! I say yes."

It was very warm in here. And edge of sunlight ran across the damp tile floor as one of the big doors was pushed open from outside. Hal Ormiston marched in, accompanied by a gush of band-music partly stilled when he closed the door again.

"I want you to take these," said Hal, walking up to Garth and extending a still-crumpled packet of two five-pound notes. "I shouldn't have picked 'em up in the first place. Now have 'em back, will you?"

Even the imperturbable Abbot opened his eyes wide, so that the glass fell on its cord. Hal's face remained in shadow; Garth could not read his expression. The young man was dressed, as they said, up to the nines; he wore a cream-coloured suit with black pique edging to pockets and lapels, a tall collar, and a broad blue cravat which (Hal would have said) was in the best bounds of good taste.

"No," Hal almost snapped, "and I won't call you 'Nunkie,' either."

"Thank you. That at least is a relief. But by all means keep the money if it fulfils any pressing need."

"There you go again," said Hal. "Let *me* be fair, for a change. I don't think it's ever occurred to you how infernally offensive you can be. Oh, not with your patients! They're elderly and decrepit. But you don't understand younger people; you rather detest younger people. I think you must have been born old."

"Well, perhaps that's true."

"Your car has been repaired," Hal said. "I persuaded a friend of mine here in Fairfield to repair it even on a Sunday. And I came down from London just for that purpose. Now, my respected ancient! Will you have the ten quid, or must I put it in your pocket for you?"

Such is human nature that Garth responded instinctively.

"Keep it, I tell you! Keep it and welcome! I should be only too glad to think this remarkable change . . ."

"Oh, I haven't changed. It's you who've begun to change, maybe a good deal for the better."

"Hal, will you tell me just what . . . ?"

"Yes. Old Bet—Lady Calder, that's to say—is in trouble. I didn't guess how serious trouble until I had another talk with Inspector Twigg not half an hour ago. That close-mouthed devil never says what he's about when he first asks you to testify. And I want to help. Still, whatever your high and mightiness thinks, I've got *my* feelings too!"

"Young man," interposed Cullingford Abbot, lifting the eyeglass with some distaste, "were you so very anxious to help when you made an anonymous telephone-call to the Ravensport police-station?"

"If I don't choose, my good Mr. Abbot, I never admit anything."

"You don't have to admit anything, young fella-me-lad. From a question your uncle asked not long ago, he knows it as well as I do. Anyone who telephoned the police-station to report a murder . . ."

Hal's voice went high and thin.

"Who said anything about a murder? *I* never did!"

"Any such person, young man, would have telephoned to Fairfield and not Ravensport. But you had just driven a Scotland Yard official to Ravensport. And you thought that would be better, I fancy. Eh?"

"I was angry. Who wouldn't be?"

"Ah!" murmured Abbot.

"My pious uncle has been carrying on with old Bet. He pretends he hasn't been, but he has. I thought it might be amusing to say they'd find something 'unpleasant,' just as a Fairfield gossip would, if they called at the cottage late at night. I didn't say *then*. I said late at night. Some thick-witted sergeant got the message garbled, that's all."

"That's all, is it?"

"Yes! I'm sorry I did it. Here."

Whereupon Hal made a movement of blinding swiftness, a quicker move than any of which Garth would have thought him capable. He darted forward, pushed the folded banknotes into Garth's side pocket, and darted back again. The glow from a glass case touched his face.

"But they were already talking about hypocrisy," snapped Hal, "while the old Queen was still alive. . . . It's not one, two, three with the hypocrisy there is now. You take Marion Bostwick, for instance."

Until then Garth had not realized that the band-music had changed to a medley of light-hearted tunes from Gilbert and Sullivan. He had not realized an aquarium could contain so many eyes, all of which seemed to be fixed on them.

"Young man," Abbot asked in a dangerously restrained voice, "what is this you tell us about Mrs. Bostwick?"

"Mind your eye, Mr. Policeman! I said nothing at all against Marion, if that's what you mean. Maybe that's just the trouble."

"Indeed?"

"You heard me. I was talking about hypocrisy. They brought her home from India when she was fourteen; a handsome piece even then, so I'm told. I met her four years later, in '05, at least three months before Vince Bostwick set eyes on her. If there's one thing that girl keeps saying, over and over and over, it's how fond she is of young men. Ask Dr. David Garth if Marion doesn't say that."

Garth did not comment. He stared at the floor, listening hard for every word.

"Well, she's lying," shouted Hal. "I've tried hard enough since she was married; and so, I happen to know, has Michael Fielding. At first I thought she must have peculiar sexual tastes, but . . ."

"'Sexual tastes,'" repeated Abbot. "'Sexual tastes.'"

And it was the raffish-seeming Abbot, of all people, who seemed most outraged by these words.

"Young man," he said in a still-restrained voice, "has no one ever told you we are not accustomed to speaking of ladies in that way?"

"Yes; quite often. Follow my point about hypocrisy? Since you're old enough to know better—"

"I am old enough to be your father," said Abbot. "But I am still capable of giving you a hiding you'll remember for six months."

"You do, Mr. Cullingford Abbot, and you'll pay me something handsome to keep it out of court afterwards."

Abbot's eyeglass dropped on its cord. It is a sober fact that his hands lunged out for Hal's throat.

"Steady!" said David Garth. *"Steady, I tell you!"*

"What's the matter with you, Nunkie?" Hal appealed to him. "I've apologized, haven't I? I'm trying to do my best for you and old Bet, aren't I?"

"Hal, you'd better go. Stop a bit, though! If it were necessary, would you swear to what you've just informed us? That both you and Michael Fielding made the most gallant attempts on Mrs. Bostwick's virtue, and that she resisted both of you?"

"Garth," said Abbot, "have *you* lost all decency and good manners too?"

"Quiet! Hal, would you and Michael mind testifying to that?"

"Michael would mind, you can bet. He's got more parsons in his family than in twenty pages of *Crockford*; and he's going to be a doctor like you. Still, if I get something for my trouble, I've got no objection."

"You will get something for your trouble, I promise. (Steady, Abbot!) That's all, Hal. Thank you."

Hal stalked out, leaving the door open. Abbot caught it

and slammed it, again partly blotting out band-music. Then there was a hard-breathing pause.

"Sorry," Abbot growled after a moment. "Silly of me. Lost my temper."

"That's all right."

"You dealt with me." Abbot said, "as I dealt with you last night when you wanted to wring Twigg's neck. Well, turn-about. All the same! 'Sexual tastes.' Spoken openly like that! What's the world coming to?"

"Michael Fielding, it would appear, is not quite the young innocent I believed. The cards will have to be dealt a little differently for this conference of ours. We can't have Marion Bostwick there; and certainly we can't have Vince."

"H'm. This scheme of yours, I trust, includes an explanation for an impossible murder?"

"Oh, yes. That's the awkward part."

"Tut! The point need not be stressed. It will be difficult, yes! But—"

"I did not say it would be difficult; it is not difficult at all. I said it will be awkward."

"Are you aware," inquired Abbot, again restraining himself, "that you are now talking exactly like that damned Prince Ahriman in your own stories?"

"Forgive me." Garth looked at his watch. "Abbot, we must make haste. The train will be here. With any sort of luck, we should be approaching one part of the truth. Are you ready?"

Serene sunlight dazzled their eyes in the parade. A spatter of applause from spectators standing or sitting twenty deep round the bandstand, greeted the end of the Gilbert-and-Sullivan medley. It was not too little applause to sound frigid or perfunctory; it was not too much applause to sound extravagant; it mingled with sky and sea and the nature of things.

Cyclists rang their bells in the parade as two formally dressed men, Cullingford Abbot and David Garth, walked through formal gardens, past brilliant bands of flowers, towards the turrets of the Palace Hotel beyond Victoria Avenue.

Though clearly Abbot was brooding about something, it did not remain quite the black thundercloud of before. When a child rolling a hoop caromed into him, and retreated with a frightened cry of "Please, sir," Abbot dived into his pocket. What he gave that child was not a sixpence but a gold sovereign. And then, when they had almost reached Victoria Avenue, the band struck up "Land of Hope and Glory."

Perhaps not a person round the bandstand failed to straighten in pride as the slow, solemn notes smote out against drowsy afternoon air. Abbot stopped dead. Glowering, he touched his companion's arm.

"Look here," he began in a rush. "I've jeered a good deal at Fairfield and what it represents. So have a number of us who fancied ourselves as wits. But in my heart of hearts I like it."

"Well?"

"Don't you understand? I said I *like* it."

"There's no reason why you shouldn't like it, except that this is strange talk to hear from you of all people. You, the advocate of the twentieth century? You, the apostle of advancement and progress?"

"Of scientific progress, yes! My father believed in that, just as I do. It's an altogether different matter. Fairfield may belong to the past—"

"Fairfield isn't the past, Abbot. Ravensport is the past. Fairfield is the present, very much the present; it's everyone here who insists on living in the past."

"Then what's the future?" Abbot walked to the edge of the kerb and swung round. "Not Bunch? Don't tell me it's Bunch? Not that blasted place with machines grinding out mechanical laughter on the pier, and people stamping on each other's toes just to prove nobody's got an advantage over anyone else?"

"Yes, possibly Bunch. Nothing ever remains the same. We can't expect it to."

"I don't expect it, really. But, my God, Garth, how I dislike it!"

"Perhaps, in my own heart, I like it no better than you. That doesn't alter the fact that the child grows into the adult, and everything changes."

"You think so? There's one thing at least that doesn't change. Listen!"

And Abbot nodded towards the bandstand. Brassy with massed instruments, almost relieved of pomposity by its deep feeling, the music threw a spell over every listener.

Land of hope and glory, mother of the free,
How shall we extol thee, who are born of thee?

It threw a spell over the cynical Abbot too. Top-hat rakish but eyeglass glittering, he stood with his shoulders back as though at attention.

Wider still and wider, shall thy bounds be set—
God, Who made thee mighty, make thee mightier yet!

Slow, inexorable, the triumphant paean soared to its end in a cymbal-clash and such a thunder of applause that half Fairfield seemed to be joining in as the bandmaster bowed.

"Come!" said Abbot, suddenly sneering at himself and snatching off his hat as though about to kick it like a football. "That's enough of such nonsense. We've work to do. Besides," and he pointed across Victoria Avenue, "besides, unless I've gone blind, Mr. and Mrs. Bostwick are going into the hotel at this minute. We can't stop 'em. Also, that's Lady Calder in the landau coming from the direction of Parliament Street; so the young chap beside her must be Michael Fielding. If you're anticipating an explosion, my dear Garth, you'd better prepare for one."

The explosion occurred sooner than any of them expected.

13

"I don't think I understand, Doctor."

"You don't, Mr. Fielding?"

"No, sir! I'm only too happy to assist you in any way I can, of course; but you didn't say much on the telephone."

"Was it necessary to say much, Mr. Fielding?"

Marion intervened. "Really, David, if this young man *can't* help you, he can't!"

Vince said, "Marion, my pet, don't chatter."

Betty Calder and Cullingford Abbot remained quiet, watching.

In the lounge of the Palace Hotel, under a high and gaudy roof of mosaic glass, the six of them sat round a table as though waiting for tea. A fountain splashed in the centre of the lounge, amid palms that seemed to have grown to an unusual height.

There were other details Garth would afterwards remember: Marion's white dress and Betty's of dove-grey, and Marion in a pose he suspected of being imitated from Mrs. Patrick Campbell on the stage. Both wore hats heavy with a close-lying plume. But individual doubts or fears were lost under the glances now being turned on Michael Fielding, who looked as though he had passed a worse night than Garth.

And Michael knew this.

He had been careful to put on sober Sunday black, with a very high collar. You seldom noticed the ugliness of his features because of a real charm which gave him his usual air between brashness and timidity. Michael's coarse sandy hair contrasted with brilliant hazel eyes like those of a matinee-idol.

"Sir—!" he began in a rush.

On the table stood three silk hats, emblems of respectability, together with Michael's own billycock hat and Vince Bostwick's silver-headed walking-stick. But Michael need not have lowered his voice. Despite its gilded cornices and all the frippery, this lounge-hall was so large that they might have been sitting at Euston Station. A few guests had already ordered tea, well out of earshot. Another man slept outright in a red plush armchair. The fountain tinkled monotonously.

Then Michael rose to his feet.

"I don't think this is quite fair," he cried. "What do you want of me, sir? Why did you bring me here?"

"Michael," and Garth dropped the formal style of address, "I'm trying hard not to be unfair. I don't even want to embarrass you. It's only—"

"Half a minute, old boy," interrupted Vince, leaning forward to rap his knuckles on the table. "Nobody else has been spared embarrassment. Marion and I haven't, and we're not guilty of a dashed thing. Now are we, old girl?"

"No, we most certainly are not." Marion lifted one shoulder like Stella Campbell in *The Notorious Mrs. Ebbsmith*. "I don't even know why we're here and I find it quite, quite intolerable!"

"That's precisely it, sir," Michael said with pale earnestness. "Nobody's done anything. You're going too far."

It was this air of injured innocence, common to all of them and doubtless reasonable enough, which nevertheless scraped Garth's nerves raw. He looked up at Michael.

"I told you on the telephone, did I not, that Glynis Stukeley was murdered late yesterday afternoon?"

"Yes, sir, you did. Anyway, a name like that was in this morning's newspapers."

"Michael, I am not setting a trap. The police know you were very well acquainted with the lady before she died."

There was a startled silence. Marion craned round to look at Michael too.

"You?" she said incredulously. "You? Why, you funny little man! How perfectly extraordinary!"

And she began to laugh. Michael had gone as white as a ghost. Marion, instantly seeing the error, became so decorous that she might have been praying.

"Governor," said Michael, "I met her. Yes, that's true. We've all met one or two women, I daresay, it would have been better if we hadn't met."

"Now there," observed Cullingford Abbot, "we have a short history of mankind expressed with admirable terseness."

"Abbot, for heaven's sake! I'm grateful to you for backing me up, but this is difficult enough to handle without a parade of your epigrams."

"Humblest apologies, my dear Garth. I myself have one or two ideas I should like to express presently. However, as a mere policeman, I apologize for butting in."

"I only meant—!"

"I know what you meant, man. Get on with it!"

"Michael," said Garth, "you're not very well off, are you?"

"No, Governor, you know I'm not. Don't hold that against me."

"You knew Glynis Stukeley never granted her favours, I take it, without expecting something in return?"

"Governor, what do you mean by 'granted her favours'?"

"There was never anything between you two?"

"Nothing, so help me!"

"You never once went to bed with her? And, in order to get to bed with her, you never did at least two things she persuaded you to do?"

Again the fountain tinkled during a funereal hush.

It is hard to say what effect those words might have created if they had carried to the ears of two elderly ladies seated at a table some thirty feet away, or of the waiter in the striped waistcoat who was marching towards them with a tea-tray. Even at their own table the words had a galvanizing effect. Marion Bostwick rose up.

"Vince," she said in a stifled voice, "I'm leaving. Whether or not you accompany me, I'm leaving. I don't mean to stay here and be insulted."

"Marion," said Vince, flinging his head round, "now just who is insulting you?"

"Vince, you fool! Once David's started like that, you can't tell where he'll stop or what he'll say next. Unless you go with me, my precious darling, you may learn more than you learn from listening outside doors in the middle of the night."

Vince also rose up.

"What the hell do you mean," he asked in a whisper, "by 'listening outside doors in the middle of the night'?"

Betty Calder pressed her hands over her eyes.

The necessity for keeping their voices lowered, in this church-like atmosphere under a dome of mosaic glass, tended to heighten feelings while restraining them. Marion, straight and magnificent in the white dress, raised her eyebrows at Vince. Without a further word she turned round and walked in a foam of rustling underskirts towards the door to the foyer.

"Forgive me," said Vince, taking hat and stick from the table. "I'll follow her, I suppose. I always follow her."

He stood for a moment irresolute, with a baffled look on his face. Then he had gone too, instinctively on tiptoe even over soft carpet.

"Garth, you clever swine," said Abbot, suddenly bouncing up and just as suddenly sitting down, "did you do that on purpose? Did you drive 'em away? Was that the game? Hey?"

But neither Garth nor Michael Fielding paid any attention.

"Listen to me, Governor," the latter was pleading. "If you can possibly believe I killed Glynis Stukeley, you must be out of your mind. At the time she must have been killed on Saturday afternoon, I was talking to a solicitor."

"A solicitor?"

"Well, anyway, dash it," and Michael made a fighting

gesture, "a friend of mine who's articled to a solicitor. He said—"

"Michael, I am not concerned with what you were doing on Saturday afternoon. I want to know what you were doing on Friday night."

"On *Friday* night?"

"Yes. After Mrs. Bostwick's telephone-call, I left Harley Street to go to Hampstead. What did you do following that?"

"I locked up the house and went home to my own lodgings, that's all."

"Did you meet anyone afterwards?"

"No, sir! Not even my landlady in Great Ormond Street. I went to bed."

Standing very straight, speaking over Garth's head, the frightened Michael here turned a little sideways as though he risked staring at Medusa.

"I didn't know she was your sister, Lady Calder! Word of honour! I never dreamed . . . !"

"Mr. Fielding, I do beg you won't distress yourself so much." Clearly Betty was resisting an impulse to cry out. "Nobody could call Glynis a dear one of mine. They're saying I killed her."

"Yes, Michael," Garth struck in, "they are saying just that. Think about it."

Michael moistened his lips.

"Lady Calder, pray do accept my apologies. You can't know everything, or you'd forgive me. When you turned up with Hal Ormiston on Friday night, I couldn't believe my eyes!"

"Why?" demanded Garth. "Because she looks like her sister? Or because you and Hal frequently compete for the same woman?"

"Sir, I—"

"David, do please let him alone! He's terribly young!"

"He is old enough to assume a few responsibilities. Do you think I enjoy doing this?" Garth paused. "Betty, be good enough to answer the questions you answered yesterday. Your sister arrived at Fairfield on Saturday morning. You had not told her you expected me, nor did you tell her of a note that arrived later in the post. Yet she knew I would be there. When you protested at her going for a swim, her words were: 'What's the matter, ducky; don't you want your young man to meet me?' Is all this true?"

"Yes, of course!"

"How did Glynis know you were expecting me?"

"David, *I* can't answer that!"

"No, but perhaps Michael can. May I have the note, please? And its envelope?"

Betty took both from a heavy mesh-bag. Garth spread them out on the table.

"My stationery, you observe. The note reads, 'My dear, I shall be with you at six o'clock on Saturday. Yours unalterably.' This was done on my private typewriter. The envelope is postmarked London, West at 12:30 A.M. on Saturday. Did you ever see these before?"

"No, Governor. I swear I didn't!"

"Michael, don't lie to me," Garth said wearily. Then he struck the table with such sharpness, as Vince had done, that one of the elderly ladies looked round and a waiter drifted forward. "You are the only person who had access to the personal typewriter in my living-quarters at Harley Street, as you have access to everything else of mine. I don't hold it against you—"

"You don't hold it against me?"

"No; what harm was done? But don't lie."

"David," cried Betty, who was staring at him, "you said that *you* . . . ?"

"I was compelled to tell you so. I lied then, if you like, but Michael must tell the truth now." And Garth looked up steadily at the young man. "You wrote this note, did you not, at Glynis Stukeley's request? And there was something else you did?"

"No; that was all!"

Garth still looked at him.

So desperately in earnest can people become that their gestures seem to be those of the wildest exaggeration. Michael, knocking one of the hats off the table, bent forward and leaned both hands flat on the table-top so that he was staring back at Garth from less than ten inches away. The red plush armchairs, the dome of mosaic glass, the forest of palms round a splashing fountain, all held them poised in an incongruous frame.

"I wrote the note; very well!" Michael was not really screaming; he only seemed to be. "For the life of me I can't tell you why she wanted me to write it . . ."

"Can't you? You're a perceptive young man. Can't you even guess?"

". . . but on my oath, sir, that's all I did. Nothing but the note! Nothing else!"

"Would you take that oath if Glynis Stukeley were alive?"

"Yes, I would."

"Will you take it before Lady Calder now? Betty—"

He reached out towards the left, as though to touch Betty's arm and attract her attention, a moment before he glanced round. But Betty had gone.

There was nothing at all mysterious in this, as he realized after an instant of sheer superstitious dread. Though she did not fear being "insulted," as Marion presumably did, Betty had loathed these proceedings; she shrank from them as though from a fire. With Garth's attention fixed on Michael, and Abbot also entranced like a spectator at a tennis-match, she could have slipped away unnoticed towards the foyer.

And yet everything, or so it seemed to Garth, now began happening at once in the death-quiet lounge of the Palace Hotel.

Two waiters in striped waistcoats were approaching the table, one from the direction of the dining-room at the far end and one from the direction of the foyer. Not far behind the second waiter came Detective-Inspector Twigg.

Garth got up, cursing under his breath. Michael retreated.

"Sir," began the first waiter, addressing Abbot deferentially, "can I bring you anything?"

"Unless you can bring me enlightenment—?"

"Sir?"

The second waiter, with Twigg close behind him, had approached Michael Fielding and was speaking to him in a rapid undertone.

"What lady?" Michael demanded rather wildly. "Where?"

And then, as the quick whisper continued, Michael's face took on an eager expression.

"Sha'n't be two minutes, Governor," he assured Garth. "This may settle a good deal. You'll excuse me, won't you?"

It did no good to protest. Not for the first time Garth saw the game being taken out of his hands; it was as though Twigg, massively marching with bowler hat in hand, covered Michael's own retreat towards the foyer.

"Now, Doctor, what's all the fuss and hurry? *I'm* never in a hurry, am I? You just sit down, Doctor, and we'll take care of you in good time. Ur! Quite a posh place, this is. Afternoon, Mr. Abbot. Sorry I haven't had the chance to see you today, bar that word or two over the telephone."

"Does it ever occur to you, Inspector," inquired Abbot, with a snap behind closed teeth, "that you can interrupt most damnably at the wrong time?"

"Oh, ah? Very happy to apologize, sir, if you'll tell what I'm interrupting."

"Dr. Garth—"

"The gentleman's been asking questions, has he? Thinks he

can give the police a bit of help, perhaps? Maybe even thinks he can get to the truth before we do?"

"And if he does?"

"Well, sir, I'm sure that's natural to people like Dr. Garth." Twigg laughed with much smoothness. "It's natural for him to try it on in a lot of ways."

"Inspector Twigg," said Abbot, suddenly getting up, "what would happen if only once, just once in your tidy universe, you happened to be wrong?"

"Oh, I can be wrong, sir! I daresay I can be wrong about a lot of things. But I'm not wrong about this. Now, by your leave, we'll get back to serious business and I'll ask the questions. Maybe you hadn't heard, sir, I've been put officially in charge of this case?"

"And perhaps you had not heard," said Abbot, leaning down to strike the table with his fist, "that you will still take your orders from me whenever and however I choose to give them?"

"What might those orders be, sir?"

"If you are still so determined to question Lady Calder, or Mrs. Bostwick either . . ."

"Lady Calder? Mrs. Bostwick? Why, bless your innocence, sir," and Twigg's heartiness rang like a benediction, "but who's been telling you all that? I never did see much we could learn from Mrs. Bostwick. And Lady Calder? I've already heard what I want to hear about *that* young-lady-with-a-past, if you'll pardon the expression; and a lot of it there is and very interesting it is too. No, sir! The one I want to see now is Dr. Garth here. That is, if Dr. Garth's got no objection? Eh?"

"I have no objections," said Garth, "and it would scarcely matter if I had. All the same, who was the woman?"

"Woman? What woman?"

"That was what Michael Fielding wanted to know. Not two minutes ago a waiter came in here with a message for him, presumably that some lady wanted to see him out there somewhere. You've met Michael; you saw him in Harley Street last night. And you were so close behind the waiter that you must have overheard the message."

"Well, Doctor?"

"Well, who summoned Michael out of here at that particular time? Why was he summoned?"

"And that's supposed to be important, is it?"

"No; probably it isn't. But you might at least ask the waiter. He must take fifty such messages in an afternoon. If you delay much longer he'll have forgotten."

"Now I'll tell you what it is, Doctor," said Twigg, with a different shade of red sweeping into his face. "You've delayed me and obstructed me and tried to flummox me just about long enough. Fair's fair; I've finished." His voice grew more hoarse. "You try it just once more, and you'll find yourself in Queer Street. You'll find—"

"Stop," Abbot interrupted sharply. "My dear Garth! You don't seriously mean young Fielding is in danger?"

"No, I honestly don't think he is."

"Ah!" murmured Twigg.

Garth, lost in a concentrated attempt at fitting together every factor in his mind, seemed miles away. He looked down at the note on the table.

"Last night," he added, "I did wonder if there might be another act of violence. I was questioning Mrs. Bostwick in the middle of the night, when somebody crept up outside the door of my sitting-room to listen. It's no use going after your notebook, Mr. Twigg. In the first place, I don't know who it was. In the second place, I think now I was only suffering from a fit of the horrors."

Twigg changed colour again.

"In danger?" he repeated after Abbot, and shook the note-book in the air. "That young man? At tea-time on a Sunday? At the front of the biggest hotel in Fairfield, with a band-concert going on smack outside the door?"

"Mr. Twigg, I said I had changed my mind. The murderer killed once because this particular murderer was badly fright-ened. That's why it usually happens, surely?"

"Never you mind why it usually happens. If you knew more about murderers in real life, Dr. David Garth—"

"I know quite enough about them," replied the pale-faced Garth, "to have testified half a dozen times at the Old Bailey. Glynis Stukeley was killed because the murderer grew fright-ened. That's all there was to it. It won't happen again. It can't happen again. Unless, of course—" Garth stopped. "By the way, Mr. Twigg, was it at the Old Bailey you learned I had written a number of foolish stories under the name of 'Phantom'?"

"God's truth, Doctor, do you want to drive me up the pole? Haven't I got enough on my mind already? Mr. Abbot! Sir! I appeal to *you.*"

"And I say to both of you," snapped Abbot, with a ruthless and glittering calm, "that you'll have me ejected from this hotel as an undesirable guest unless you both moderate your voices and try to behave. Is that clear?"

Twigg had been wrong on one point, at least. The band-concert was over. Groups of other guests had begun to stalk or drift into the lounge, searching tea, amid a burst of talk which was no less loud because they moved so slowly. Otherwise, with Twigg and Garth again at each other's throats, the outburst could not have gone unobserved.

"Is that clear, I say?" demanded the inexorable Abbot. Garth bowed and sat down.

"Very well," said Abbot. "If you have any further questions, Inspector, this is the time to put them. If not, shall we end these proceedings now?"

"I have further questions, sir, thanking you very much. Nothing's ever ended quite as easy as the doctor may think it is."

"Or as I think it is, perhaps?" inquired Abbot, suave behind his eyeglass. "Never mind! What are the questions?"

"Doctor," said Twigg, corking himself down after an obvious and violent effort, "you've been asking. 'What woman?' And you seem to think I ought to be asking it too. That's as may be. But there *is* one woman, and not Lady Calder or Mrs. Bostwick either, I've been almighty interested to meet this very day."

"Mrs. Montague, you mean?"

"Ho, now!" said Twigg. "If that's the invalid lady who near got herself killed on Friday night, I think we can give her a rest too. No, Doctor! I was referring to a Mrs. Hanshew, Mrs. E. Hanshew," and Twigg looked at his notebook, "now staying with her married daughter at number 72 Acacia Avenue in Bunch. Does that name mean anything to you?"

("Look out! Look out!")

Garth had no reason, offhand at least, to think himself vulnerable here. But the hunt was up again, and he was the quarry. Alertness tapped out a warning just in time.

"Mrs. Hanshew? That's Lady Calder's housekeeper, I believe?"

"You 'believe' she's Lady Calder's housekeeper? Lummy, Doctor, can't I ever get a plain answer to a plain question? You *know* she's Lady Calder's housekeeper, don't you?"

"Yes. I know it."

"Oh, ah! You've met Mrs. Hanshew any number of times, I daresay? She's acted as a kind of chaperone, like, when you and Lady Calder and other people have gone for a swim? Or had these life-saving exercises on the beach?"

("Look out! Look out!")

"If it pleases you to call her a chaperone, Mr. Twigg—"

"Never mind what pleases me or don't please me. Just answer plain questions, if you don't mind. Do you know, Dr. Garth, what I was doing in the train going back to London last night?"

"Not being a star-reader or a crystal-gazer, Mr. Twigg,

I'm afraid I do not. Why don't you try asking plain questions for a change?"

"I laid myself open to that one, didn't I? All right! Then I won't ask you; I'll tell you." Twigg allowed a pause. "I was reading a book called *The Mystery of the Yellow Room.*"

14

Though the footsteps of hurrying waiters made no noise
on that soft carpet, the whole lounge stirred to a shuffle and
rattle of tea-trays. George Alfred Twigg, Garth was thinking,
had an oblique form of attack that always took you from an
unexpected side. He studied the edge of the table, wondering.
It was Cullingford Abbot who jumped into the breach.

"*The Mystery of the Yellow Room?*" Abbot demanded.
"Where'd you get a copy of that? You didn't take the one
from Lady Calder's house."

"No, sir, and I didn't need to," Twigg said with dignity.
"It's in the *Daily Mail* Sixpenny Series. You can buy one at
any railway-station bookstall. And I did."

"Why?"

"Lummy, Mr. Abbot, why does anybody buy a book? I
wanted to see what was in it. Have you read it, sir?"

"No; but I'm beginning to believe I should have. Did you
find anything helpful in one of your despised police romances,
Inspector?"

"Rummy kind of laws they've got in France, sir, if that
book's any example. Rummy ways of conducting a trial, too.
And liberties allowed to journalists that'd make your hair
stand on end.

"You see, Mr. Abbot—" but Twigg's cold eye was on Garth
as he spoke—"it's about an old scientist and his daughter
who's a scientist too, if you can believe that. They're working
on some queer business called 'the instantaneous dissociation
of matter,' like as if you could have people wiped out by a
bomb (ho!) that wouldn't even leave a trace of 'em afterwards."

"Well?" asked Abbot. "Is someone killed by a bomb?"

"No, sir."

"Then what's the application?"

"I'm trying to tell you!" Twigg was still watching Garth.
"The young lady in the story (she's not so young, either) sleeps
in a little room with yellow wallpaper, all locked up like a
strong-room but locked on the inside. In the middle of the
night they hear screams, the sound of a struggle, and one or
maybe two revolver-shots. When they break in . . ."

Abbot looked sour. "They always break in, it seems. Yes?"

"The young lady's not dead, but it looks as though she may
be a goner. Bruises on her throat from being choked, a wallop

over the head, and bloodstains everywhere: including the print in blood of a man's hand against the wall. But there's nobody in that room except the victim, and it's still locked up on the inside."

"H'm. Is that supposed to help us with this affair?"

"Sir, I'm dead certain the solution does! Have you read the book, Dr. Garth?"

"Yes." Garth glanced up. "Yes, I've read it."

"Now what, Doctor, would *you* say was the important point about the solution?"

"The same point, I suppose, you have already chosen for yourself."

"Oh, ah? And what might that be? Care to tell us?"

"With pleasure." Garth rose to his feet. "But I should like to be quite certain about your reading habits. Since you mention the trial scene, you must have read the book through to the end?"

"Never you mind how far I read it! That's no concern of ours now!"

"On the contrary, it is very much our concern. You are unlikely to have read a book of nearly a hundred thousand words in the short railway journey between Fairfield and London. Mr. Twigg, why don't you admit you prepared this ambush beforehand in the hope of trapping me in any blasted way you could?"

"I'm asking the questions here, Doctor! What's the important thing about that solution?"

"The identity of the murderer, I should say. The murderer is one Frédéric Larsan, an official police-detective who only pretends to be solving a whole series of crimes he has committed himself. That, no doubt, is the point to which you refer?"

"God's truth," yelled Twigg.

Only a sharp word from Cullingford Abbot cut him short. Briefly Abbot turned away, perhaps to hide a smile, for it was a face of poised cynicism he turned back under the queer, vari-coloured light of the lounge.

"That *is* the point?" Garth inquired.

"Well, no," said Twigg, suddenly regaining all his blandness and looking rather more sinister than before. "No, Doctor; that's not the point and you know it's not. And *I* can be a comical fellow too. Maybe I'd better begin."

"Will you accept my assurance." Garth said desperately, "that I never felt less humorous in my life?"

"Oh, ah? Then what's the game?"

"Mr. Twigg, I can't speak for the working of police minds. I don't know how they work. But your illustration of the

Yellow Room is nonsense, both practically and aesthetically too."

" 'Aesthetically,' " Twigg said in a stupefied kind of way. " 'Aesthetically'. Ho!" The word seemed to madden him as another word had done last night. "Now what's this 'aesthetically,' will you just tell me that?"

"I mean you can't have it both ways. You can't select one part of some fictional story that seems to support your theory, and disregard another part that totally contradicts it. The situation at the Yellow Room is not in the least like the murder at the pavilion; and Lady Calder has no connexion with either."

"Then I'll ask you a question about Lady Calder. How many bathing-costumes has she got?"

"What's that?"

"You heard me, Doctor. How many bathing-costumes does Lady Calder own?"

Once more the oblique attack swooped at him. Fear, never far from Garth where Betty was concerned, invaded his whole mind. He could feel he was being outmanoeuvred at every step; he began to wonder if even Twigg's rages were contrived; with great clarity he saw he could not continue to match himself against the police—and yet, somehow, he must manage it.

"Yes, Doctor? We're waiting."

"I don't know how many bathing-costumes she owns," Garth said truthfully. "I never asked her."

"But she's got more than one? You'd agree to that?"

"More than one? Yes, I think she has."

"Oh, ah! Now the lady don't like other women using her bathing-costumes? Or her bathing-robe either, if it comes to that?"

"And again I don't know the answer," Garth said truthfully, "because we never discussed that subject."

"And again I do know the answer," said Twigg, "because I had a bit of a word with Mrs. Hanshew this afternoon. What does Lady Calder say about the bathing-costume her sister was wearing late Saturday afternoon? She *says* Glynis Stukeley found that bathing-costume, all unbeknownst to her, and put it on all unbeknownst as well. Lady Calder says that, don't she?"

"Very well. What if she does?"

"Then she's not telling the truth. She kept those things locked up. Mrs. Hanshew will swear to it. If Glynis Stukeley found a costume in that house or a bathing-robe either, she could only have got 'em because her sister gave 'em to her.

"That's one small point against the lady, Doctor. The bicycle is another one. She keeps that bicycle in a little shed against the north side of the house, near a cycle path up to the main road. She *says* she was out cycling up to the time she met you at just past six o'clock, and she *says* she passed young Mr. Ormiston. Young Mr. Ormiston swears, as flat as a man can swear it, she didn't do anything of the kind.

"And what about the piece of sash-cord that was used to strangle that Stukeley woman? Is it likely a total stranger walked into the house looking for a weapon to use? Or just hoped he'd find one? Or did find one in a back bedroom where some workmen had left it when they were repairing window-cords at the back of the house a week ago?"

"Just a moment, Mr. Twigg! Can you prove the sash-cord came from that back bedroom?"

"Oh, ah. We can prove just that. Mrs. Hanshew swears it did."

Cullingford Abbot sat down and began to whistle between his teeth. A roar of conversation filled the lounge. Twigg extended his hand.

"Now you listen to me, Doctor. You don't want me to question Lady Calder: is that it? All right; I'm not questioning her! You want a chance to defend her yourself: is that it? All right; I'm giving you a chance. Suppose you were in charge of this case, what would *you* do?"

"If you mean that . . ."

"I mean it. Try me!"

"In the first place," said Garth, "I should read a book called *By Whose Hand?* In the second place, I should ask what has happened to Michael Fielding."

"Michael Fielding? Oh, lummy, are you at THAT foolishness again?"

"Well, where is he? He said he'd come back, but he hasn't. There's his hat on the table in front of you. Where is Michael himself?"

That was the moment at which Garth saw Marion Bostwick.

He was looking past Twigg's shoulder towards the east side of the lounge, where high door-entrances of polished inlaid wood opened into the foyer. Marion stood at one of these doors, head raised, facing inwards, in her white dress. She did not seem to be scanning the lounge, but rather to be waiting. She was alone. "On Friday night, Mr. Twigg," Garth said abruptly, but keeping his eyes off Marion, "I made a promise to a certain person. I have not yet broken the promise, although in justice to Lady Calder, it may soon be necessary."

"Oh, ah? What promise, Doctor?"

"That remains to be seen. If you are not going to find Michael Fielding, I am. Now excuse me."

And he strode off towards the foyer.

Twigg bellowed out something behind him, lost under the babble of talk. Cullingford Abbot's voice struck in. But Garth paid no further attention.

He could not hurry, lest he attract attention. It seemed to take several minutes, and took in actual fact six or seven seconds, to reach the florid line of doors. What Garth tried to remember was the face of the waiter who had brought Michael that message; and yet, as with the faces of most waiters, he had not even observed it at the time.

The foyer was pretty well filled. Festoons of electric lights shone on polished wood in a hall kept sombre to heighten its ornateness. Round the walls, a dozen feet up, ran a frieze of twenty-odd panels each painted dramatically to show some fighting ship of the Royal Navy at full speed under smoke; the central panel, just above big doors leading out to Victoria Avenue, was of the latest dreadnought-class battle-ship added to the fleet.

But these struck the only dramatic note.

The hall-porter stood at his desk beside a clamouring telephone, and ignored its ring. Two lifts, each propelled by a white-gloved operator pulling at a steel cable, made stately journeys up and down six floors. Round the foyer, like carriages in Hyde Park, moved a slow and ceremonious parade of ladies' hats.

They were larger than they appeared, these hats, because of the narrow brims; they bloomed with flowers or flat-lying plumes. All the women were gloved, and most of the men too. It would present a fingerprint problem to Twigg if—

And now Marion had disappeared too. Or, at least, Garth couldn't see her.

Where the devil *was* Michael?

It was as though all those hats, with the stolid faces beneath them, impeded Garth and kept him powerless. Then past him swam a figure he thought he knew, a figure in a striped waistcoat; and, though he could not call out, he stepped squarely in front of that figure and made it stop.

"You're the one, aren't you?"

"Sir?"

"Aren't you the waiter who carried a message, about fifteen minutes ago, from some lady to a young man who was with me in the lounge?"

Cold outrage froze out at him like the glances of passers-by.

"No, sir, I am not. Any message of that sort, sir, would have been carried by a page-boy. If you will excuse me, sir—"

"Just a moment, please! Are you on duty here, or in the lounge?"

"Here, sir."

"How long have you been here?"

"About half an hour, sir. Now if you will kindly—"

"Then you must have seen him, at least. There weren't all these people in the foyer then." Garth gave a rapid description of Michael. "He was in some haste. He wore no gloves and carried no hat." Unobstrusively money changed hands. "Can't I refresh your memory? Didn't you see him at all?"

The waiter turned away, struggled, and turned back.

"I *might* have taken a message from a lady, sir. It sometimes happens."

"Who was the lady? Can you describe her?"

"No, sir, I cannot. I would not have looked at the lady, sir. She was just a lady."

"Look here, man. I am not a jealous husband trailing his wife. This is a matter even more important than that. Here, let me refresh your memory a little more!"

Suddenly, under his breath, the waiter became all too human.

"I can't take any more money, sir," he said in an anguished hiss. "It wouldn't do any good, anyway, not if you was to give me ten pound. We're not allowed to notice 'em, and I didn't. And she spoke behind my ear. Honest to God."

"Then how do you happen to remember at all?"

"Because the lady asked him to meet her in the Grotto, sir."

"What's the Grotto?"

"That's the billiard-room downstairs. It's not open on Sunday."

"If it's not open on Sunday, how could he meet the lady there?"

"I don't mean it's locked. But the covers are on the billiard-tables and there aren't any lights to see by. Sir, you've *got* to excuse—"

"One last question! Did the young man go down there?"

"Yes, sir. He went down alone."

Sunday or no Sunday, there were shapes from the realm of nightmare that stretched out again to touch David Garth. The hall-porter's telephone went on ringing. The waiter dived away and disappeared.

This foyer, so full of feminine presence, held a scent of perfume or flowers or both. On the wall of polished wood, with an arrow pointing along a corridor towards the north, a sign in gilt Gothic lettering said, "To the Grotto."

Halfway along that corridor the electric lighting ceased.

Sunday had closed down its law at the proper boundary. But the carpets remained deep, the corridor wide. Garth, hurrying still farther along that corridor, might have been in darkness if somebody had not left open a window of mosaic glass at the end. A little dwindling daylight, at past five o'clock on the north-east side of the hotel, showed him the shape of a newel-post. The staircase led downwards, with another arrow and another gilt sign, "To the Grotto."

"Michael!" Garth said aloud.

He expected no answer, and got none.

The staircase, broad and carpeted, faced back in a northerly direction as you stood at its top. At the left-hand side, along the panelling of the stairwell, hung boards mounted with those improbable-looking fishes which seem as though they must be dummies and can never have been caught. But their eyes were conspicuous, as had been the eyes of the fish in the aquarium.

Light ended at the foot of the stairs.

Garth ran halfway down; then he hesitated, and walked slowly the rest of the way. A rather low archway, as the entrance to the Grotto or the billiard-room or whatever else they might call it, opened on darkness.

He cried out, "Michael!" And then, in a louder voice, "Who's there?"

There was no time to wonder what might happen if he met someone he had no wish to meet in the dark. For he knew beyond any question someone was there, without being able to identify the rustle or movement that told him he knew.

Standing in the doorway, he took a box of matches out of his pocket and struck one. He shielded the flame until it burned steadily, but it showed him nothing except the edge of a covered billiard-table a little distance away.

At his left, just inside the doorway what looked like a flattish wooden box was attached lengthwise to the wall. The keyhole of the box gleamed just before the match went out. Garth's gloves were thin, and the box unlocked. His fingertips pried it open, and someone's voice cried out at him as he pressed down the electric switches one after the other.

Three canopies of light shone out softly over three covered tables in a low-ceilinged, stone-floored room with grottoesque arches round the walls and more boards showing stuffed fishes like a frozen aquarium. Beyond the first billiard-table stood Betty Calder.

Never before had he seen Betty in a rage, but she was in a rage now.

"What are you doing here?" she screamed at him. "What do you want? Can't you ever, ever let me alone?"

"What am *I* doing here?"

"Yes!"

Possibly she saw the shock in his face, at what he feared or almost feared. It may have been that even Betty's rage was curiously ineffectual or else that she could never hate enough even though she loved. In any event, when she struck the edge of the table with her fist, it was as much in sheer despair as with any other emotion.

"Oh, what's the good of our going on? What's the good of our thinking we can ever be happy? We aren't being frank with each other even now, are we?"

"No, Betty, we are not being frank with each other."

"And we never can be! We never can be! Why don't you go away and let me alone? Even if I did want her dead—"

"Good God, Betty, do you know what you're saying? Where's Michael Fielding?"

"*I* don't know where he is! How should I know? And I don't care either!"

"You will care, my dear. You will care very much if that young man is dead and Twigg finds us together again at the wrong time."

Betty's lower lip had gone down so that her mouth was pulled almost square over the fine teeth. Nobody could have called her face evil or ugly, but it seemed almost so in the shock she clearly felt. The hat under a short flat plume, the dove-grey dress and short dove-grey jacket with its pearl buttons, added grotesque formality to that loss of control.

"Dead? What makes you say he's dead?"

"He has disappeared, at least. Some woman summoned him out of the lounge hardly a minute after you yourself had gone. Betty, it wasn't you who summoned him?"

"No!"

"He's known to have come down here alone. Did you see him?"

"No!"

It was cool and almost damp in this billiard-room. Round the walls its grottoes of twined stone made alcoves inside each of which a very dim electric lamp was set over the board of each prize catch so that you could read in white letters who had caught the fish and the date on which it was caught. But Garth was staring hard at the near edge of the billiard-table behind which Betty stood.

Something, all but unnoticeable against the dark-grey canvas covering even when the canopy-lights shone down on it, caught and held his eye.

"Betty—"

He strode forward, whipping off his gloves and stowing

them away in his pocket at the same time he took out a handkerchief. He touched the edge of the table with his forefinger. Then quickly he brushed his hands on the handkerchief and put it away.

"Go gently, now," he said, "and try not to lose your head any further. But this," he tapped the edge of the table, "this is a bloodstain. Betty, where is Michael Fielding?"

15

"I don't know. I never saw him. You must be mad if you think I did."

"How long have you been down here?"

"T-two or three minutes. Not longer. That's all."

"If there is anything else, Betty, you needn't fear to tell me."

Betty drew a deep breath.

"Yes," she said, "I'm quite aware I needn't. I know you'll protect me. You're already protecting someone else, aren't you?"

The soft voice had also gone out of control, becoming a gasp. Garth stood staring at that waxen pallor and the dead-looking brown eyes. It would do no good to tell her that a woman, any woman, can choose the worst possible moment for displays of hurt or jealousy carried to the edge of raging spite.

"I see," he said. "It was you outside the door of the sitting-room last night. You heard what I was saying to Marion Bostwick."

"Yes, I heard. All of it. Even after the second time you nearly caught me."

"Betty, can you possibly understand . . . !"

"No, I can't. Up to then I was blaming myself and hating myself for how badly I'd treated you. After that it was rather funny. Have I ever been as bad as your dear, dear friend Mrs. Bostwick? Have I ever been one-tenth as bad? Now I'm going to tell you what really happened on Saturday."

"No, you are not."

"I'm going to tell you—"

"And I say you are not," shouted Garth, circling round the table to stand over her. Betty's grey gloves went up in the air like claws about to scratch; but this was a futile gesture too. "I can guess already, and there is no time. If anything has happened to Michael Fielding, it will be enough to explain your conduct today."

"Do you imagine I care about explaining my conduct today?"

"You should. What are you doing down here? In a billiard-room, of all places. Why did you run out of the lounge?"

"I came down here because it's the one place in this awful hotel where a person can be alone on a Sunday. Alone,

alone, utterly and entirely alone. Did you never want to be alone and hide your face away from everyone? No, I don't suppose you did. You're one of these self-sufficient persons. I knew you didn't trust me; I knew that since yesterday evening. But I never guessed how little you trusted me until you showed that typewritten note to your Mr. Michael Fielding and said you were 'compelled' to lie about having written it to me."

"You heard what I was telling Marion last night? And yet you never said a word about it today? Until a trifle like the note brought on these hysterics?"

"A trifle, is it? You call the note a trifle? My God, how I hate you! I've never hated anyone so much in my whole life."

"Betty, be quiet!"

"Yes, strike me! Why don't you? I know you'd love to strike me; I can see your hand go up; why don't you?"

"Be quiet, I say! We must find Michael; we've got to find Michael! In another minute——"

In another minute, he knew, there would have been a burst of sobbing which he could have ended only with a savage slap across her face. And this was precisely what he wanted to do; it frightened him that he should so much have wanted to hit Betty or shake her until her teeth rattled.

Abruptly Garth turned away, looking round the room and wondering.

And he felt the sweat start out on his forehead. Here in this so-called Grotto they seemed lost in an undersea world, without even a sound except the noise of his own footsteps. He hurried towards the alcoves, each with its spectral fishing trophy that looked glazed or varnished with one open eye.

Perhaps they were glazed or varnished; he was not enough of a sportsman to know. Each alcove, in addition, contained a small round table and a bench covered with padded green leather. He searched each of them, moving slowly; he looked under the benches and up over his head at twisted stonework. Then he returned towards the billiard tables.

"There's nowhere else to look," he said. "Michael is not here."

"Are you surprised? Maybe he vanished. Maybe I made him vanish, like that witch-woman in one of the books you gave me."

"For the last time, Betty, let there be no more of this. That's a part of the trouble, which you had better understand here and now. I not only gave you those books; I wrote quite a number of them too."

"Oh, what in dear heaven's name are you talking about *now?*"

"Just that. I may have made a bad job of protecting you. But I am not going to have you hanged because I wrote half a dozen stupid novels about impossible crimes."

"Don't apologize. You needn't. You've done other things, haven't you? You've done quite a wonderful job at protecting your dear, dear Mrs. Bostwick?"

"What's this," interrupted a new voice, "about his dear, dear Mrs. Bostwick?"

From the corner of his eye, only half a second before that voice spoke, Garth noticed for the first time the invasion of another light which may have been burning a good deal longer. The archway-entrance to the billiard-room was brilliantly illuminated from outside. The stretch of wine-coloured carpet leading to the stairs was also illuminated; the wine-coloured carpet on the steps, the brass stair-rods, the polished walls on either side, all shared this glow. Vincent Bostwick, silk hat held across his chest and silver-headed stick under his left arm, stood at the foot of the stairs.

"Yes, madam?" demanded Vince. "May I ask what you were saying?"

Betty did not move, her face now completely expressionless. But Garth covered the distance to the archway in three long strides.

The whole corridor above the staircase was illuminated, from crystal chandeliers against its ornate ceiling. Marion Bostwick stood halfway down the stairs, at the left side by the handrail, her blue eyes as expressionless as Betty's.

Vince said, "I was asking—"

"Yes," interrupted Garth, his own temper simmering. "But we thought you had gone, Vince. We thought you had both gone. We thought you always followed Marion."

"My dear old boy," Vince said in a different tone, "so I had. That's why I came back. Marion hadn't gone, it seems. She thought you were about some odd sort of game down here and I bribed an attendant to turn on these lights."

"Now why should Marion have thought I was about some game?"

"Well, old boy . . ."

"Don't let him bully you, Vince," cried Marion. Round her mouth twisted an expression partly of fear and partly of cruelty. She made a magnificent figure on the staircase, white dress against wine-coloured carpet and polished-oak wall; but that look round the mouth dominated everything else.

"Don't let him bully you," she repeated, leaning forward. "You're forever allowing everyone to bully you. I won't have it, Vince! We needn't be afraid of anything David says."

Vince flung his head sideways.

"There are times, old girl, when you lack elementary decency. There are times, in fact, when you lack it in more senses than one. I don't propose to make a row here, which is evidently what you want me to do."

"Then, *I* will, Vince dear. Be sure I will!"

"Try it, Marion," said Garth.

He was never to learn what might have happened, or what Marion might have said. Two other figures appeared at the top of the stairs—a young man white-faced and stumbling, an elderly man with a heavy grey moustache, gripping the young man's arm just above the elbow—and stood looking down at the other three below.

The light of the crystal chandeliers beat on these two newcomers. The elderly man, teeth showing in a kind of frozen violence, was Cullingford Abbot. The young man was Michael Fielding.

"Go down there," Abbot snarled to his companion, releasing Michael's arm. "Go down there, I beg, and explain yourself. Once before this afternoon, pray believe me, I was prepared to deal with a youth of your age. I am prepared to do it again. Go down, sir!"

And Michael tottered down the stairs.

His appearance, which should have provided a shock of anticlimax, was not anticlimax at all. The look of his eyes, the pinched nostrils, the almost unnatural gloss of his high collar, told Garth there might be worse events in waiting.

In the suddenness of that apparition, too, Garth failed to see Marion's expression as anyone might have failed to see it. Marion, Vince, and Garth were all looking upwards. Betty had run out to the archway and was also looking up.

Abbot, at the head of the stairs, drew a handkerchief from his sleeve and mopped his lips like a suave conjurer. Replacing the handkerchief in his sleeve, he raised his right hand in a gesture of direction to some person unseen. The chandelier lights went out; every light went out, so that there remained only the faint glow from the billiard-room. Behind Abbot's back Garth could see a square of dwindling daylight from a window of mosaic glass still pushed up halfway; and (he had not observed this before) a vertical edge of daylight from a side door that was slightly ajar.

Michael stumbled in the sudden gloom, and all but fell on the stairs. Vince stood to one side. It was Betty who spoke first.

"I hope you're satisfied," she said, turning to face Garth under the archway. "I hope they're satisfied too. I hope they're all, all satisfied!"

Then she ran.

Garth had one glimpse of the hopeless despair in Betty's

face before she ran blindly up the stairs, holding up her skirts and hearing Marion's laughter as she fled past. He did not try to stop her. His present emotions (and they were complex) centred first on Marion Bostwick and then on Michael Fielding.

"Now, my dear Garth," continued the harsh voice of Cullingford Abbot, as he descended the stairs at a somewhat strutting walk, "let us clear up certain misunderstandings."

"By all means."

"First: I have got rid of Twigg. Pray don't ask me how; but for the moment I have got rid of him and he won't trouble you. Second: in these alarms and excursions you have been making an ass of yourself."

"I am not satisfied of that."

"No?" In leisurely fashion Abbot set the glass into his eyesocket. "Twigg was on the point of invading the hotel with constabulary to find you. My good friend the Secretary (call him Secretary, please; not hotel-manager) was frantic. Yet all I did was go into the . . . all I did was go in to wash my hands. And there was the young man you were looking for, as hale and unharmed as you see him now."

"Yet I am still not satisfied." Garth swung round. "Michael, what happened?"

"Yes, Michael," Marion Bostwick cried from the stairs. "What happened?"

Michael had run in one direction as Betty had gone in the other. He had run into the billiard-room. He stood with his back to the nearest table, silhouetted against its canopy-lights, with a wild and hollow and incredulous look on his face.

"So help me, Governor, I think you must be dotty." Michael's voice went high. "Happened? Nothing happened. It was a have."

"A what?"

"A have. A joke. A not very funny joke, either. You were there yourself, weren't you, when that waiter sneaked up in the lounge and whispered to me?"

"Yes, I was there. What did the waiter say?"

"He said some lady wished to speak to me privately 'in the Grotto' (those were the words he used) about something to do with 'the affair.' Well, naturally, what did I think at first?" Abruptly Michael swallowed as though his throat hurt him. "I thought he meant the murder case, and I told you so. I didn't even know what the Grotto was supposed to be, though there are signs and arrows all over the place."

"Did he tell you who the lady was?"

"No. He swore he hadn't seen her. Then, on the way, I

began to wonder. That word 'affair' can mean more than one thing."

"Ah!" breathed Cullingford Abbot, who was standing beside Marion Bostwick and brushing his moustache. "Whereupon you imagined a fair charmer yearning for an assignation, I daresay? Don't you rather fancy yourself, young man?"

They had all crowded after Michael, who made a badgered ducking motion of his sandy-haired head. Tension only grew with those words.

"Whatever I imagined, I didn't think it for long. In this place? In a billiard-room? Anyway, not a soul turned up. I waited here for eight or ten minutes in the dark. Then I knew I'd been had, and I left. It's not the cleanest spot in the world, as you can see for yourself?"

Here Michael appealed directly to Garth.

"Governor, why all the rumpus? Is everybody else dotty too? I'd no more gone for a wash and brush-up than that old gentleman with the eyeglass charged in at me as though I'd stolen the crown-jewels. I'm sorry if I spoke a bit sharply and told him to mind his own business. But I've been through a great deal today."

"You may go through still more," Abbot told him, "unless you behave yourself. However! The apology is accepted. No harm has been done. You do see that, Garth?"

"See what?"

"That no harm has been done!"

"What do *you* say, Michael?" Garth asked softly. "You met nobody here in this room? And no harm came to you in the dark?"

"Deuce take it, Governor, what harm could have come to me? I'm all right; don't you see that? My collar isn't even wilted. And what's the matter now?"

"I am wondering," Garth answered after a pause, "why you should mention your collar at all. Some people carry a spare collar for hot Sundays. There is a fairly large bloodstain on the canvas cover of that billiard-table about four inches from where your right hand is resting now."

"Governor—!"

"You were attacked, weren't you? And frightened nearly out of your wits? As a medical man yourself, will you permit me to examine your throat and nostrils?"

Michael ran round to the other side of the table, as though to put its length between himself and the advancing Garth. But a poisoned atmosphere seemed to have affected the breathing of most persons here. Marion stood very straight, mouth and eyes disdainful; Vince leaned on his walking-stick and stared at the floor.

"Young man," Abbot asked curtly, "is this true?"

"No! No! I swear it's not!"

"If you let the murderer frighten you out of speaking, Michael," said Garth, "you may well get an innocent woman hanged. Did you observe Lady Calder? Does that prospect please you so very much?"

"Governor, for God's sake!"

"And if you let David Garth frighten you into anything, my poor Michael," Marion Bostwick said with superb assurance, "you're a far more futile person than I ever thought you were. *We* owe him nothing! *We* needn't be afraid of him! All he's concerned to do is protect his fancy woman at the beach-house. Isn't that so, David?"

Garth took two more steps towards the billiard-table before turning back.

"Marion," he said, "don't make it war. For old friendship's sake, don't make it war."

And up went Marion's shoulder.

"David, dear, what utter stuff and nonsense you do talk! And the most high-flown kind of rubbish too. 'War'?"

"War between us. I've been trying to avoid that."

"Oh, la-di-da! I have not the least idea . . ."

"Then Vince has, if you haven't."

"I have a good many ideas, you know," said Vince, flinging his head round and studying Marion in a dispassionate way, "that even my damned talkativeness keeps to itself and only dreams about. Marion, my pet, I should have a little care. You think you don't need David any longer. You think he won't dare give you away or he'd give away Betty Calder too. You're skating like a maniac, my sweetest love; but have a little care. I warned you once you could never think two moves ahead."

"Really, if we are speaking of maniacs," said Marion, "I think I must be surrounded by them. Michael, do tell these poor people! Was there anybody in this room when you came down here a while ago?"

"No, Marion, there was not."

"Did anyone attack you, dear Michael?"

"No! No! No! And there aren't any bruises on my neck, either."

"If all one wants to do is get at the truth, and please believe that is all I want to do," Marion's yearning was like that of a fleshier angel, "it's never so awfully difficult as people think. This *is* the truth! You must see it's the truth. You're a stupid lot of fools if you don't! Mr. Abbot, don't *you* see it's the truth?"

"Abbot—" Garth began with some violence.

"Now if you interfere—" Marion almost screamed.

Their voices rang out and clashed amid the stone grottoes. Michael stood rigid behind the billiard-table. Vince was again staring at the floor.

"Listen to me, all of you," said Cullingford Abbot.

There was a sudden silence.

Again drawing the handkerchief out of his sleeve, Abbot dabbed at his mouth and also at his forehead. He hesitated. He stalked towards the archway as though leaving them, and then stalked back again.

"Up to twenty-four hours ago," he announced, "I should have said blandly I knew how to meet any situation. Well, I don't know how to meet this one. I am not God. Still less, despite my grandiose statements, am I the C.I.D. either. Garth, Twigg brought some news."

"Oh?"

"The inquest on Glynis Stukeley has been arranged for tomorrow at Fairfield Town Hall. Had you learned that?"

"No, of course I hadn't. What will the police do at the inquest?"

Abbot thrust the handkerchief back into his sleeve.

"I can't say. By which I mean Twigg won't tell me." His expression sharpened. "They may get the inquest adjourned. On the other hand, considering Twigg's present mood, they may bring evidence to get an inquest-verdict of wilful murder against Lady Calder and have her held for committal before the magistrates."

"A trial is as close as that, is it?"

"I fear it is."

"Won't Michael be asked to testify?"

"Tut!" The eyeglass loomed hypnotically. "This young man's affair with Glynis Stukeley, legally at least, had nothing whatever to do with the murder late yesterday afternoon. Young Ormiston will not be called, if it comes to that; nor will Mr. and Mrs. Bostwick, even if they knew anything. The only certain witness will be Lady Calder herself, as the next of kin. And probably you, who discovered the body."

Shadows seemed to be closing amid the grottoes, as though an undersea world pressed closer.

"That's what I wished to ask." And Abbot made a nervous gesture. "Garth, have you any evidence aside from psychological evidence? Suppose the police take the second course? If at this moment you had to brief counsel in Lady Calder's interest, could you prevent a verdict of wilful murder?"

"No, I could not. Much of what Twigg says is probably true."

"To put the matter crudely, then, you're dished?"

"At the moment, to put the matter crudely, I am worse than dished."

Across Marion's face travelled the edge of a smile, hardly more than a quirk at the corner of her mouth before it disappeared. You might not even have believed it had existed there against the radiance and health of her twenty years. But Vince Bostwick saw it. So did Abbot.

"Indeed," the latter said flatly. "I had hoped . . ."

"Look here!" he went on, with an even fiercer gesture. "In this duel going on between you and Twigg, both of you have struck and parried with meanings that were just out of sight. Nothing was ever above-board. Nothing was ever quite what it seemed. And yet I followed that duel pretty well, I fancied, until . . ."

"Until when?"

"Just before you left the lounge, Twigg asked you how you yourself would conduct the case. You recommended him to read a certain novel called *By Whose Hand?* Do you remember that?"

"Of course I remember it."

"Well, it won't help you. I have read that book too. The apparent witch-woman, who has been ensnaring and befuddling a much older man, is of course no witch-woman at all. She is innocent. Her 'impossible' crimes are only tricks devised by the real murderer, another woman of cold and astute nature who has been trying to fix the blame on her. I asked Twigg what he thought of your statement. Twigg said he agreed with you."

"Twigg agrees with me?" Garth echoed incredulously.

"Yes. He had copied in his notebook some words from the last chapter of that novel. Let me see if I can quote." Abbot threw up a hand in concentration. " 'I did not succeed,' says the real murderer, 'but I might have succeeded. It's all a question of law. They can't convict you of any crime unless they can show you how you did it.' "

Garth lowered his head. He did not see Marion, or Vince, or even Abbot's hypnotic eye. Twigg had backed him into a corner at last, and used just the wrong part of his own case.

"Well, my dear fellow? Are those words in the book?"

"They are."

"Has Twigg even a measure of right on his side? And, if he has, how do you mean to meet the charge?"

"I don't know." Garth looked up. "God help me, I still do not know. And yet, before it is too late, I have got to find some way."

16

The train reached Charing Cross towards dusk of a fine evening in June. David Garth, emerging from the station, raised his hand towards one of the new motor-cabs in the rank outside.

Once more the atmosphere swept over him: the tarry smell of wood-paving after a day's heat, the remnants of sunset beyond Trafalgar Square, a soft traffic-rumble punctuated only by the jingle of hansom-bells and the *putt-putt* of an occasional motor-car.

But Garth was far from being in the same mood he had felt only four nights ago.

This was Monday, June 17. A porter followed him from the station, carrying a heavy suitcase and a hat-box: his luggage from the Stag and Glove. Nor was he in evening-clothes this time. He wore the professional uniform of top-hat and frock coat in which he had attended the inquest at Fairfield this afternoon.

The inquest. Yes.

Briefly, in that unreal twilight, he wondered if Inspector George Alfred Twigg might not loom up again in front of him. Perhaps he hurried a little. But he saw only familiar things: the shops at the other side of the Strand, and the "Golden Cross," and Morley's Hotel facing Trafalgar Square.

Then the cab-engine sputtered and exploded into life as the driver swung its starting-handle. His luggage was flung up beside the driver.

"Number 31b Harley Street."

Now for the test!

"Very good, sir."

Sitting back in the cab, all that chuttering way through streets half-deserted when theatre-curtains had gone up, he tried not to think. But several times he touched the many sheets of folded paper he had put in the inside breast pocket of his coat. They were not typed, those sheets; he had written them by hand, laboriously, through the long night before the inquest. And images stabbed through.

In Upper Regent Street, just above Piccadilly Circus, the lights of the Café Royal rolled past on his right. He wondered whether Abbot held court in the big blue-and-gold room where, at the other side of a glass screen, more Bohemian elements drank at marble-topped tables.

Farther on up Regent Street, towards his left, posters outside the Polytechnic advertised a new French cinematograph entertainment called *The Pumpkin Race*. That film was worth seeing, people said; one small incident precipitated a wild chase through the streets of Paris which might have been grim if it had not been so hilariously funny, though Marion Bostwick declared she would die and lose her soul before she paid as much as four shillings for any animated-picture show.

Well, Marion! Now, Marion!

But he was not obliged to lock up his thoughts—not entirely, at least—when the cab turned into quiet Harley Street towards his own door. Twilight had become darkness. At the kerb stood Vincent Bostwick's 20-horsepower Daimler landaulette, painted white with red wheels, its head-lamps burning and Vince's chauffeur-engineer at the controls.

Vince himself stood on the pavement near a street-lamp, fretfully smoking a cigarette. And Vince rose at the newcomer as Garth paid off the cab.

"Yes, old boy? What happened at the inquest?"

"All in good time, Vince."

Unlocking the front door, Garth carried his luggage inside and closed the door with a hollow slam. That familiar hall, with its antiseptic white woodwork and its black-and-white tessellated floor, seemed even more bleak when he switched on the light.

"There was nothing on the newspaper-bills," said Vince, dropping the cigarette on the floor and grinding it out underfoot. "You see—"

Nowadays it was much the fashion to wear white tie and white waistcoat with a dinner-jacket as well as with tails. Clearly Vince had been dining at his club, and dining well. Though he was no less lazy and lounging, the wine brought out a blue vein at his temple and etched deeper the fine little aging lines round his eyes.

"You see," he went on, "I didn't dare ask a friend of mine in Fleet Street. Marion and I aren't concerned in this, so far as anyone knows yet; and I can't have the Yellow Press on our backs. What happened at the inquest?"

"They adjourned it."

"Meaning what, exactly?"

"The only testimony was Betty's formal identification of her sister's body as the next of kin, which has to be done as a matter of law. Immediately afterwards Twigg got up and asked the coroner for an adjournment. There were no other witnesses. They didn't even call me."

"Oh? Then all your troubles are over, aren't they?"

"Hardly," Garth said with restraint. "It only means Twigg is waiting to jump. And now Betty has run away. That may be just what he is waiting for."

"Betty has run away? Where?"

"I wish I knew. She's not at the cottage and she's not at Putney Hill. At least, nobody answers the telephone at Putney Hill."

Garth hesitated, his mouth a line of worry. Only one light still burned against the height of the hall. It was too oppressive with silence when nobody spoke and too full of echoes when you did. Abruptly he led the way to the back room they called the little library.

This was a little better, after he had touched the electric switch beside the door. Four bulbs, in shades like glass flowers, glowed out above shabbily comfortable Morris chairs and smoking stands, and glass-fronted bookcases with enamelled designs on their doors. Books gave a certain warmth; so did the reflection of lights in glass. But no decoration could remove the atmospheric chill of that house.

Garth glanced at the little writing-desk to the right of the fireplace. Then he looked back at Vince.

"For the moment, however, that must wait. Look here: since you and Marion were returning to town anyway, I asked you to execute a commission for me. Well? Where is he?"

"Michael?"

"Yes; who else? Couldn't you find him?"

"I could find him easily enough, yes. But I couldn't bring him here. He's locked up at his lodgings, with a doctor standing guard and two mysterious clergymen as well." Vince's eyes grew fixed. "Steady, old boy! Is Michael so important?"

"Yes, Vince. You know he is."

"It's just possible the fellow's really ill! After all, Michael's not the only person who's been offering a medical excuse for not being questioned."

"If you refer to Mrs. Montague," Garth said curtly, "I had a word with her this morning before the inquest. I also had a word with Colonel Selby. Both of them are going to be very useful."

"Last night, David, you said you needed some kind of inspiration to find a way out of this. Have you found a way out?"

"Yes, I think so. I even hope so. Where's Marion tonight?"

Vince opened his mouth to speak, and evidently thought better of it.

Here in this little room, with the door closed against traffic-noises from the street outside, it was as though they were buried at the heart of the Great Pyramid. Every colour seemed to acquire sharpness from the intensity with which they looked at it. Vince removed his collapsible opera-hat, folded it together, and flung it into a Morris chair.

- "Old boy, ever since Saturday morning I've been wanting to tell you something."

"Yes?"

"On Saturday morning," Vince stared at the floor, "that fellow Abbot was questioning Marion at Hyde Park Gardens."

"Yes?"

"Marion was repeating her story about—about Glynis Stukeley attacking Mrs. Montague at Hampstead on Friday night." Vince still stared at the floor, flinging out words. "Marion was going to Abbot about *you*. She said you seemed to doubt her story about the attack, and said she couldn't understand why on earth you doubted it."

"Yes. Well?"

"Then Abbot appealed to me, and I said I couldn't understand either. In other words, I let you down after you'd supported both of us. I've always felt like smiling when people use words like 'cad' or 'rotter' or the like; but it's not really so very funny. I was in a blue funk, and I let you down."

"Vince, forget all that! No apology is necessary."

"All the same . . ."

"I greatly appreciate," and Garth struck his hands together, "I greatly appreciate your schoolboy code of ethics. I'm afraid I share that code. But this matter has grown too desperately serious; it's going to end in a smash."

"Yes. That's what I meant. David, what are you planning? If you expect me to support any scheme against my own wife . . . !"

"No! I don't expect that. Even the law doesn't expect it."

"What's the game, then?"

"Can you bear it if I speak frankly?"

"Old boy, I only hope to God you will."

"It's not easy to decide how much of this affair you must have guessed already and how much of it will still shock you when you hear it. At the same time, you've lived with Marion for two years. Your worst enemy couldn't call you a fool."

"Has it ever been observed," said Vince, with one eye on a corner of the carpet, "that Marion's favourite word is 'fool'?"

"No, I disagree," Garth said sharply. "Her favourite word is 'old.' She even calls *you* old. Do you remember?"

"David, I admit to being a good deal of a fraud. Most of my ideas in this life have come out of books, out of E. F. Benson and *The Dolly Dialogues* and all the rest of the airy persiflage we're supposed to keep up. Any other ideas (yes, you've hit it!) are from schoolboy ethics and from these accursed stories about mysteries. By the way, there's a rumour going round—don't ask me how it started!—that you yourself are a fellow called 'Phantom.' Is it true?"

"Yes."

"Well, I can't say I'm surprised. I've suspected it once or twice. But that doesn't help us with Marion." Vince's tone changed. "And I warn you, if you're planning anything against Marion . . . !"

"Whatever I am planning, you have my promise no harm will come to Marion. It's only that we had better face a few facts about her. In some ways she's not unlike the late Glynis Stukeley. She is greedy, she is unscrupulous, and she's not entirely normal."

"Is this some of your damned Viennese psychanalysis?"

"No. For the most part it's plain common sense, as any experienced G.P. could tell you. Glynis Stukeley only wanted money. Whereas Marion inspired somebody to commit murder."

"I deny—"

"Deny it or not, it's true." Garth raised his voice. "She may not have done so knowingly or consciously, though I'm not even sure of that. But she won't suffer for it. She can't suffer for it. Whatever happens and whatever life is wrecked, Marion will go on her way in all serenity after she has wept and howled a little. That's her nature. Both her guardians have known it from the beginning."

"David, what are you going to do?"

"Very shortly I am going to Hampstead. Should you care to accompany me—"

"If you mean to see Mrs. Montague and Colonel Selby, that's no good. They're still at Fairfield."

"On the contrary, they are in London. They returned this afternoon at my special request."

"To give Marion away? To tell the whole blasted world that . . ."

"Haven't I already assured you, Vince? No harm can come to Marion. She is safe. She's as safe as—as you are yourself. Possibly I can't expect you to help me. But it will save a great deal of trouble if you answer a plain question. Where is Marion now?"

"I don't know."

"Vince—"

"I tell you, I don't know," shouted Vince. "She nipped out of the house as soon as we returned this afternoon, and I haven't seen her since. That's why I had dinner at the club. And you tell me your friend Betty Calder has run away? It's odd, isn't it, it's devilish damned odd, that both those two women should have chosen to make themselves scarce on the same day?"

"Yes," answered Garth, suddenly struck by a new thought, "it's odd. It may not be devilish damned odd, but it *is* odd. I am wondering . . ."

"What?"

Outside, in the hall, on its table beside the stairs, the telephone began to ring.

It may have been the wine he had drunk, or it may have been the inhuman stridency achieved by the ringing of a telephone in a silent house, that made the blue vein stand out farther at Vince Bostwick's temple.

Garth opened the door to the hall. And, at the same moment, someone began to ply the knocker of the front door. Garth, on his way towards the telephone, stopped and hesitated on a wire of nerves between the two.

"Answer the telephone, will you?" he called over his shoulder to Vince. "If it's a personal or professional call for me, say I'm out. I'm out to anyone except Betty. Or to Marion, of course, though that's unlikely."

"Why don't you answer the blasted telephone yourself? Is it less important than some joker at the door?"

"It may be less important, yes, if the joker happens to be Inspector Twigg with some new trick for us."

"They don't like each other, do they, do they?"

"Who?"

"Marion and your—Marion and Lady Calder."

"No, they don't like each other. Answer the telephone!"

The strident ringing was cut off a second before Garth, gritting his teeth, opened the door. But he need not have worried; or, at least, he thought he need not have worried. Outside stood Cullingford Abbot.

Evidently Abbot had been holding court as usual at the Café Royal. Like Vince he wore a dinner-jacket, under a short cape whose scarlet lining gleamed by the light of a street-lamp as he flipped back the edge. A barrel-organ was tinkling through a side street; the chauffeur-engineer at the wheel of the white Daimler landaulette seemed to be whistling in time to it.

"Ah!" said Abbot, lifting the eyeglass. "They told me you lived here as well as kept your consulting-room here. I could not be sure a light on the ground floor meant anything, or that I was wise to dismiss my cab. Still, I see you own a second motor-car."

"Motor-cars are too expensive a toy for me to own more

than one. The Daimler belongs to Mr. Bostwick. However, pray come in."

Vince was saying something to the telephone in a low and urgent voice. Abbot's expression sharpened to alertness as he swept off his hat.

"My dear Garth, is anything wrong?"

"I've lost Lady Calder. That's to say," Garth corrected himself quickly, "I don't know where she is. Mr. Bostwick has been having the same difficulty with his wife."

"Tut! Then we all have our troubles. I've lost Twigg."

"That's a great pity, isn't it?" Garth spoke not without sarcasm. "Our Inspector Twigg, I should think, would be a difficult man to mislay."

"It *is* a pity, sir, when I don't know what he's doing and I want to know. Er—"

Abbot paused as Vince clashed the telephone-barrel back on its hook. Garth swung round.

"Yes, Vince? Who was it?"

"Colonel Selby. He wanted to speak to you. I said you were out." A slight roar became noticeable under Vince's tone. "Well, old boy, isn't that what you told me to say?"

"I didn't mean—"

"No; stop; fair play!" Vince hesitated, moistening his lips. "He wants you to go up there at once. I said I'd go instead. I suppose it means we'll both go?"

"It does indeed mean that. Why did he want to speak to me?"

"He wouldn't say. No, it's nothing devilish, if that's what you're thinking! He said it wasn't important; it could wait. Anyway, we'll both go in my car."

"Yes. If you remember, Vince, we made a similar journey on a summer night just over two years ago? When you first introduced me to Marion?"

"David, what in hell is happening? How is it *you* know Colonel Selby? Wait; stop; of course! You said you'd spoken to him in Fairfield today."

"That's not altogether it, Vince. I now have his permission to tell you. On Friday evening he called on me professionally."

"Professionally?"

"My profession, I should say. About some person whom he believed, in his own view at least, to be insane."

Vince put the tips of his fingers on top of the telephone table, and looked back without speaking. Cullingford Abbot, though not an easy person to ignore at any time, had to draw Vince's attention by a loud throat-clearing.

"Mr. Bostwick," he said, with somewhat ominous suavity, "you may perhaps remember having met me. In my own small way I do represent the police. And there seem to be several things about which Dr. Garth has not informed me. Sir, may I beg leave to accompany you in the car?"

"Sir," replied Vince, "you may. There are things Dr. Garth hasn't told me either."

Vince strode to the still-open front door, and made a gesture to the chauffeur at the wheel of the Daimler.

"All right, David! I won't ask you. But does this mean we're approaching the end of the road?"

"Yes, Vince," said Garth. "I think we may be approaching the end of the road. One moment!"

"If we're bound to go through with this," and Vince was his old casual self again, "let's get on with it. What's the trouble now?"

"I have a small errand first. No, wait! I shall not be long."

The chauffeur had climbed out of the car, carrying its starting handle. Motioning the others to remain where they were, Garth returned to the little library.

He went quickly to the writing-desk by the fireplace, but he did not at once sit down. He could hear, against a quiet night, the creak and thump, creak and thump, as that starting-handle wrenched against a reluctant motor. It might have symbolized Garth's own state of mind.

From his inside pocket he took out half a dozen sheets of writing-paper folded lengthways, and weighed them in his hand as though he weighed them in a scales: the uncertainties, the risks, the horrifying consequences that might follow a wrong decision.

And there must be no wrong decision. There must be no mistake now.

Then the car-engine roared into life, settling to a steady throb. Garth sat down. He took a long envelope from the rack, slipped the folded sheets inside, and in firm characters wrote someone's name across the envelope.

PART IV

THE DEADFALL

Derby Street, on the E. side of Parliament Street, leads to *New Scotland Yard*, the headquarters of the Metropolitan Police since 1891. The turreted building, in the Scottish baronial style, was designed by Norman Shaw, and is impressive by the simplicity of its outline and the dignity of its mass.

—BAEDEKER'S *London and Its Environs* FOR 1908

17

"Come in, Doctor," said Colonel Selby.

The foyer of the house loomed out of shadows. Its bronze Diana on the newel-post of the staircase, holding up an electric light seldom found in classic mythology, seemed no less fusty than walls panelled to head-height in oak and papered above with some material like dark-red burlap.

But no such fustiness could apply to Colonel Selby himself. Iron-grey and balding, thick-set and clean-shaven, he faced them with a bearing of power and authority only slightly tempered with fright.

Behind those eyes, Garth knew, would be a kind of fanatic: over-dogged, over-scrupulous, in the smallest detail of conduct. His professional costume, the uniform of retirement, was the same frock coat with silk lapels, set off by white waistcoat and broad black cravat, he had worn on Friday evening.

"Come in, Doctor," he repeated. "Got to open the front door myself. Sorry! Blanche (Mrs. Montague, that's to say) dismissed the servants—"

"*Again?*" Garth was thinking. Alarm shot through his mind. But the next words reassured him.

"For the time being, that's to say, while we were in Fairfield. They're not back yet. Didn't expect to be back ourselves."

"That's my fault, I'm afraid."

"Not at all! Best thing that could have happened, maybe." The heavy voice hesitated. "Hullo! I wasn't expecting . . ."

"What's got into everybody?" demanded Vince Bostwick. "You were expecting me, surely? I spoke to you on the telephone not so very long ago."

"Oh. That! Yes, to be sure. When your voice answered, my boy, I'd an idea the doctor himself wasn't very far away."

"Then you must be a ruddy mind-reader!"

"Think so? Not necessarily."

"Anyway," said Vince, "I don't believe you've met Mr. Cullingford Abbot here. Mr. Abbot is—"

"On the contrary," interposed Abbot, his eyeglass gleaming, "I've had the pleasure of meeting this gentleman at the Oriental Club. Your servant, Colonel Selby."

"Your servant, sir." By instinct Colonel Selby straightened up stiffly. But some repressed emotion made his face swell. "Yes, I remember," he added, towering above Abbot as the latter entered. "You were the one who telephoned here on Saturday morning, weren't you?"

"I was."

"Spoke to my manservant before he left? Asked if you could have a word with Mrs. Montague?"

"I did. It might be pointed out, furthermore," retorted Abbot, "that I have not yet exchanged one word with the lady or so much as had a glimpse of her even at Fairfield."

"And now, I daresay, you want to thrash the whole matter out? Well, never mind. Maybe that's best. Come in, please. Come in, all of you."

Colonel Selby glanced at the door of the drawing-room, which was uncompromisingly closed. Unsure of himself, unsure of all things, he hammered the heel of his hand against his forehead. Then he led them to his den at the back of the foyer.

The green-shaded gas-lamp was burning on his desk, in the den. Its light shone on brown-leather chairs and was reflected in the glass of a rifle-cabinet above which loomed so many bound copies of *The Field*. The tiger-skin lay by the fireplace. Round the walls, high up, animal-heads bared their fangs against dark wallpaper obscurely patterned in dull gold.

"Look here," Colonel Selby went on in a conciliatory tone, addressing Abbot. "I had rather, of course, the police didn't question Blanche just yet—"

"Indeed? If you have something to hide—?"

"Hide? What in blazes do you mean by that, sir?"

"One moment!" said Garth.

It may have been the effect of the animal-heads, like a gallery of frozen violence. It may have been the fact that three persons had committed suicide in this house. Certainly Garth felt the tainted atmosphere as soon as he entered the foyer. So, plainly, did Abbot.

For the first time Abbot had encountered someone who could match and outface him at his own game of authority.

Though Colonel Selby might be less intelligent and far less sensitively perceptive, he had an advantage that did not lie in mere height or bulk. Yet it became clear that Abbot, moustache lifting above his teeth, could give as good as he received.

"Mrs. Montague," said Colonel Selby, "is prepared to answer any questions from Dr. Garth. She is not at the disposal of any Scotland Yard jack-in-office who chooses to intervene. I won't try to prevent her being questioned, mind! Maybe that's best. Still! There can be no harm done, can there, if Dr. Garth goes upstairs and speaks to her first?"

"Yes, I think there can be," Abbot said coolly. "Dr. Garth has already spoken to the lady today, I believe?"

"Yes. At Fairfield. What of that?"

"He has had his chance," said Abbot, "and he has failed. Even if the twenty-four-hours' grace to Lady Calder and Mrs. Bostwick had not expired some time ago, I made no promise about Mrs. Montague. What I did make——" again the moustache lifted above the teeth—"was a foolish promise which has earned me only a reprimand from the Commissioner. At my age, sir, I do not enjoy being treated as a schoolboy. Now it's time to use my own wits."

"One moment!" Garth said again.

Reaching into his inside pocket, he took out the envelope across which was written the name of Mrs. Blanche Montague.

"There is no need for anyone to question her," Garth went on, "if we permit her to make her own response. Colonel Selby, will you undertake to deliver this to Mrs. Montague?"

"What is it? Will it upset her?"

"Yes," Garth answered honestly, "I am bound to admit it will upset her. But it is the only way out."

"What is it, I asked?"

"It's a statement of certain facts known to her, and, I think, to you as well. I can only hope it will be persuasive. Will you take the statement, Colonel Selby? And make sure she reads it?"

"*I* will take the statement, by your leave," said Cullingford Abbot.

Garth swung round.

"No, Abbot, you will not. If we are to avoid scandal and a good deal worse, no one must see this except Mrs. Montague and Colonel Selby."

"Aren't you forgetting, my dear fellow, that I represent the Commissioner of Police?"

"No. Nor am I forgetting we must wreck no more lives than we need. Well, Colonel Selby?"

"Avoid scandal, you said?"

"I can't swear it will. I can only hope so."

"Then give it me," said Colonel Selby, stumping forward and thrusting the envelope into his own breast-pocket. "Mind! If you don't want anybody else to see this, I can't hand it over now. Marion's with her—"

"Marion's with her?" exclaimed Vince Bostwick.

Abbot's face had gone rather grey at this apparent treachery on Garth's part. Vince, who had been standing by the rifle-cabinet with his back turned and his hand on its ledge, moved slowly round as though supporting himself.

"*Marion* is with her?" he repeated.

"Yes. They're up in Blanche's room with the door locked. God's thundering guns," said Colonel Selby, "but what's so very surprising about that? Before she married you, Vincent, this was the girl's home. Where else should she go if she's unhappy? We—we may not approve things we hear of. And preach sermons, maybe, at ourselves and everybody else. When the pinch comes, though, we stand by our own. Got to! What else can we do?"

"May I beg, Colonel Selby," snapped Cullingford Abbot, "you will spare us your own brand of prosing?"

"Now look here—"

"I assume, sir, you refuse to hand over that envelope in your pocket?"

"By God, sir, you assume dead right."

"Then would you mind taking me to Mrs. Montague at once?"

Colonel Selby nodded curtly. He had marched forward, with a bald and lowering forehead, when a new thought struck him.

"Got your legs?" he asked. "Good! Up the staircase; first door on the landing at the head of the stairs. Can't miss it. You'll hear 'em talking."

Nodding in reply, eyeglass turned over his shoulder almost as though his neck were dislocated, Abbot left the study with a noiseless step. Colonel Selby breathed noisily.

"No, Vince," Garth said; "stay where you are."

"I was only—"

"*Vince, stay where you are.*"

Anguish flowed in that garish room under the animal-heads. In contrast to most of its decoration was the old swivel-chair before their host's neat desk, with the light of the gas-lamp shining on it. Colonel Selby groped for the swivel-chair. It creaked underneath him as he sat down, his hands suddenly pressed over his eyes.

"Colonel Selby," continued Garth, looking steadily at Vince, "this is not a pleasant time for anyone. I am loath to disturb you. It's only that you telephoned me a while ago. Vince couldn't or wouldn't give me a message."

"Oh. Yes. To be sure." With an effort the other seized and found thought in a kind of physical action. He rose to his feet, his face smoothing itself out. "Probably nothing in it. But you can't tell. Not now! Not any longer! Er—at Fairfield today, Doctor, I had the idea (sorry!) you were interested in this girl Lady Calder."

"Yes. I am very much interested in her. Why do you say that?"

"Well! When she called here tonight . . ."

The atmosphere changed again.

"Lady Calder is here?"

"Yes! Steady! Called here about an hour ago, wanting to see Marion. Marion answered the door. Things didn't seem quite right between 'em. They went up to Marion's old room, and seemed to be having a bit of a slanging-match." Colonel Selby made a gesture. "Never interfere between two women, Doctor; you'll soon learn that when you live in the same house. Anyway! It's not what I wanted to tell you."

"What did you want to tell me?"

"This police-officer, chap named Twigg . . ."

Garth stood very still. "Yes?"

"He got here ten or fifteen minutes later, and *I* answered the door. Said that fellow Abbot sent him. Well! No reason he *shouldn't* be here, but he seemed to be trailing your friend."

"Yes?"

"Just then Marion and Lady Calder came downstairs. Pretty little thing, too. Like the other one, only honest-looking. Twigg went at her in a stalking kind of way, like a beater through the bush after a tiger, and shooed her into the drawing-room." Colonel Selby broke off. "Damme, Doctor, what's wrong? *I* can't see to everything."

"No. I beg your pardon. Where are they now?"

"Still in the drawing-room, I daresay! Why not?"

"And Mrs. Bostwick?"

"Marion ran back up the stairs to Blanche's room." Sweat stood out on Colonel Selby's forehead. "Later I wondered—"

"Yes. So do I."

"I told you it wasn't all gas and gaiters, didn't I?" interposed Vince Bostwick, pointing a long finger. "I told you it's not easy when you lose your head and your heart and everything else that keeps the world steady and the rest of us sane. Possibly you believe that now, old boy. Or don't you?"

Garth did not answer.

Flinging open the door of the den, he went out into the foyer more quickly than Abbot had moved. Vince, to do him justice, could not maintain a kind of cynical frenzy that went into his question; Vince's expression changed, and he followed.

The foyer had never seemed so ominous in its quiet. Garth ran to the door of the drawing-room. He knocked, and knocked again, before opening that door too. The drawing-room was empty.

Golden-oak furniture and starched lace-curtains mocked him under the pale lamps. The tiger's head—had they spoiled the tiger's hide in skinning it, so that only its head remained for a trophy?—opened fangs above the mantelpiece. Garth ran back to Vince, who was standing in the middle of the foyer.

"Vince, you're acquainted with this house. I'm not. Go up and look in 'Marion's old room,' wherever that is. Look in at Mrs. Montague's room too. Betty and Twigg are here somewhere. We've got to find them."

"Now take it easy!" Vince was already embarrassed at his own outburst. "She's been questioned before, hasn't she? Anyway, why imagine they're here? Probably they've gone."

"Oh, no. They haven't gone. If you imagine that, you can't anticipate Twigg's tactics when he's moving in for a kill."

"Don't use words like that! Dash it all, didn't you say no evidence was given against her at the inquest?"

"Yes. I should have seen that was a part of the game. Twigg wanted her to think the worst was over just before he jumped at her to get a confession."

"Confession?" Vince shouted. "Are you admitting that woman's guilty after all?"

"No, she is not. She didn't kill her sister. But that won't save her. Partly due to my own asinine attempts to make her story better, no jury on earth will ever believe what she says. Go and look for her, won't you?"

"Aren't you coming too?"

"No. Not for a moment." Garth's eyes roved round. "It's not likely, but it's just possible—"

"What is?"

"Go on!"

And now Vince was running, up the staircase with its carpet and its brass rods. Garth walked straight past that staircase and to the back of it, where the door with the bolt led down to the cellar.

The bolt was not pushed into its socket. Turning the knob, Garth yanked the door open. Just inside, where a flight of wooden steps led down between whitewashed stone walls into earth-smelling depths, one sickly electric bulb burned at the foot of the stairs.

Though he ran down the steps, he tried to tread softly so as to make as little noise as possible. He was almost certain he heard voices, and sure of it an instant later.

The underground corridor which led to the kitchen carried sounds with the effect of a whispering-gallery, though the heavy door of the kitchen was closed. A very faint line of light showed under the sill.

Both the voices he heard were unmistakable.

"Now, miss (oh, ah; beg pardon; it's 'my lady'; but no matter o' that) now, miss, I'll just remind you of something. It wasn't me that brought you down here. It was you that brought me. Eh?"

"Yes, it was."

Betty's voice sounded clearer and firmer than he had heard it since the whole twisted affair overtook them.

"Just to tell me this cock-and-bull story?"

"It happens to be true."

"Let's see if I've got it straight," said Twigg. The pouring scepticism of his voice increased with each word. "On Friday night, you expect me to believe, Mrs. Bostwick tried to kill her own aunt? A nice lady like Mrs. Bostwick?"

"A 'nice lady.' Is that what you think she is?"

"Oh, ah. That's just what I think. But never mind me. Your sister, you say, was never in this house at all. She never went out through this door at all. Nobody went out through this door. Mrs. Bostwick made it up, after Mrs. Bostwick tried to kill her aunt?"

"That woman isn't her aunt! They're not related."

"I'd appreciate it, miss, if you made up your mind what it is you want to tell me. How do you know Mrs. Bostwick did this?"

"She admitted it!"

"Who'd she admit it to? To you?"

"No."

"Who was it, then? Who'd she admit it to?"

"To somebody else. I—I can't tell you who it was. I mean I won't tell you!"

"Now *you're* shielding somebody, eh? Have you ever been in this cellar before?"

"No."

"That's very interesting, that is. What did you think we could discover, just by standing here and looking at a door to the outside, like? There's not one grain of sense in any of this, is there?"

"I hoped—"

"What did you hope? Why did you follow Mrs. Bostwick here tonight?"

"Because she wasn't at her home. I thought she'd probably come here, just as she did on Friday."

"That's not what I asked you. What *reason* did you have for coming here?"

"I came here," Betty answered in a clear voice, "because I am tired of being too weak-willed to stand up for myself. I came here because yesterday I was jealous, and I behaved like a beast and a bitch to the only man I ever cared for in this world. If Marion Bostwick tried to kill this so-called 'aunt,' she probably killed Glynis too. No matter how much you try to stop me or how much you sneer, I am going on trying to make that woman admit it."

Garth walked forward and opened the door, resisting an impulse to fling it open so that it would crash against the inner wall.

"It's not necessary to go on trying, Betty," he told her. Then, controlling another savage impulse which could have blunted his wits and addled the wariness that must protect them both, he looked round at the man facing Betty.

"Mr. Twigg," he said, "I think it is time you and I had a reckoning."

18

The kitchen, a large cavern with a glass-panelled half-underground door, remained as dingy as when he last saw it.

Only one pale-yellow electric bulb, hanging gauntly from the ceiling over the drainboard beside the sink, brought out whatever could be seen of the expressions on faces. It barely dispelled shadows. It must have summoned blackbeetles to the corners. But at least it was better than the rush-light which previously had been burning on the big cooking-range built into the flue of the chimney.

Betty and Twigg faced each other across a large table with a marble top and a chopping-block. Both craned round. Twigg wore his bowler hat on the back of his head, and his gold watch chain quivered as he straightened up with a good deal of dignity.

"You think that, Doctor?" he asked in his hoarse voice. "Maybe I think so too. But what you'd like or I'd like is no odds to anybody. I've got a duty to do."

"So have I."

"And all's fair in that duty. Just you be kind enough to clear out of here—"

"No. State your case against this lady. State it here and now. If you're right in any point you make, I'll acknowledge it and so will she. State your case!"

"Ho! And have you twist everything up?"

"Is it so difficult? Can't you protect yourself?"

Some of the colour drained out of Twigg's face.

("That was a dirty one," Garth was thinking. "Let it be!")

Betty, clearly convinced these two would fly at each other's throats (as it is quite possible they would) ran away from the table and over to the sink. She stood with her back to the drainboard, under the light, watching them.

"By jing!" whispered Twigg, achingly tempted. "By jing! Maybe you're the one who can't protect yourself, eh? Now that Mr. Abbot's not here to back you up?"

"Maybe I can't. Ask your questions. I'll tell the truth."

"*You'll* tell the truth? When this woman's going up for murder, and you're probably for it as accessory after the fact?"

"Does it honestly strike you, Mr. Twigg, that the question of my own arrest weighs so very much with me?"

"No; I'll give you that. You're daft! Where a doctor of your reputation's concerned, and a woman from the Moulin Rouge—"

"Keep your moral judgements out of this, Mr. Twigg," Garth said in a very soft voice. "If you're going to use the advantage, I implore you, keep your moral judgements out of this."

Suddenly, like duellists, they began circling round the table and the chopping-block.

"You admit you've got something to hide, Doctor?"

"Yes."

"And that woman's got a whole lot more to hide?"

"Yes!"

"Ah!" Twigg's colour went up. "Maybe you do halfway mean it. We'll see. Maybe you're not such a stuck-up—!"

"And you're not such a pig-headed—!"

Both of them stopped at the same instant.

"What beat me," said Twigg, "what beat me from the very minute Mr. Abbot and I walked out on the sands and saw you two standing by the pavilion, was something I didn't begin to understand until much later. Because why? Because none of that business seemed to be sensible no matter what happened."

It was a measure of Twigg's absorption in the problem that he had lowered his guard; once committed, he trusted the word of the man who had fought him at every step; he might have been arguing to another officer of the Criminal Investigation Department.

"Thinks I to myself, 'That woman killed her sister, right enough. And the doctor's shielding her. Still and all, why do they keep on telling a story that makes 'em look even guiltier than they are?'"

Here Twigg looked the other man in the eyes.

"We'll allow you two were interrupted, Doctor, before you could work up a proper story. We'll allow sand is tricky stuff to mess about with. We'll allow Lady Calder's flighty; easy to upset, and acts too quick. Even so! She's not simple—"

"Simple?"

"Simple in the head! Like the village idiot!"

"Yes?"

"She's got plenty of imagination; maybe too much. Oh, ah! She tries to imitate you and think like you think. And you're not simple, Doctor, not by a jugful, even if you do write those stories I'll admit now I read! Never mind how I learned you write 'em. Secretaries to a literary agent can tell things, specially when the doctor is a witness in a trial at the Old Bailey, and a secretary in the audience says, 'Oo-er!'

"But how did a brown-and-yellow bathing-robe get from the house out to that pavilion, when it wasn't carried by the woman who went out for a swim at four o'clock? I got the answer next day, handed me on a plate. And the night before I'd been all wrong, letting you half-flummox me, until I saw the kind of books that were all over Lady Calder's sitting-room and specially that book about the near-murder in the Yellow Room."

Garth braced himself. Twigg saw it, and pounced.

"I asked you next day what was the point of the Yellow Room as compared to the real murder we'd got here. You tried to flummox me again, didn't you?"

"Yes!"

"You said it was because the murderer was the official detective investigating the case?"

"Not the official detective, necessarily."

"What's that, Doctor?"

"I was trying to deceive you, and I admit it! What more do you want?"

"But that wasn't the point, was it? In this Yellow Room business, I mean, they heard screams and shots and whatnot in the middle of the night. But the murderer wasn't there at that time. He'd attacked the lady in the afternoon, and left the bruises and the bloodstains. She hid 'em all, and pretended nothing had happened. In the night it was only a nightmare that got her. She dreamed she was being attacked again. She jumped up screaming in bed, and grabbed a revolver and fired at nothing; then she fell and cracked her head on an overturned table. There never was any murderer in the Yellow Room. Is that true?"

"Quite true."

Garth glanced quickly over his shoulder towards the open door to the cellar corridor behind him.

"Oh, ah! And there never was any murderer in that pavilion, either. Leastways, at the time we thought there was. Isn't that true too?"

"Quite true."

"At four o'clock in the afternoon," said Twigg, "a woman in a bathing-costume walked down the beach and out into the water. Mr. Abbot and young Mr. Ormiston saw her from some distance away. Mr. Ormiston thought it was Lady Calder. Then he changed his mind oh, ah, like witnesses keep on doing!—and said it was Glynis Stukeley. But it couldn't 'a' been Glynis Stukeley. Lady Calder don't like people using her bathing-costumes, and keeps 'em locked up so they can't be used. The woman on that beach *was* Lady Calder."

Twigg flung his head round.

"Fair's fair, miss. You heard what the doctor promised! It was you in that bathing-costume and nobody else. Now wasn't it?"

"Answer him, Betty!"

"But I—"

"Answer him, Betty! Tell the truth!"

"It *was* you, miss. Now wasn't it?"

"Yes," Betty whispered.

"Ah!" said Twigg, but with no other pounce of triumph. Red-faced, inexorable, he turned slowly back to Garth. "Admit that, Doctor, and I've got the two of you just where I want you."

"You think so?"

"I know so! 'Course she went for a dip! 'Course she pulled herself up on the porch of the pavilion afterwards! But she didn't stay there any two hours. She never did before, they tell me. And why should she this time? She was as mad as hops and wild with her sister. She stayed there just long enough to make a small pot of tea and drink one cup of it on the porch, ten minutes maybe, and back she went to the house. The fingerprints she left on the cup and the teapot—"

"They could have been old fingerprints, Mr. Twigg."

"They could have been, Doctor. Do you think they were?"

"No, I do not."

"Ah!" said Twigg.

Betty, her back to the drainboard, was gripping its ledges at either side.

"And she didn't leave any footprints when she went back to the house, did she? The tide was still too high. Any footprints would have been washed out clean. Or else they'd be so close to the top they'd have dried enough to be taken for old footprints made on any day you like. There wasn't a print within thirty feet. And nobody'd been strangled—not yet. Nobody was thinking about murder—or maybe not. Agreed?"

"Yes! Agreed! Get on with it!"

"This murder, now, wasn't done in the pavilion at all. Not on your life! Where was it done, Doctor?"

"It was done, in my opinion, in the back bedroom assigned to Glynis Stukeley. Pieces of sash-cord were lying ready to a murderer's hand."

Betty let out a cry. Garth started towards her, across the

dingy kitchen under the sickly yellow light. Then he changed his mind and backed away.

"Oh, ah!" Twigg said relentlessly.

Whereupon he paused, tapping his finger-tips on the marble top of the table.

"What time was that? In exactness, what time when Lady Calder gets from the pavilion back to the house? Maybe fifteen or twenty minutes past four. To go as near as we can by the medical evidence, it's not for a good bit more than an hour that the murder's done.

"But that fits in. Lady Calder's got to go upstairs to her own room; get out of her wet bathing-costume; get into her day-clothes again. And that takes time, or it takes my wife time. Afterwards she goes down to her sister's room. The quarrel breaks out; the real quarrel; the honest-to-God quarrel; the one that ends with a rope round the neck.

"Lady Calder told a lot of the truth in her story. You bet she did! In the parts we could get answers to from other witnesses. Glynis Stukeley *did* get to Fairfield by a morning train. There *was* a letter for her in the afternoon post: typed address, London postmark.

"You were getting there at six o'clock, weren't you? That's another reason why she wouldn't have stayed out at that pavilion, where she admits she was. She didn't want her sister to meet you.

"But the row blew up. And what happened to her is what's happened to a whole heap of murderers before they know how to stop. The lightning's struck. It's all over. There's the victim dead. They're scared to the soul. What'll they do next? Suppose you tell us, Doctor, about the evidence of what did happen next?"

"No," snapped Garth. "No, I will not. You're making too much of rather a pathetic triumph."

"I'm doing me duty, that's what I'm doing, and don't you ever forget it. I'm no swine. I don't like singing big. But I'm cornering a murderer and there it is." Twigg broke off. "What's got into you? Why do you keep looking back over your shoulder?"

"As you would say, Mr. Twigg, it's no odds. Forget me! Here, will you smoke? Will you have a cigarette?"

They were grotesque words, as though Garth's judgement had slipped as his hands almost slipped. He had not forgotten this time, as at Fairfield, to fill his silver cigarette-case. The case flashed out, wabbled, and all but clattered to spill on the table.

"Smoke?" said Twigg, controlling himself. "No, Doctor.

Thanks very much, but I will not." They looked at each other strangely, as though both hesitated and wondered. "If this is some more of your games, by jing, I wouldn't try it on! What happened when she'd done the murder?"

"It's your story. Why don't you tell it?"

"Oh, ah. That's just what I will. Do you know why I will?"

"Mr. Twigg—"

" 'Because there,' thinks I to myself, 'just *there* is where the light went out in the case. Those two, the guilty woman and the doctor, weren't acting together. They didn't know it, but they were acting independent-like. And they didn't mean to, but they flummoxed each other.'

"Here *she* was," said Twigg, glancing round towards Betty and back again, "standing over her victim, alone in the house. It's nearly twenty minutes to six o'clock. You'll be there at six. Nobody'll believe her if she swears she didn't do it. But you're different. You're high and mighty. They'll take your word (won't they?) if she convinces *you* she couldn't 'a' done it? She's got to do that, or she thinks she has. For she can't say, 'I've just done a murder,' to the man she still hopes to marry.

"Two witnesses saw her go out on the beach at four o'clock, All right! Why not prove it was her sister? Why not prove Glynis went to the pavilion, and was strangled there, and never came back? No matter what they suspect, they can't prove anything if they can't think how the trick was worked. You taught her that, Doctor. Maybe you didn't mean to, but you taught her that. If she's got the nerve to go through an unholy-awful fifty or sixty seconds at the right time, she may fool everybody.

"And she very nearly did.

"There's several parts to a scheme that can be put together in a very short time. She can strip the clothes off her sister, chuck the clothes into a cupboard, and dress a dead body in her own wet bathing-costume and rubber bathing-cap. She can dust the sand off the rubber soles of her bathing-shoes and put those on the body too.

"What else do we know about this innocent-faced girl (ho!) who's standing over there now? In Harley Street, on Friday night it was, I overheard you telling Mr. Michael Fielding. She's a member of the Royal Life-Saving Society. Time after time she's done exercises to carry a 'drowned' body, slung round the shoulders in what they call a fireman's lift, from the water to the beach and the grass verge round the house. So she can take a dead body in the other direction.

"Any trouble there? None that *is* trouble.

"A wool bathing-costume stays damp a long time. She

won't want to get herself touched with damp and give the show away, specially since she's got on a silk blouse. But she can wrap the body in something, can't she? And there's nothing better than her own serge bathing-robe, with one of Glynis Stukeley's handkerchiefs stuck in the pocket to make the flummery look better.

"Now what'll happen, as sure as guns, is a visitor who knows her habits gets to the house at six o'clock and thinks she's not there because she won't answer a hail?

"I'll tell you: he'll think she's at the pavilion. Where else could she be, when she goes for a bathe every day the weather's fine? That's what young Mr. Ormiston thought, when he turned up first. He wouldn't go on out there; no, not him! But you'd go like a shot, Doctor. That's just what you did.

"If she could get you to go on out ahead of her while she's still scared-stiff-determined in the house with a dead body, she could do the trick. That pavilion might have been hand-made for it.

"It wouldn't 'a' worked if Mr. Ormiston had stayed there. But he didn't. He nipped away in a blind rage. There's just one other thing she had to do. What was it, Doctor?"

Nobody answered. Twigg's voice echoed through the cellar rooms as though through a cavern.

"What was it, I'm asking you? She couldn't admit she'd been at the house all afternoon. That'd dish her for sure. She'd be the murderer more than ever. What other bit of flummery would cover her tracks and make her story sound solid-sure?"

"If you mean the bicycle . . ."

"Yes, Doctor, I mean the bicycle. Where was it kept?"

"In a shed built against the side of the house."

"Where? Opening on the grass, wasn't it? Near a cycle-track? And not twenty feet from the room where her sister'd been killed? Yes or no?"

"Yes!"

"She wheeled out the bike and dropped it on the grass. She went back to the room for a dead body. She must have looked near crazy, just like she's looking now, but they'll all do that if the hangman's after 'em. She picked up that dead body, and she walked out across the sand from the place where she dropped the bike.

"She followed you, Doctor. There are two rooms in that pavilion. You couldn't go into both of 'em at once. Which-ever one you chose, she'd choose the other one. The sand was too firm and hard-packed to show the weight of one woman carrying what she did carry. You didn't make much noise inside, you tell me. She didn't make any noise at all. God's truth! When I thought of why she didn't, I could have killed you myself for letting you near hocus me with a lot of talk about her not being inside because there weren't any traces of sandy footprints. When she got as far as the steps what did she do?"

"There is no need—"

"You bet there's not! But I'll tell you. She kicked off her shoes."

"What I meant—"

"Just inside," said Twigg, "I'll tell you what else there is. There's a big canvas screen, built out at right angles between the doors of the two rooms. In the old days bathers of opposite sexes couldn't even see each other go into their dressing-rooms. If you looked back or round from either room, you couldn't have seen her go in or out the door of the other room.

"You had to move slow; it was dark and at first you weren't sure. She could move quick. A few seconds, that's all! A few seconds to put down that nice, beautiful burden on the floor. And hang up the robe. And nip out to the steps again.

"She put on her shoes there. She stepped backwards out on the sand. If she had to scuff up the last two footprints she'd made, her skirt would hide it until she could get you to walk down the steps and mess up the tracks still more. Then she was ready, waiting and listening, to sing out your name and call you to the door. She was out of breath and untidy. But what of that? She could say she'd been riding a bike. She didn't have to tell you she'd been carrying the body of the sister she strangled."

"Stop," Betty screamed. "Stop this. If you want a confession—"

"*Betty, be quiet!*"

"I don't care. I can't bear any more."

"Ah!" said Twigg. His hard breathing gradually slowed down while he craned round to look at Betty. He strolled towards her. "Well, now, miss," he added, dusting his hands together in an expression between leisureliness and contempt, "I don't think we need a confession. I think we've got enough against you already. Still! You offered it. And while we're about it, Doctor," he flung his head round, "we'll have one from you too."

"A confession of what?"

"You guessed what she'd done, didn't you? While you were out at the pavilion, standing over Glynis Stukeley's body for the first time, you guessed what this woman had done?"

"I promised to answer questions, Mr. Twigg. There was no promise to counter vague generalities. State a precise question or for God's sake hold your peace."

Twigg spun round.

He studied the other with sudden attention. Then he lumbered back to the marble-topped table.

"You guessed she'd messed about with the evidence, didn't you? You guessed she'd brought a dead body from the house to the pavilion?"

"Yes. I guessed that."

"Oh, ah! And you told one thumping lie in your testimony, in the hope of shielding this woman here?"

"Yes. I did."

"Oh, ah! I'll just lay a tanner you told the same lie to her too, and you both pretended to each other, and never admitted the truth of it even between yourselves."

"No. We never admitted it. Even between ourselves."

Suddenly Twigg looked a little shamefaced, glaring first at Betty and then back at Garth.

"Why did you have to go and do this? Either of you? It's not so easy, is it? It's easy to think up these fancy stories. It's not so easy when you learn what murder's like, and find you've only made a fool of yourself after all?"

"I greatly fear," answered Garth, "that is true too." His tone changed. "Now another word of warning, Inspector. I have badly misjudged you. You are an honest man and you are not a bad fellow. But nothing on earth is of less importance than your personal vanity or mine. And I ask you again to carry the triumph no further."

"Ho! That's a lot of brag and bounce, ain't it? Now we know this woman's a criminal—"

"Who says she is a criminal?"

"Don't talk soft! We know she committed the murder!"

"Who says she committed the murder?"

Garth stood motionless, as though listening, his head partly turned towards the corridor and the open door behind him.

"Inspector," he went on, "you are a first-class police-officer. No mechanics of a crime will ever baffle you. What you have completely overlooked is the motive. You still don't see the real reason why the victim was killed."

"I don't, eh? She was killed because her sister couldn't put up with her any longer!"

"Oh, no. It's not quite as simple as that. And the murderer was a man."

"God's truth! Are you trying to tell me it's another man who's been mixed up in a blackmailing relationship with Glynis Stukeley?"

"Not exactly," said Garth, "though that enters into it. The murderer is a man who for years has been engaged in a sexual relationship with Marion Bostwick."

"Marion Bostwick?" yelled Twigg.

"Listen!" said Garth.

There was someone else moving in the cellar.

Garth went over at Betty's side and put his arm tightly round her. Twigg lifted his head.

The noise they heard might at first have sounded like the scuttle of a rat. Yet it was not a rapid movement. Slow footsteps on gritty stone approached from the direction of the cellar stairs. Those footsteps began to run only as they neared the door; and then the newcomer stopped short as he appeared in the doorway.

Violence and despair entered with him. His right hand hung at his side, but it held an Eley's revolver. He looked at each of them in turn, with eyes so wide open that a ring of white showed round the iris.

"I'm the man you want," said Colonel Selby. "I strangled that woman at the beach-house. And nobody else is going to suffer for it."

Holding the revolver in both hands with trigger-guard outwards, drawing the hammer back to cock, he rammed its muzzle between his teeth and up hard against the roof of his mouth. There was no time for Twigg to interfere. Garth could not have interfered even if he had wished to do so. He had time only to seize the back of Betty's neck and force her head downwards. She did not see what happened when Colonel Selby pulled the trigger.

19

Distant clocks were striking the hour of one in the morning when Inspector Twigg, Cullingford Abbot, and David Garth entered Garth's consulting-room at number 31b Harley Street.

First Garth switched on the four bulbs of the chandelier. Their light lay bleakly over the broad desk, over chairs of black padded leather, over a mantelpiece on whose ledge the bronze clock was flanked by a silver-framed photograph of Garth's parents at one side and by a silver-framed photograph of Betty Calder at the other. The room was haunted by a vague smell of drugs or antiseptics.

"Sit down, gentlemen," Garth said. "This profession of mine I chose for myself. It has a thousand compensations. But tonight has not shown me one of them."

He himself sat down behind the desk. Abbot occupied the big chair facing it. But Twigg, too restless, paced and lifted his fist.

" 'Sexual relation,' " Twigg was saying. " 'Sexual relation!' " He flung the words away from him, as though he would stamp on them and blot them out as too shameful to exist. Yet he could not resist repeating them. "With Mrs. Bostwick? Ever since she was fourteen years old?"

"Tut!" Abbot said acidly, though even his eyeglass appeared subdued. "Can you honestly claim you never suspected it?"

" 'Sexual relations.' God's truth! It's not *right*."

"Possibly not. But such things happen. It's refreshing to hear that you, a policeman of twenty years' experience, have never encountered them."

"Encountered 'em? Oh, ah! I've encountered 'em often enough. I began in K Division, and that means the East End. But among the gentry——"

Twigg stopped short. Abbot raised his eyebrows.

"The gentry? Your hated gentry? Is Saul also among the prophets?"

"All I meant——"

"If you may be said to have a fault, my dear Twigg, it's that you regard these queer animals as being either much worse or much better than they really are. Have a little charity. Try to think that the ranks of the damned may be not so much different from yourself."

"Look here, Doctor." Twigg turned to Garth with a fierce and lowering embarrassment. "If you'd just mind *telling* us? Eh?"

"You have heard the main facts, Inspector. There is very little else to tell."

"The main facts, perhaps," agreed Abbot with some malevolence. "Otherwise there is almost everything to tell. And you know it."

"It will be held in confidence, I hope? Colonel Selby is dead. Nobody else has read that statement I gave him. Is there any reason why Vince Bostwick should ever hear one word more about it?"

"Oh, it will be held in confidence. If the police were inclined to tell all they knew, many people (including your obedient servant) would not sleep well at night. Still! In the interests of Mr. Bostwick himself, is that wise?"

"I don't know! I don't know! I only wish I could decide!"

"You are too young, Garth, to remember the Bravo case in '76. Nearly all the explosion of tragedy was caused by the fact that a very handsome young woman would *not* give up her affair with a man more than old enough to be her father. Those were Mrs. Bostwick's feelings too, I take it? That caused the tragedy?"

"In part, yes. But only in part."

"And the other part? Let us hear it!"

Garth leaned back in the chair. Then he leaned forward again, elbow on the desk, shielding his eyes with his hand.

"Two years ago," he said, "a close friend of my own age married a girl of eighteen. She had been brought home from India at fourteen by a guardian who was then (at a guess) in his middle fifties. About this girl there was some disturbing quality not easy to identify. Nor could the household, Colonel Selby and Mrs. Montague and their ward Marion, be called altogether a usual one. Mrs. Montague, though she permitted a telephone in the house, refused to have their names included in the directory. The wedding was a hasty, ill-arranged affair; neither Colonel Selby nor Mrs. Montague attended the ceremony at Hampstead Town Hall.

"Something had gone wrong there. It concerned Marion; nor was I prompted entirely by what Vince would call my Viennese inclinations to suspect a matter of a sexual nature. As I told Vince long afterwards, any experienced G.P. could have seen that.

"Though Vince deeply loved his wife, it became plain they were not happy and that she was restless to a dangerous point. The only clue appeared to be her constant, monotonous harping on the matter of how much she liked 'young' men, which was not true. On so many unnecessary occasions did she drag in references to how 'old' people were, *à propos* love or marriage, that it was revealing. I wondered—"

"You wondered if the lady protested too much?" inquired Abbot. "A point made by a somewhat older psychoanalyst than any in Vienna?"

"Yes. Others noticed it too; it need not be laboured. Marion, Vince, and I attended the opening night of *The Merry Widow*. Afterwards, again in that same restless state, she began questioning me about my work. She asked me what I should do if someone came to me and told me she was 'abnormal and unnatural and apt to be locked up in a madhouse' to keep her from committing a murder.

"At the beginning of the following week Colonel Selby telephoned Michael Fielding and asked for a professional appointment so that he could see me here, away from his house and the members of his household. On Friday night he asked me much the same question."

"And he was talking about her?" asked Abbot.

"Oh, no," retorted Garth. "He thought he was talking about himself."

"He 'thought' he was talking about himself?"

"Yes."

Garth leaned back in the chair.

"Even now, when Colonel Selby is dead, I should not reveal any word ever spoken in this consulting-room if it were not necessary to explain a crime to the police. But that was a revealing interview.

"The man was shaken, badly frightened, at the end of his nervous resources. He said that he wanted to state a hypothetical case, and changed this to saying he was talking about someone he knew.

"Every doctor knows (and sometimes dreads) that opening. When a patient approaches some very embarrassing subject, and begins by insisting it is a hypothetical case or someone else's case, almost invariably he is talking about himself. On many occasions it will take time and delicacy to get the truth.

"Colonel Selby was talking about himself—and his relations with Marion Bostwick. The man was horrified. Because he could not keep away from a woman so very much younger than himself, because it had happened time after time when he had sworn it shouldn't happen again, he thought he must be tainted and insane. He was over-conscientious, over-dogged, thoroughly scrupulous. . . ."

Garth sat up straight.

"Don't scoff," Garth added sharply, as the familiar look

of benevolent cynicism crossed Abbot's face. "I mean just what I say. If he had not been all of that, he would never afterwards have admitted he killed Glynis Stukeley and then shot himself."

There was a pause.

"I beg your pardon," said Abbot. "You are quite right, of course. I am not myself fond of bad taste, though I am always displaying it. Go on."

"Colonel Selby was not to know it had happened to many other men besides himself. Up to then he had lived in the relatively (I say relatively) uncomplicated world shown to us by Mr. Kipling. Above all he was never to guess that the driving, motivating force in the sexual affair was the girl herself, Marion, who brought about all the trouble and will get off scot-free."

Again there was a pause.

"Colonel Selby wanted to tell me of this affair on Friday night. He was nerving himself to tell me, especially since he and Marion were both being threatened by a blackmailer. But the interview was interrupted. It was interrupted by two things, occurring one after the other, though at the time I could understand only the second—and more obvious—interruption.

"The telephone rang out in the hall. We could hear Michael's voice talking to Marion at the other end of the line, using her name, while she cried out about some then-unnamed calamity or catastrophe. Colonel Selby sprang up in a worse state of nerves. He said he could not go on with this; he broke off abruptly, and took a hasty departure. The mention of Marion's name had influenced him, of course, as I thought. But another incident, which I failed to interpret then, had just influenced him far more.

"Abbot, he was sitting in the same leather chair you are occupying now. Just as the telephone rang, he looked away from me. He looked over towards the fireplace. Before any mention had been made of Marion Bostwick's name on the telephone, a change went over him; while he was looking round, his fingers tightened with some violence on the arms of the chair. Abbot, look round now. Look at the fireplace and especially the ledge of the mantelpiece above. What do *you* see?"

Abbot craned round. Twigg, who had been pacing, stopped in the middle of the consulting-room and also followed the direction of Garth's gesture.

"So!" Abbot whistled, turning back. "A silver-framed photograph of Betty Calder. Or would it seem to be—?"

"Exactly. To a man who was being blackmailed, wouldn't it seem to be a photograph of Glynis Stukeley?"

"Oh, ah!" said Twigg, rubbing his forehead. "Oh, ah!"

"I don't say it made Colonel Selby suspicious of me as a part of any plot against him. But he must have decided I had some very odd friends or relatives. Certainly he would change his mind in haste about giving me his confidence.

"At the time, however, I had never heard of Glynis Stukeley; I knew nothing of plots or blackmail; his behaviour, though observed, was forgotten and went uninterpreted until twenty-four hours later.

"The same applies to a similar fact which Colonel Selby mentioned to me almost as soon as he marched into this room. Out in the waiting-room somebody had left a copy of a novel, unfortunately a novel I myself had written, called *By Whose Hand?* It had been left open at the frontispiece, and Colonel Selby was glancing at the book before he saw me. The theme of that novel, as you both know, is the influence exercised by a young woman—apparently of supernatural attractiveness and other powers—over a man very much older than herself."

"So he thought you were getting at him? Or somebody was getting at him?"

"Oh, no!" said Garth. "Not then. Not until afterwards."

"What's that, Doctor?" demanded Twigg.

"If he had thought any such thing at the time, he would have bolted before he even saw me. Nor would he have been so quick to mention the book at the beginning. You see, Colonel Selby was no reader. If you look at his study, his den, the place where a man's most instinctive tastes are revealed, you will find nothing in the way of books except bound copies of *The Field*. He had not read the book. He could have gained very little idea of its contents by glancing at it while he waited. He knew only that it was strange, queer (as everything was beginning to seem to a bedevilled man), and that it upset him.

"On the other hand, it very much occurred to me as confirmation of my own theories. Colonel Selby's secret was his passion for Marion Bostwick and hers for him. Someone knew this (who?) and had left the book there (why?) so that he should find it; and the person who left it there must be someone attached to my own household. On these puzzling notes he left my consulting-room in a panic.

"Up to the time he left I had heard nothing of a blackmailer or blackmailing tactics. Immediately afterwards I began hearing of little else. You, Inspector, drove in to the attack by saying the blackmailer was Betty Calder. You, Abbot, confirmed this over the telephone. You added that Betty must have been having an affair with Vince Bostwick. Then came news of the strangling assault on Mrs. Montague."

Garth paused.

Briefly, while Twigg stiffened and Abbot grimaced at the edge of the desk, old antagonisms flared and burned.

"Considering all we now know, Inspector," Garth asked, "will you acknowledge the person who nearly killed Mrs. Montague was Marion Bostwick herself?"

"Oh, ah! I'm bound to. Will you acknowledge something too, Doctor? When you take a dislike to somebody, I tell you straight, you're an uncommon hard man to get on with. God's truth! You didn't say 'Inspector' then. You had a way of saying, 'Mr. Twigg,' with a sting in the tail, like, that fair drove me wild whenever I heard it. Will you admit that too?"

"Willingly. I mention the attack on Mrs. Montague only to emphasize what happened when Glynis Stukeley appeared in the case."

"Fair enough, then. Well, sir?"

"Well! The enigmatic Glynis, who loved torturing people almost as much as she loved money, was blackmailing somebody. Who was being blackmailed? It was not Vince Bostwick; everyone agreed she had never been near Vince. She was not even asking money from Vince, a very wealthy man, as the price of silence about somebody else's conduct.

"This raised the obvious corollary question: from whom was the blackmailer asking hush-money, and why?

"Every trail led to that house at Hampstead. Mrs. Montague, a morbidly respectable woman, hastily dismissed the servants on Friday evening. Whether or not Glynis had gone to the house too, it was plain she had been summoned or had invited herself; Marion described Glynis's clothes too accurately for this to have been invention. Clearly Mrs. Montague wanted to confront Marion with Glynis. When Glynis failed to appear, she shouted 'whore' at Marion and all but caused her own death. Colonel Selby, who was supposed to be at his club, was in fact at my office nerving himself to ask advice. The conclusion seemed inescapable that the two persons being blackmailed were Marion Bostwick, the wife of a wealthy man, and Colonel Selby, who was at least well-to-do.

"Then, next day, came the murder.

"I have concealed several things from you, gentlemen—"

"By jing, you have!" said Twigg. "But it's the part about the murder I want to hear. You walked in there and found the body. How'd you tumble slam-bang, first crack out of the box, to that trick of moving the body from the house to the pavilion? How'd you guess Lady Calder had done that? How'd you reason it out?"

"I did not reason it out."

"Ho?"

"If you were ever to write such fiction, Inspector—"

Twigg lifted both fists.

"I am quite serious," said Garth, looking up in such a way that the other hesitated. "My main concern has been and will always be to protect Betty Calder. Let me see if I can explain it in another way."

He brooded for a moment.

"It was a very bad matter of seconds when I discovered Glynis Stukeley's body and thought it was Betty's. The relief, to find it was not, became a shock like that of pleasure. Under the surface of the mind began a train of associations with things I had seen. They were not conscious thoughts, any more than they are conscious thoughts just before a story-idea comes to us fully worked out.

"If they had been conscious thoughts, while I moved from the body to the robe against the wall and back, they might have gone in the following sense. 'Suppose Betty did this?' I knew, of course, she could not have committed murder; she was incapable of that. 'But suppose she had; how could she have done it?' The absence of footprints outside, the big canvas screen hiding the door of one little room from the door of the other room: these factors unconsciously gathered in a mind used to the tricks of fiction. They provided an explanation, which later proved to be the true explanation, in a shorter time than it takes to tell.

"At that point I reached out, touched the teapot, and jumped back as though I had been burnt. I had not been burnt. The teapot was stone cold. I jumped back, smashing a cup, because at that instant I heard Betty's voice calling my name.

"It was as though a nightmare were coming true. If she *had* done this, she would be just *there*. The very fact you later used so devastatingly—that she could not have known I was inside the pavilion, unless she had been there to see me go in—confirmed my fancied reconstruction. The first thing I saw was a bicycle, just where it would be if she happened to be spinning a lie to throw off suspicion.

"After which, I, the experienced in fiction, botched everything in fact.

"No doubt I should have hurried her away from there immediately. No doubt I should have challenged her; ex-

plained what I suspected; and, if I insisted on joining the
lies, found a more helpful one. I can only tell you that in her
state of mind then it seemed far more necessary to reassure
her, to support her, to give strength to a woman near collapse
after what she had done. So I told her, as well as the police,
the one thundering lie I did invent."

"Oh, ah! About the tea being still hot?"

"Exactly. It would prove, if it were believed, that the
murderer must have been inside the pavilion and strangled
Glynis Stukeley there. But it was futile. You and Abbot
arrived too soon. The subject of tea could not be mentioned
until the tea would have been cold anyway. I can hardly
blame you if you fail to understand."

Twigg, fists on hips, looked him up and down.

"Well, Doctor, I'll tell you what it is," he said. "You did
wrong. You now admit you did wrong. Apart from that,
God's truth!" And Twigg drew a deep breath. "You must
think nobody was ever human except yourself, or ever made
a fool of himself over a woman either, if you imagine for
one minute I CAN'T understand."

"Amen!" said Abbot. "But I am interested in another
aspect of this. Who or what made you make up your mind
Colonel Selby must be guilty?"

"You did. During a talk we had at Betty's cottage later
on Saturday evening."

"H'm. I fancied something of the sort. You said I re-
minded you of someone. Was it of Colonel Selby?"

"Yes. Not in your personal appearance, as I told you. You
are short; Colonel Selby was tall. Colonel Selby was clean-
shaven; you have a moustache almost worthy of Napoleon's
Grande Armée. He was going bald; you have kept your hair.
There were similarities much more striking.

"Abbot, you have copied many of your mannerisms from
Sir Edward Henry, who formerly was head of the police in
India. The military carriage of the shoulders, the military
style of speech, the curtness, the handkerchief in the sleeve.
You smoke Indian cheroots and you're a member of the
Oriental, a military man's club. You and Colonel Selby
shared a certain near-dandyism of dress. Above all, you both
had a fondness for violence and for much younger women—"

"Just a moment! Hold hard, there!"

"Can you deny this?"

"Whether I deny it or not," Abbot returned with acid
politeness. "I suppose I should take it as a compliment. In
your eyes, evidently, the late Colonel Selby was an admirable
character."

"Admirable?" Garth repeated. "Hardly that. I rather liked the man. Before he lost his head and committed murder, I would have helped him if he had allowed it. However, just because no sermons are being preached, let's not hold him up as an example for other men of uncertain age.

"In fact, that is a part of the solution. To have seduced a girl of fourteen, no matter how physically mature she may have been, was as irresponsible as it was brutal and callous. In a girl more sensitive than Marion, who is not sensitive at all except where her safety is concerned, it could have caused psychological harm beyond repair. It's true she was all too willing. It's true he turned her into the driving force determined to continue this affair whatever happened. This very violence of his, when he did lose his head, was what most appealed to her own. She complained (you recall?) about the lack of it in other men. Do you also recall what occurred when you and I were talking in Betty's sitting-room on Saturday night?"

"Probably. Which particular occurrence?"

"You were pacing back and forth in front of a mantelpiece with a number of silver-framed photographs on its ledge. Quite by accident I indicated a photograph of Betty and Glynis together. You turned round to look at it, just as Colonel Selby had done here in my consulting-room. . . ."

"Ah! And it unlocked memory?"

"*That* was the memory I had been trying to pin down. *That* was why he ran away from me. Already he had given enough indications of his character. If he were sufficiently frightened, he would not hesitate to kill. 'If Blanche ever suspected—!' he had said in this room. Note, from what you told me, that both Colonel Selby and Mrs. Montague were in Fairfield on Saturday. But they were not staying in the same house. Mrs. Montague more than suspected; by that time she must have known. She was with relatives. He was at the Imperial Hotel, and could have gone out unobserved to Betty's cottage."

"Yes. If he knew Glynis was there."

"Remember what else you told me. Glynis Stukeley had attached herself to (of all people) Michael Fielding. Why? The main reason, of course, must have been her wish for a spy-post close to me. I was next in line for amiable blackmail if, as Glynis believed, a reasonably well respected neurologist was carrying on an amiable intrigue with her sister.

"But Glynis could not resist her passion for torturing people. She kept a close eye on all her victims; where was the profit in her game unless she did? She could have learned from Michael, well ahead, that Colonel Selby would see me on Friday night. Michael alone could have left a copy of *By Whose Hand?* in the waiting-room.

"Colonel Selby did not understand what the book meant. But she thought he would. 'My eye is upon you,' she would be saying; and, as Glynis saw the matter, it must disturb him all the more because he would not be able to imagine how a reminder appeared there as though by magic. If we are seeking the real witch of the low-tide, we must look at Glynis Stukeley herself.

"In the same way, she persuaded Michael to forge a note from me, saying that I should be in Fairfield at six o'clock. It was to disturb Betty, to keep Betty in a state of apprehension, while Glynis appeared to enjoy the spectacle."

"But how did she learn you were going there at that time? Or Colonel Selby was going there earlier in the day?"

"In my opinion," said Garth, "because Colonel Selby had made up his mind to kill her."

"Tut! I don't see—"

"You will in a moment. On Saturday night, as I think you do know, I had in some fashion to prove what I believed in order to defend Betty. The first thread to be followed was an interview with Marion; she herself brought it about at the Stag and Glove.

"Marion *had* attacked Mrs. Montague. Her much-cherished lover *was* Colonel Selby, though she did not use his name. I did not believe she herself was concerned in the murder of Glynis, or even guessed—at the time—it was Colonel Selby who had done it. The interview was interrupted by a footstep outside the door, which she mistakenly supposed to be her husband's. I learned nothing very coherent after that. The first thread snapped.

"A second possibility of proof lay in a talk with Michael Fielding. The good Glynis might have betrayed to him the reason why she wanted that book left in the waiting-room. When I questioned Michael next day at the Palace Hotel, and said I knew he had done one other thing besides forge a letter, his demeanour showed Glynis had told him. But he would not admit it. The second thread snapped."

"Doctor," interposed Twigg in a hoarser voice, "somebody had a try at strangling young Mr. Fielding in the billiard-room at the hotel. Lummy! Was it Colonel Selby? Could Mrs. Bostwick 'a' put him up to doing that?"

"She did," Garth replied. "But Colonel Selby, now more than ever horrified at what he had been doing, could not go through with it. Michael might have seen—possibly did see—his assailant's face. By that time he was far too frightened to speak. My third and last thread had snapped too."

He waited, looking at the desk, and then raised his eyes.

"Let me recapitulate briefly a compressed and ugly series of events. When I left the house at Hampstead, not very late on Friday night, Marion and Vince were still there. Colonel Selby returned, presumably from his club. After the assault on Mrs. Montague, these two victims of the blackmailer, Colonel Selby and his ward, took serious counsel on what must be done.

"All this is conjecture, I acknowledge! But it is probable.

"Colonel Selby confessed to Marion he had visited me without giving anything away. He did mention the red-bound book invitingly left open. When Marion reads, she reads Vince's favourite books. If Colonel Selby up to then did not understand the meaning of the story, Marion did—and told him.

"Very probably she confessed to him she had burst out against Mrs. Montague. The blackmailer, Glynis Stukeley, was moving ever closer. At any moment this situation would end in catastrophe from somebody's word or deed unless Colonel Selby acted.

"Matters had fallen out so that a pattern could be arranged. In Marion's hearing *I* had said I meant to visit Betty in Fairfield late on the following afternoon. There is only one train that would get me there: the 5:32 at Fairfield station. Meanwhile, Mrs. Montague was awake and crying out to be taken away from the house. She did not *fear* Colonel Selby; she had no reason to do so; she was only horrified at him. She had relatives in Fairfield. He could take her there, provided he did not stay in the same house.

"In short, why was everybody at Fairfield the next day? Because Colonel Selby saw a covering screen in bringing together as many innocent persons as possible; and Glynis Stukeley must be lured to her sister's house and killed.

"Lured, how? Because she could not resist the bait.

"Glynis, as we know by Marion's confession, was sitting in a cab and watching the Hampstead house on Friday night. She longed beyond any dream of bliss to know what had taken place there. She saw me arrive, and Vince soon afterwards, and then the police.

"No doubt the presence of the police drove her away. To where?

"Remember, she had persuaded Michael to leave the book in the waiting-room for Colonel Selby, and to remain there afterwards until Michael heard from her. Since I was at Hampstead, she thought it safe to make a quick call at Harley Street. She could learn the result of the cat-and-mouse game with Colonel Selby; she could telephone one of her victims at Hampstead and discover what happened inside those maddening walls.

"She telephoned from Harley Street—and spoke to Colonel Selby, whose plan had been prepared. If she had not telephoned to him, he would have telephoned her at her lodgings later.

"They were all going to Fairfield next day, he said. Glynis could not resist that. Particularly she could not resist the news that I was going 'late in the afternoon.' Before she left Harley Street, she persuaded the frantic Michael to write that forged note. If those two had remained much longer, they would have met me coming home. But, as we can tell by the hour of the postmark on the letter, they were away in good time.

"You know the result.

"Colonel Selby had no intention of throwing any blame on Betty, who (let us admit it) brought the blame on herself. She was in the house, upstairs, when the murderer arrived and left unseen. Nor do I need to repeat what Betty herself did."

Twigg cleared his throat, and seemed in some danger of being strangled by his own collar.

"But what about Mrs. Bostwick?" he demanded. "Doctor, are you sure Colonel Selby and Mrs. Bostwick didn't work out that scheme together? With her egging him on?"

"No, I am not sure," Garth said curtly. "It is only that I do not think so. Colonel Selby was the sort of man who believes all business-affairs, including murder, should be carried on the shoulders of the man alone. On Sunday, however . . ."

"Oh, ah? On Sunday?"

"Marion, even after the interview late Saturday night, did not think I knew enough to be a serious danger. She will never confess where a third party can hear her; in that respect she is a far stronger vessel than was her late lover. But she heard that Michael, who might know the truth because he might know the meaning of the book, was to be questioned in her presence.

"Abbot, do you recall how abruptly she left our gathering in the lounge of the Palace Hotel? It was not because I tried to drive her away, as you thought. On the contrary! I was approaching the question of the book, but I had not reached it. She left because she learned Michael was another of Glynis's conquests. What Glynis knew, Glynis's men were apt to know. What Michael knew, I might get from him.

Marion's secret—as yet, she thought, one of adultery alone —was in great danger.

"She had already taken counsel with Colonel Selby. He was at the Imperial Hotel, just next door to the Palace in Victoria Avenue. More than that! A side door in the corridor, at the end of the billiard-room wing, was closed when I went down to the billiard-room but open shortly afterwards. Some-one had slipped from one hotel to the other."

Abbot grunted.

"*I* remember," he said. "Mrs. Bostwick spoke her real thoughts at last? And frankly asked the murderer of Glynis Stukeley to silence Michael Fielding? But she must have suspected, at least?"

"Oh, yes. By that time she suspected. I think she suspected from the time she talked to me the night before. Colonel Selby tried. And he could not go through with it. There is a limit."

"As to that," Abbot murmured, "one wonders."

"*I* wondered," said Garth. "They had frightened Michael so much that I could not persuade him to speak. He might never speak. You told me the inquest was next day; that Betty might be arrested; and I was desperate. Then it oc-curred to me, last night, that the person who might be forced into speech was Colonel Selby himself.

"Already his conscience gave him no second's peace. The attempt on Michael showed that. In his code you do many things; you commit adultery and you commit murder. But you do not let an innocent person suffer for it, and you do not dream of letting a woman suffer.

"You know what I did. I had talked both to him and to Mrs. Montague this afternoon, to make sure of my ground. Already I had prepared a full statement of what I knew, or thought I knew. I would hand this statement to him in the presence of a third person, having hinted—not too broadly —what was in my mind. I would tell him to give it to Mrs. Montague, though in fact it was intended for him alone. Of course, he would read it first. If I were wrong in what I believed, he would roar out and tell me so. If I were right . . .

"Well, I had hoped to have Michael there for more ques-tioning and possible identification. That failed. But it was not necessary. Luck (if it can be called that) put in the ugliest possible position the woman with whom I have the honour to be very much in love. I had to stress all this when I spoke in Colonel Selby's hearing. I had to make you, Inspec-tor, present your full case and to admit its damning features.

I had to make sure he would follow me. And then I had to wait."

For the second time since Garth had seen him, Twigg's face lost much of its colour.

"But, God's truth, Doctor! You'd got no evidence! No jury evidence at all!"

"No. I had not. That was why I had to do it."

"And suppose something had gone wrong? That house was a ruddy arsenal of firearms! Suppose something had gone wrong?"

"Ask any surgeon, Inspector, what would happen if he began to think of all the things that could go wrong at an operation. No piece of surgery would ever be performed."

"And you only began accusing him," said Twigg, "when he started walking towards that door with a gun in his hand? And—"

Twigg stopped. He glowered. He took several paces towards the fireplace, and several steps back. He pushed back his hat.

"Doctor," he said in a tone of repressed ferocity, "you said several things about me tonight. You said 'em to my face."

Instinctively Garth stiffened.

"Yes? And if I did?"

"We'll never see eye to eye, you know. And you'll never make a good copper in all your born days. But, God's truth! You might offer me that cigarette-case again, Doctor. You're not so bad yourself."

FINE MYSTERY AND SUSPENSE
TITLES FROM CARROLL & GRAF

☐ Bentley, E.C./TRENT'S OWN CASE	$3.95
☐ Blake, Nicholas/A TANGLED WEB	$3.50
☐ Boucher, Anthony/THE CASE OF THE BAKER STREET IRREGULARS	$3.95
☐ Boucher, Anthony (ed.)/FOUR AND TWENTY BLOODHOUNDS	$3.95
☐ Brand, Christianna/DEATH IN HIGH HEELS	$3.95
☐ Brand, Christianna/FOG OF DOUBT	$3.50
☐ Brand, Christianna/TOUR DE FORCE	$3.95
☐ Brown, Fredric/THE LENIENT BEAST	$3.50
☐ Brown, Fredric/MURDER CAN BE FUN	$3.95
☐ Brown, Fredric/THE SCREAMING MIMI	$3.50
☐ Buchan, John/JOHN MACNAB	$3.95
☐ Buchan, John/WITCH WOOD	$3.95
☐ Burnett, W.R./LITTLE CAESAR	$3.50
☐ Butler, Gerald/KISS THE BLOOD OFF MY HANDS	$3.95
☐ Carr, John Dickson/THE BRIDE OF NEWGATE	$3.95
☐ Carr, John Dickson/CAPTAIN CUT-THROAT	$3.95
☐ Carr, John Dickson/DARK OF THE MOON	$3.50
☐ Carr, John Dickson/DEADLY HALL	$3.95
☐ Carr, John Dickson/DEMONIACS	$3.95
☐ Carr, John Dickson/THE DEVIL IN VELVET	$3.95
☐ Carr, John Dickson/THE EMPEROR'S SNUFF-BOX	$3.50
☐ Carr, John Dickson/IN SPITE OF THUNDER	$3.50
☐ Carr, John Dickson/LOST GALLOWS	$3.50
☐ Carr, John Dickson/MOST SECRET	$3.95
☐ Carr, John Dickson/NINE WRONG ANSWERS	$3.50
☐ Carr, John Dickson/PAPA LA-BAS	$3.95
☐ Chesterton, G. K./THE MAN WHO KNEW TOO MUCH	$3.95
☐ Chesterton, G. K./THE MAN WHO WAS THURSDAY	$3.50
☐ Crofts, Freeman Wills/THE CASK	$3.59
☐ Coles, Manning/NO ENTRY	$3.50
☐ Collins, Michael/WALK A BLACK WIND	$3.95
☐ Dickson, Carter/THE CURSE OF THE BRONZE LAMP	$3.50
☐ Disch, Thomas M & Sladek, John/BLACK ALICE	$3.95
☐ Du Maurier, Daphne/THE SCAPEGOAT	$4.50
☐ Eberhart, Mignon/MESSAGE FROM HONG KONG	$3.50
☐ Eastlake, William/CASTLE KEEP	$3.50
☐ Fennelly, Tony/THE CLOSET HANGING	$3.50
☐ Fennelly, Tony/THE GLORY HOLE MURDERS	$2.95

☐	Gilbert, Michael/THE DOORS OPEN	$3.95
☐	Gilbert, Michael/GAME WITHOUT RULES	$3.95
☐	Gilbert, Michael/THE 92nd TIGER	$3.95
☐	Gilbert, Michael/OVERDRIVE	$3.95
☐	Graham, Winston/MARNIE	$3.95
☐	Greeley, Andrew/DEATH IN APRIL	$3.95
☐	Hughes, Dorothy B./THE FALLEN SPARROW	$3.50
☐	Hughes, Dorothy B./IN A LONELY PLACE	$3.50
☐	Hughes, Dorothy B./RIDE THE PINK HORSE	$3.95
☐	Hornung, E. W./THE AMATEUR CRACKSMAN	$3.95
☐	Kitchin, C. H. B./DEATH OF HIS UNCLE	$3.95
☐	Kitchin, C. H. B./DEATH OF MY AUNT	$3.50
☐	MacDonald, John D./TWO	$2.50
☐	Mason, A.E.W./AT THE VILLA ROSE	$3.50
☐	Mason, A.E.W./THE HOUSE OF THE ARROW	$3.50
☐	Priestley, J.B./SALT IS LEAVING	$3.95
☐	Queen, Ellery/THE FINISHING STROKE	$3.95
☐	Rogers, Joel T./THE RED RIGHT HAND	$3.50
☐	'Sapper'/BULLDOG DRUMMOND	$3.50
☐	Symons, Julian/BOGUE'S FORTUNE	$3.95
☐	Symons, Julian/THE BROKEN PENNY	$3.95
☐	Wainwright, John/ALL ON A SUMMER'S DAY	$3.50
☐	Wallace, Edgar/THE FOUR JUST MEN	$2.95
☐	Waugh, Hillary/SLEEP LONG, MY LOVE	$3.95
☐	Willeford, Charles/THE WOMAN CHASER	$3.95

Available from fine bookstores everywhere or use this coupon for ordering.

Carroll & Graf Publishers, Inc., 260 Fifth Avenue, N.Y., N.Y. 10001

Please send me the books I have checked above. I am enclosing $_____ (please add $1.00 per title to cover postage and handling.) Send check or money order—no cash or C.O.D.'s please. N.Y. residents please add 8¼% sales tax.

Mr/Mrs/Ms _____

Address _____

City _____ State/Zip _____

Please allow four to six weeks for delivery.